PERPETUUM

RALPH WAYNE BOLDYGA

Edited By: Kristin Campbell @ C&D Editing
Printed By: RALPH WAYNE BOLDYGA
Printed in the United States of America
First Printing Edition, 2024
ISBN 979-8-9901937-0-3

Dedication

To all inhabitants of Earth, now and forever.

The events described in this book are fictional; however, some literary license was used to incorporate current events and recent technological achievements. The names of institutions and places described are all fictional, no matter how similar they may seem, except for US political office holders and geological points. Dates of death and future political achievements of all characters are all random and fictional.

I have nothing but warm feelings for all the people's names used in this book. Each holds a special place in my memory.

Acknowledgement

A special thanks to my wife for holding down the fort while I typed out my manuscript. She endured endless hours of stories about time jumping.

A word of gratitude goes out to my editor. She really had to work very hard to make my manuscript publishable.

This book and related subject matter that I plan to publish in the future are all the product of my dreams. Having always been a daydreamer, I resolved to take notes in my later years so that I may share them with readers such as yourselves. I hope you enjoy and find motivation within the content.

Contents

Introduction

Hi,

Let me introduce myself. I am Maximilian Hickman. Everyone calls me Max.

As a reader of this book, I hope you agree to become an agent for planet Earth and join forces with me and my descendants to stave off the imminent destruction of biological life. This book is not written for financial gain or to entertain but to enlist a force of agents who act on behalf of planet Earth and all mankind. Trust me when I say that all mankind, and all living things, will need to be protected in the future.

I know I don't need to point out the obvious to an agent apprentice like yourself, but I will say it, anyway. We all share the same ball of life. It does not matter what religion, ethnic background, or country you reside in or, for that matter, your political beliefs. There is only one ball of life as we know it, and we are all interdependent, no matter how much that may bother you. I ask that you, as an apprentice agent, should you decide to accept the mission, work with my army to do what you can to save us all.

Obviously, you have a question now. *What are you talking about, Max? I just picked up this book because I was looking for adventure, or a pleasure read. I did not sign up as an agent.*

Sorry, reader, but you did. Until you can wake up on a planet other than Earth, you are an agent apprentice. Like it or not. Now, you may decide to ignore your mission assignment, but I hope you will not turn a blind eye to the cause. You will become a full-fledged agent when you finely start working to ensure the planet will be there for your descendants.

It really doesn't matter if there is only one person who buys this book and becomes a full-fledged agent or three-hundred million decide to join our force. It's all about the agent doing the most he or she can. Just one agent in the right place, with the right political power or influence, can change everything. You might say, *Yes, but I have no power. I am just one person of meager means.* You may ask, *How can I change anything to help planet Earth?* I say to you that you don't know who your descendants will be. Who you will influence and who you will enlist by having them read this book. Who will you share this story with. Each action will cause a chain reaction that may just be the right combination to save us all.

You are still reading. You want to know what I am talking about, don't you? So, let me do my best to share this story with you, for the assignment is perpetual. There is no backing out once you cross this line. At the end of this book, I will give you a chance to register and hear about the continuing mission. You will also be given an opportunity to follow the mission and join the force of the future.

CHAPTER ONE

YOUNG DESCENDANT

13.19.17.17.10| TZLOK'IN DATE: 1 OK | HAAB DATE:
8 SEK | LORD OF THE NIGHT: G8

It was Saturday, March 26, 2405, on a beautiful early spring morning, but not as cool as it used to be when I was a child back in the 1970s. It seemed, over the years, the weather had changed a bit in the Mid-Atlantic area with March temperatures now averaging 80° Fahrenheit (26.666° Celsius) compared to 60° Fahrenheit (15.555° Celsius) from back in the day. We used to anticipate planting our gardens with the purchase of seeds and, as I could recall, it had been the time we would start cleaning our fishing tackle in preparation of the spring fish runs of yellow perch and rock fish that would spawn in the Chesapeake Bay and its tributaries. Those days were now long gone.

Now, our food was grown in hydroponic indoor gardens, under artificial lights and in balanced atmospheres. Tasteless food that had all its nutrients added as an afterthought was all one could find to eat. It wasn't much better than eating grass, in my opinion, but vegetables could no longer grow in the open air and soil, leaving us with no other choice. I truly missed the taste of garden-grown tomatoes that had ripened on the vine, topping my sandwiches, and a fresh green salad. The fish no longer spawned in the freshwater rivers. Fortunately, you could still catch ocean fish, though. The mighty Chesapeake Bay no longer existed, either. It had been swallowed up by the Atlantic Ocean back in the 2200s.

The rising waters had forced the people who had once lived along the coast to move inland. Even the capital of the United States, Washington DC, had to be abandoned. The capital had eventually been relocated to Lexington, Kentucky.

I was an old man now, born in the 1960s, and it was time for me to pass the torch to one of my most promising descendants. Not only that, but I felt responsible for keeping all of humanity alive.

I had held my secrets for generations, knowing that if others discovered what secrets I possessed, man would destroy himself within a few years and plague the universe forevermore.

This young descendant of mine seemed to be the only person whom I could find capable of withstanding the temptation of releasing the knowledge that I was planning to unload upon him. He had the technical and mental aptitude to understand all the finite details and the implications of the power he would hold. I must confirm that I could trust him not to abuse the power. I prayed to God that his soul be honest and true to his word.

As written by Plato, "Mankind will never see an end of trouble until lovers of wisdom come to hold political power, or the holders of power become lovers of wisdom." I believed this descendant of mine was a man who was a lover of wisdom, and he was about to be offered the ultimate power.

Today, I was expecting my great-forty-five-times-grandchild, Scott Hickman, to visit. It had been hard to convince him to physically make the trip. He had wanted to meet me virtually, but I had let him know this meeting was way too important, so I had insisted we meet face-to-face, in the flesh.

Scott was twenty-five years old now and really didn't feel he needed to spend any time with an old man whom he had only met a few times in the past, at local events. To Scott, I was just a genetic mutation to whom he aspired to somehow inherit some of my longevity.

He was a single man, a graduate of the US Naval Academy, which was now located in Capon Bridge, West Virginia, on the shores of the Atlantic. Seemed the mountain valleys of West Virginia made excellent deep-water ports for the United States' Atlantic fleet. Anyway, Scott had graduated with honors, with a major in quantum physics and a minor in nuclear chemistry. He held the rank of Commodore and maintained a top-secret, Yankee-white security clearance, which was the highest in the land. He knew how to keep classified information secret, and he had advanced encryption training.

With the super quantum computers of today, almost any code ever written in my lifetime could be broken in hours. The only way I was able to keep critical information a secret was to keep it in my head. I didn't keep any critical information on my electronic devices, and I didn't communicate about the secrets I held electronically. At my age, there was a huge risk of losing everything. One trip, fall, or knock on the head, and all would be lost. Besides, time was of the essence, as the calendar counted the days.

Alexi identified Scott as he approached and announced the message throughout my dwelling, "*Scott Hickman is approaching your front door. Scott Hickman is approaching your front door.*"

"Thank you, Alexi," I told her, although I knew she was not a real person, and went to the door to greet him.

It was 1100 hours (11:00 AM). Perfect timing, as expected of a military man.

"Scott, welcome. Please, come in."

He responded with a, "Sir, yes, sir."

Scott reminded me of myself in my youth. He was about six-foot-two (187.96 cm), with light brown hair that was closely trimmed and dressed in his Navy officer's uniform. Clean shaven and in good physical shape, Scott seemed a little reserved. It was obvious he was not quite sure why I had insisted on his physical presence. He knew who I was and that I was really old. He also knew he was a direct descendant. However, our relationship was quite distant, though Scott did not know exactly how distant. Out of respect, and to avoid upsetting our living relatives, he had honored my request that he make his visit in person. I had set up our meeting for a Saturday because I understood that he was a busy man and, being a man in his position, could not easily get away during a normal weekday.

"Please, take a seat at the kitchen table and just call me Poppy. I need a minute to disable Alexi and my entire in-house network. We don't need her listening in or, for that matter, any of my appliances to start collecting information about our conversations and sharing everything," I told Scott. "By the way, will you turn off your mobile phone?"

Scott just snickered a little, as if to say "*really?*" but appeased me by carrying out my request.

I then started to explain. "I need a successor. A successor who will not abuse power and can keep life-dependent secrets. I am not talking about my life, and not just your life, but more than American lives—life for all things that exist on Earth. I am talking about information wielding so much power that it is beyond any other power on Earth, or anything you can even comprehend."

Scott shook his head, got a cocky smile on his face, and said, "Poppy, sir, do you need me to send you to a senior home or assisted living center? I understand you are very old, and Nana, Mam passed many years ago. Do you need my help? You can even move in with my mother and father. I already have their approval." He raised his hands in a placating gesture at the furious look on my face. "The family has been expecting this day would come. But don't worry; I, and the rest of the family, will take care of you if you need help and don't want to go into a center."

I could feel my blood pressure rising, and I was sure he saw the frustration on my face as my voice started to quiver and crack with anger, but I tried to keep my cool. I doubted they even knew what cool was anymore.

"Son, would you like to live a long life, like mine? To know more, do more, and explore more than anyone else on Earth, besides myself?" I asked. "This is an important question. You can earn a hundred doctorates and contribute to all the sciences that have ever been and all the sciences that may ever be. You can live a *really* long life. You can explore the farthest reaches of our galaxy and possibly galaxies beyond. I am serious, son; do you want this? And no, I don't need a nursing home or assisted living center. If you even suggest it again, I will make sure you were never born."

Of course, he could see on my face that I was not really threatening him with that, but he was doing his best to read me.

"Son, I will need a yes or no. Before you answer, however, there are things you need to consider. You will need to pledge to me that you will never share this information with anyone else, besides myself, until you near your end. Not a wife or girlfriend, kids, friends, or commanding officers, or anyone—ever! You must pledge not to use this power to hurt or destroy, and you must pledge to work with the US government to keep our democracy strong and our country secure. You will be forbidden from using the power and knowledge to just accumulate wealth and political power; however, reasonable use of the information to comfortably support yourself and family would be acceptable and expected. You will be making a covenant with God Almighty, and you will be struck down if you violate it."

I continued, "Please, think about what I am saying and take my old age and everything else you know about me into consideration. You need to understand that I work closely with the CIA and the executive branch of our government.

"Think about what I am saying and let me know if you are in. If you are, you will need to clear your calendar for next weekend and spend it here with me. Tell everyone you are going to go fishing with your poppy if they ask. You and I will need to spend some time together. Otherwise, I will continue my search for a successor outside of my own family blood line."

With that, Scott rose, turned on his phone, and said, "Poppy, sir, please do not call me *son*. I have a father, and he is the only one I allow to address me as such. I am normally addressed as Commodore Hickman. However, being as we are related, and you are a civilian, you may address me by my first name." He then tucked his chair back under the table and told me, "I'll get back to you on Wednesday. I need to think about all this before pledging to make such a promise."

I then told him, "Don't communicate with me electronically or discuss this matter with anyone else. I need you to deliver your decision in person. I will accommodate you no matter the hour."

I could tell he did not like the idea of having to come out to my place again, but he agreed. He grabbed his hat, tucked it under his left arm as he shook my hand, and made for the exit.

"No need to show me out, Poppy, sir, I will let myself out." Then he was gone, leaving me to wonder if I had chosen wisely.

CHAPTER TWO

THE DECISION

It had been like watching paint dry, just waiting for the arrival of the day. At my age, you didn't normally wish for time to pass quickly, yet here I was, as anxious as a child awaiting Christmas morning, anticipating what Santa had brought.

I turned off Alexi after I had her make my coffee and prepare my breakfast—an egg and English muffin sandwich with turkey bacon and cheese. I loved the way she made them things. But no matter how good the breakfast, I did not want her recording Scott's visit. So, I shut down the home network. Simple, just pulled the plug on the router for the satellite communicator. Then I sat back, sipping my coffee. Within a few minutes, there was a knock on my door.

I thought to myself, *Wow, Scott is as excited as I am. This is awesome.*

As fast as an old man could move, I went to the door to greet Scott. However, to my surprise, it was not Scott.

A man in a blue jumpsuit uniform with a name tag "*Jimmy*" greeted me with some satellite-looking insignia over the chest pocket. "Good morning, sir. My name is Jimmy. I am with your DS (DataStream) service provider. It seems your router lost connection to the satellite this morning. I am here to fix it. It's all part of your service agreement. There is no cost; I just need to check out your router. I will have you up and running in just a few moments."

"No, no need, Jimmy," I told him. "I pulled the plug to the router."

"Sir, you should not do that. You have no phone, no television, no communications at all, and none of your appliances can service you. Your electricity will even shut off if you are down for more than an hour or so. You can't even flush the toilet without the network. Heck, they will even send a paramedic to the house, being you are a senior. Sir, you need to plug the router back in. It's mandatory to keep your system connected."

I knew what Jimmy was telling me was correct, so no need to argue. Besides, I had not had my full cup of coffee yet, so my thoughts were seriously diminished.

"I'll plug it back in—no need to worry."

Jimmy insisted it be done immediately and waited to make sure it was reconnected. So, I plugged it back in, and he started tapping on his phone.

After a few minutes, he smiled and said, "Sir, you are now connected. Don't you feel better?" with a big smile on his face.

Being the grumpy old man I was, without having my caffeine fix yet, I told him, "No!" That was about as nice a response as I could muster, and it had taken all the restraint and fiber of my soul to limit my response to that one word. I could also picture myself knocking that cocky smile off his face.

Now I was confronted with an issue I had not anticipated. It seemed I was under CIA surveillance or being monitored by some other branch of the government. Maybe everyone was under this type of surveillance now? Who really knew? But I suspected that, with a service man arriving in less than fifteen minutes without me requesting it, something was up. They had not come so fast the last time I had pulled the plug. It was almost obvious they now considered me a person of interest.

It used to be a man had some privacy, but things were quite different in this day and age. I needed to get Scott and myself out of all surveillance areas. Out of the house, away from all the streetlight cameras, away from all vehicles, doorknob cameras, and obscured from all direct satellite view. If the government was monitoring my movements, I wanted to make sure they were not obtaining any critical intel. I couldn't let them record or even lip read my conversation with Scott. I needed to take Scott out of the bounds of their surveillance capabilities. Something old-school and quick.

I got it—my old workshop in the backyard. That should work. There was nothing hooked up to the DS back there, and I had a system established to obscure my movements. So, that was my plan.

After Alexi announced his arrival, I would signal to him not to talk, take his phone, and just ask him to walk back to my old shop. There, we could have a confidential conversation.

Midday came, and I still had not seen nor heard from Scott. I had Alexi fix me lunch. It was a mystery meat sandwich with rubber cheese on cardboard bread. I thought the condiments were the best part, but no matter. It kind of reminded me of my years as a Boy Scout. There had been a camp in Baltimore County, Maryland. The camp had been great, but the food had been less than stellar. So, to keep everyone from complaining to their parents, they'd used "Pleasing" brand foods. Everyone had been required to ask for the "Pleasing" food in the chow line. If you did not ask for it by its brand name, "Pleasing," they would not serve you. If the parents asked what the kids would be eating at the camp, the camp always replied they would serve only *Pleasing* food. It had even been in the brochure for the place. That type of thing would stick with a person their whole life, no matter how long they lived.

Now I was getting worried. It was almost dinnertime and still no sign of Scott yet. The sun set early this time of year, and the shadows were starting to get long. I found myself pacing and looking out the windows for any sign that Scott was coming, although I knew Alexi would announce his arrival well before I would be able to see him myself.

Suddenly, I heard Alexi make an announcement. "*Scott Hickman is approaching your back door. Scott Hickman is approaching your back door.*"

Great, but the back door?

I went to the back door, and I could see a tall, uniformed man walking up my dock toward the house. Yes, it was Scott. Apparently, he'd decided to make his visit by boat.

I opened the door and greeted him warmly, "Welcome, Scott."

He removed his hat and tucked it under his left arm, as he seemed to do every time the hat was removed, and said, "Good evening, sir." Then he made eye contact and shook my hand.

"Please, come in." -I signaled for him not to say anything with a shush hand signal—you know, with my index finger running from my chin, crossing both of my lips, and almost touching my nose. Apparently, that symbol was no longer used. Go figure. So, I said, "Don't say anything. Just place your phone on the table, and let's go to my shop. There is something I want to show you."

He nodded that he would comply, and the phone hit the table. Then I led the way out of the house, and I could hear the back door close as he left.

My old workshop was back some ways on my property. I had about nine acres

8

on the water, with cliffs in the back stretch. The shop sat about halfway between the two points. It was a good-sized, large block building. I called it my workshop, but it was really a lab, equipped with a tunnel that led up to the cliffs.

Scott was closing in on me, and I knew he wanted to say something, so I kept ahead of him in hopes that he would not attempt to speak until we got into the shop. That worked out, as we made it without a word.

I entered the shop and turned on the lights. Scott entered behind me, and I could see the surprise and curiosity on his face. He was totally taken aback by what he saw. His mouth fell open for a few moments as he slowly turned his head, and his eyes grew wide as he took it all in.

Scott started to walk around the lab, taking in the various pieces of what might have seemed like equipment from the 1931 Frankenstein movie to him. He pointed, asking what the various pieces were, and I told him they were all third generation pieces and parts. I showed him a soundwave generator that was capable of producing three different soundwave frequencies at high energy, all at the same time.

"Initially, I had to have three different sound generators that were each the size of a New York City phone book," I explained, but that really didn't help him envision it. He had never seen New York City, had no idea what a phone book was and, most likely, didn't even understand what a real book was. I had to laugh at myself after I made the comment.

After walking around the lab for about an hour, with him questioning anything odd that he saw, I offered him a stool at the counter, which had two full life-sized ceramic manikins sitting there as well. I saw him look at the stool as though he wanted to take a seat, but he hesitated, so as not to risk soiling his white whites. Perceiving his dilemma, I took a clean white rag from a stack I kept in the lab and covered the stool. He promptly seated himself upon it.

"We can talk now, so let me introduce you to Tom and Jerry." I laughed as I pointed to the two manikins.

Scott seemed a little hesitant to even speak. He whispered, "We can talk now?"

I nodded. "It's all safe. Tom and Jerry don't gossip."

He smiled then asked, "What's this lab for, and why would you need such a lab equipped with all this strange equipment?"

"I would love to tell you, but we have an important matter to resolve first. I need to know your answer. Are you interested in being my successor or not? And will you abide by the guidelines that I gave you?"

Scott cleared his throat, stood up, and looked me dead in the eyes. "Sir, yes, sir. I would be honored to be your successor, and after considerable thought and consideration, I pledge to abide by all the guidelines, as you have requested, sir."

I replied with a tiger's growl, "Great! And it's Poppy, not sir. Got it?"

"Yes, Poppy, sir."

I decided to let him get away with the "Poppy, sir" thing. I didn't think that was a habit I could get him to break.

"Will you join me for dinner this evening? I am serving cardboard mystery meat and tasteless vegetables."

He laughed. "I actually caught a good-sized fish as I trolled to the house—mahi-mahi. We could make a fine dinner with it, if you don't mind cooking it on the grill."

Now that sounded better than anything I had expected, so I agreed to have Alexi make up some macaroni and cheese to go with it and a side of tasteless broccoli. Then I walked to the lab refrigerator, which was not connected to the DS but rather a quite retro model that I had kept alive.

"You want a beer or something to drink?"

"I would love a beer," he replied.

I pulled out one of my special homemade brews for him, popped the top, and handed it to him.

As we headed toward the door, I said, "We are not going to discuss anything outside of the four walls of this shop. Just hold all your questions and please be patient. Let's just enjoy dinner."

Now, you must understand that grilling was not something everyone did in this day and age. I was one of the few people around who actually owned a working grill. Because of this, I had a sure invite to every community, church get-together, and all the fundraisers, no matter what the cause. They always asked me to bring my grill and grilling utensils.

There were few trees or wood fuels to feed a fire with, so there was no charcoal. Burning of fossil fuels, including wood and coal, was regulated and highly discouraged. It seemed the burning of fossil fuels had caused greenhouse gases to build up and warm the Earth, and all that was tied into the rising seas. If I recalled, that had been a topic being discussed back in the 2000s. Apparently, they had decided to start regulating all fossil fuel emissions.

Due to acid rain, there were few trees remaining. The trees that could tolerate the acidic rain were those that grew in silica soils located in the lowlands. Mountain soils were full of heavy metals that leached out and poisoned the trees that grew there. With the rising sea levels, the living trees were submerged, leaving only a few trees remaining.

Now, everything was cooked on electric ranges, in electric ovens, or with microwaves. Most appliances did the cooking and cleanup, so almost no one even knew how to cook anymore, let alone barbecue.

Years ago, I had taken an old metal oil tank and ran electric heating elements through cast iron pipes to take the place of the propane gas elements. Then I had installed an iron grate, and you know what? The damn thing worked almost as good as a gas grill. It took a little longer to get hot, and the wired-up heat controllers looked a little scary, but it worked good enough for me. Just don't lick your fingers before adjusting the temperature, and you would survive the electric shock.

I walked over to the grill that was on a patio near my dock. The dock lights had turned on with the setting sun, and I could see Scott's boat at the end of the pier. I turned on the grill, and the dock lights started to wane. I was probably using more electricity than half the town at that moment.

Scott walked down the dock, toward his boat, explaining, "I want to change out of this uniform. I'll bring the fish on my way back."

"That's fine," I told him. "The grill takes some time to heat up, anyway, and I need to ask Alexi to start fixing those sides." Seeing that Scott had finished his brew and had set the bottle on one of the pier pilings, I called out to him, "Do you want me to get you another beer?"

He gave me the thumbs-up sign and continued toward his boat.

Imagine that, the thumbs-up sign had survived time, yet the shush signal was lost to history.

With that, I made my way into the house and asked Alexi to fix up four servings of macaroni and cheese and two sides of broccoli.

"*Are you sure you want four servings*?" she asked.

"Yes, Alexi, four servings. I have a guest, and we plan to indulge a little this evening. I would like it served in about an hour."

"*I will prepare four servings of macaroni and cheese and two orders of broccoli to be served in one hour,*" Alexi responded.

I headed back out the door and made my way back to the workshop to withdraw another homemade brew for young Scott.

Unbeknownst to Scott, my special homemade brew was not your normal homemade brew. It was spiked with a virus that could withstand the alcohol. This virus was basically protected by being immune to alcohol, and it had special properties—one sip, and you got a cold that basically invaded your cells and implanted an altered set of genetic code throughout your body. It would only infect males who were my direct descendants. Most of the people on Earth were safe. They must carry my "Y" chromosome genes in their bloodline for the splice to take place. Then the "X" chromosome, mitochondria DNA, was changed. If anyone else were to drink the brew, it would only give them the typical buzz with no modifications to their genetic code. Ingenious, right? I thought so. However, I had not developed it myself and had to give the credit to some of my old lab partners, Todd and Ed. I had taken their work and done some advanced research, which had yielded this designer virus.

The virus itself had a limited contagion time. The carrier was contagious for eight hours or less. So, now I just needed to make sure Scott didn't visit any blood relatives for the next eight hours. I would feed him enough beer to get him buzzed then encourage him to spend the night, so as not to risk his life trying to get home. Getting him to stay until tomorrow morning should be easy enough.

This dosing became part of the secret package; he just didn't know about it yet. This was the part that would allow Scott to live as much as nine hundred years and for his body to replace any damaged or lost parts. If Scott eventually had children, they would gain some longevity and live to an average age of a hundred twenty years, but not the nine hundred that Scott should enjoy.

Most of my lineage enjoyed a one-hundred-twenty-year lifespan, as Scott would have. None of my lineage had any idea as to why they outlived most everyone else, except that Poppy had some great genes. Good genes were what the family all bragged about. Most seemed to be free of cancer, but I didn't know if anyone had regrown a lost appendage. None that I had heard of, anyway. However, I could cut off my finger, or anything, and it would grow back in time but usually a little smaller than the original, so I didn't want to test it again. One small toe had been more than enough to convince me that the gene splicing worked well enough. Besides, it had still hurt to cut something off until it healed completely.

Scott had no choice now; he had made his decision, and I had moved forward with my plans for him without him even knowing it. No need to even tell him yet. He would wake up with a slight cold tomorrow, as the virus did its work, and then, in a day or so, it would pass, leaving him with a superior set of genes.

I could see him returning from the fish cleaning station that was located at the end of the dock next to where his boat was tied. He was now dressed in casual attire. He had a pouch of foil in his hand with two nice-sized fish fillets.

"Wait just a minute—I'll get some non-stick cooking oil and seasoning," I told him. A few moments later, we had them cooking on that hotwired electric grill.

I handed him his second brew, and we talked about family and how everyone was doing.

Just as the fish were coming off the grill, I heard Alexi announce, "*The macaroni and broccoli are done. The macaroni and broccoli are done.*" Perfect timing.

We sat down at the kitchen table, and then I said a prayer. Afterward, we shared a wonderful first meal together.

Scott had a few more beers as we talked about more family matters and history. They were store-bought beer from the house refrigerator, devoid of my bio enhancements. I could tell Scott was starting to feel them.

"Please, feel free to spend the night—I have an extra room," I told Scott. "I would hate to see you trying to navigate the boat back in the dark." The winds were starting to pick up, and the seas were a bit choppy. You could see white caps in the moonlight.

"I planned on spending the night in the boat. I put in for leave already, so I am off-duty until Monday. I figured I deserve some time. Besides, I already told everyone that I was going to go fishing with my poppy." He grinned.

I knew Scott was a sharp guy, and I could see he had been thinking ahead—arriving by boat and having the fishing poles visible and in use, cooking the fish out on the grill where all could see them. All good.

It was starting to get late, and I could see Scott was itching to talk again.

13

"Can I get another beer from the workshop?"

"No," I responded. "Let's just call it a night, being you will be around for a few days. I am an old man, and I need my beauty sleep. You can use the guest head and the rack if you like. I'll see you in the morning, Scott. Have a good night."

"Yes, sir—I mean, Poppy, sir," he replied.

With that, I left the kitchen table, telling Alexi, "Clean up from dinner, please." She generally handled all the housework and rarely did I have to burden myself with any household cleaning chores.

I also had Alexi start my shower and get the water going to the perfect temperature. I could hear Scott doing the same in the guest bathroom. Apparently, he was either feeling comfortable enough to take me up on my offer or the beer had brought down his defenses some.

Immediately after my shower, I turned in and, as usual, I was out before my head hit the pillow.

CHAPTER THREE
EXPOSURE
13.19.17.17.15| TZLOK'IN DATE: 6 MEN | HAAB DATE: 13 SEK | LORD OF THE NIGHT: G4 GREGORIAN: MARCH 31, 2405

I awoke at about 0500 hours (5:00 AM), with the announcement from Alexi, *"Scott Hickman is approaching the back door. Stott Hickman is approaching the back door."* Then I heard the door slowly open then close. Scott had let himself in.

It seemed Scott had preferred to spend the night sleeping on his boat rather than listening to me snore.

I got up with my usual vigor—s-l-o-w motion. I could hear Scott sneezing and sniffling. The virus was doing its job.

Seeming a little upset that he was feeling under the weather, Scott said, "Good morning, Poppy, sir. It seems I have caught a cold or something, but I don't understand. I've already had my yearly cold vaccination. I can't imagine how I would get a cold this time of year."

"Not to worry," I told him. "I had the same cold recently. It only lasted about twenty-four hours. If it's the same thing, it will pass." I must say, he did look bad. His eyes were red and watery, his nose was running, and he was obviously uncomfortable. "I took antihistamine, which worked for me. You want one?"

"I can't just take medication. The Navy has very strict regulations and do random testing on everyone. It's standard procedure upon returning from several days' leave."

Apparently, an antihistamine was not going to be an option for poor Scott. I could see he was breaking down fast, and he stated he might need to visit the base medic. Then I remembered my wife used to complain about how even the biggest badass men turned into children when they got a cold. Military men crumbled, and mighty leaders retreated to the safety of their beds. Scott was proving to be no different.

I decided I would do for Scott what my wife used to do for me. I would baby him for the day, knowing I could not let him leave the property—he was still contagious, and I did not want to take any chances of him running into some relative and spreading the virus. Additionally, I was not about to tell him that I was the culprit who had exposed him to this virus, on purpose, or what it was about. At least, not yet, if it could be avoided.

I asked Alexi to make Scott an herbal tea for someone with a cold. "Please sweeten it a little with some honey. And fix a poached egg and some toast with a little butter and honey. Oh, and get Scott a box of his own tissues."

Alexi complied then asked, "*What would you like for breakfast this morning*?"

"One of those English muffin sandwiches that you make so well and a cup of coffee; one sugar and a little creamer."

And Alexi delivered without delay.

I noticed that it appeared a little stormy outside. As I watched the sunrise, I could see the harbor was quite rough looking. Not a day you would want to troll around, fishing on a boat the size of Scott's. This was working out better than I could have imagined.

"It looks rough out there. Maybe we should put off fishing until tomorrow. We can just work in the shop, cleaning up my old rods and fishing gear," I told Scott.

He smiled and replied, "Yes, Poppy, sir, I agree."

It was good Scott was apparently letting me take the lead, and he had enough wits about him that he knew we were talking in code so that if anyone were listening, they would not know what we were up to. I had been worried about that because, sometimes, a person could be book smart and just lack street smarts, as I called it. Scott, however, seemed to be the whole package, which was reassuring, considering he was already on a predestined journey.

After breakfast, we collected ourselves and made ready for the day. Of course, Scott was sneezing, snorting, and blowing his nose as we made our way to the workshop. I was now confident Scott wouldn't say the wrong thing outside of the shop. He was obviously on board.

"Where's your phone? You should leave it in the house. We don't want it to get ruined by the cleaners."

He raised an eyebrow, placed the phone on the table, and then blew his nose again.

As he settled in on an old couch I had in the shop, I set the box of tissues on the small table next to him. Then I came out and asked, "You have any recording devices on you? Any electronics or tracking devices?"

"The military inserted a small transponder in my left arm, just under the skin. It doesn't record or track, just an electronic set of dog tags."

"Hmm," I pondered. "We may have to deal with that sometime tomorrow. Anyway"—I clapped my hands together—"I don't know where to start. I've never had to do anything like this before. I'm just going to start with my dilemma, and we can go from there."

Scott nodded in agreement.

"The reason I contacted you is because I need to find a successor. I always wanted my successor to be a blood relative. By doing so, it would save me a lot of work. Now, look at the calendar on the wall." I waited until he did so before explaining, "That it is a Maya Long Count Calendar with an atomic clock below it. Below that is a countdown calendar with seven hundred twenty-six days remaining. Have you ever seen a Maya calendar before?"

"I'm not familiar with the Mayan calendar, but I know the Mayan people once ruled a large portion of Southern North America, which was once Mexico. The atomic clock, I'm familiar with because the military uses them worldwide."

Nodding, I continued, "The Maya calendar at the top started at the beginning of Mayan creation, which was August 11, 3114 BCE. The Maya calendar does not contain any leap years and is very accurate for calculating long periods of time. It allows one to identify every day. Long calculations of time are not usually important to most folk, but to me, it is imperative that I use such a calendar.

"The atomic clock has been in existence since 1948, and it's as accurate a clock as I can get." Then I started to spoon feed him a little information. "I have lived almost eight hundred ninety-eight years, even though I am only four hundred forty-three years old on December first."

I could see the wheels turning in his head. He had already known I was as old as dirt, but now I was claiming to be eight hundred ninety-eight years old and, out of my same mouth, telling him that I was four hundred forty-three years old. He didn't look like he was buying it.

I continued, "I only have until that Maya calendar ticks to 14.0.0.0.0 before I expire. I know it reads 13.19.17.17.15, but those numbers don't go to ninety-nine before they roll over. I have about two years left to live—seven hundred twenty-six days.

"I am sorry to hear that, Poppy, sir,"

"No, don't be sorry or sad. I have lived ten lives compared to any mortal man," I assured him. "Now, there is something I need to share with you. You, too, will live a long life, as I have." I could see Scott was surprised to hear that. Then he kind of cracked a joke in disbelief.

"How long will my junk continue to work?"

"It will work long enough to get you into trouble," I cracked back.

"Do I have to suck blood or sleep in the dirt?"

I smiled. "No, not a requirement, but it is optional. If you want to sleep in a dirt bed or in a coffin, that is your choice. I won't stop you."

"How does it all work?" he finally asked.

"I will answer all your questions in time. Today, you are here just so I can enlighten you some. Tomorrow, we will be taking a trip." When he went to protest, I told him, "Please, let me finish. I am old, and I lose my train of thought. Please, don't interrupt. You are a serious man, and now is the time to be as serious as possible."

"I'm sorry, Poppy, sir, but I am not buying this nine-hundred-year-old crap. How am I supposed to take something like that as a serious statement? You have got to be joking. There is no way any sane man would make such a claim."

I knew then that I was going to have to sacrifice another one of my toes to prove my point. This time, not for myself but for Scott.

I took off my shoe while he watched, proclaiming, "You really are a crazy old man."

Next, I removed my sock and took out a large fish-cleaning knife that was on the shelf. It was in there to be sharpened so, in retrospect, not a good choice. But, as it was, I used it to lop off my little left toe, right before Scott's eyes.

Scott jumped up with a wad of clean tissues and went for my foot as blood pumped out, screaming at me, "What the hell have you done, old man? Are you crazy?"

"It's okay," I repeated to him over and over. "I am all right, and I'm not crazy.

Watch. Look. It hurts really bad, but it's only been a minute and has already stopped bleeding."

After a few more moments, it became apparent that it was healing itself right before his eyes. Then, over the next hour, we watched my toe start to regenerate. At the same time, I explained, "I created a virus that could extend life and allow one's body to regrow any damaged appendage or organ." I showed him my foot again, propped up in his face, with my newly grown little toe now about half the size of the original. "It will continue to grow for a few more days, or maybe a week. Although it may not grow back to full size, it will be good enough for me to live out my life."

Now Scott was in total disbelief. He had just witnessed what most people would consider a miracle. The longevity story was suddenly a fact he must reckon with. He was now forced to believe everything I told him. Not easy to do with a tissue rolled up and stuffed halfway up into his cranial cavity.

That was when I laid it on him. "Scott, you have been exposed to the same virus, and I expect you will inherit the same capabilities. That's why you are sick today. By tomorrow, you will be able to do the same thing, as your nine-hundred-year journey has just begun, less about twenty-five years. The sniffles and sneezing will subside in the next day or so, and you will feel like a million bucks once you get through this cold, as all your organs regenerate and become fresh and undamaged.

"You see, many people in history have had the gift of longevity. The Old Testament of the Hebrew Bible lists Methuselah living nine hundred sixty-nine years, Jared living nine hundred sixty-two years, Noah living to nine hundred fifty years, and Adam living nine hundred thirty years. There was also Seth living nine hundred twelve years, and Enos lived to nine hundred five years. Those are just the persons mentioned in the Bible who lived for more than nine hundred years. There are many people in history who lived extended lives. Not all of them got a full nine hundred years, but they did a lot better than the average seventy years that most folks get these days. However, you and I are the only ones, who I know of, who will be able to claim we can regenerate an organ or appendage."

"Is this the power you claimed to hold and share?" Scott asked. "The great and mighty power that can rule the world and that I can never share with others? That God will strike me down for if I should mention it to anyone?"

"What were you expecting?" I asked. "Is there something more you want?"

I could see he was excited but, at the same time, disappointed and frustrated. To Scott, my secret was supposed to be much more.

Then, after a few moments of silence and a few sneezes on his part, I told him, "No, this is not the power I spoke to you about. However, this is the result of obtaining such power. This is only one of many powers you will possess; and no, you are not free to share this with anyone.

"Now, since you are not feeling too well today, I feel we should cut our meeting short and pick this up tomorrow. It's getting near lunch, and you look like you could use a grilled cheese sandwich and a bowl of Alexi's chicken noodle soup.

"Before we continue this meeting tomorrow, we will need to gather enough food and water to last a few days and move it into the shop. I will work on that. You might want to pack a few changes of underwear. Maybe a box of tissues and some toilet paper would also be a good idea. We are going on a camping trip."

"Where are we going?"

"You will travel far tomorrow and see much. Just work on getting better for now," I told him. "Now, let's go get that lunch. And please remember, now more than ever, to be very careful with what you say, even out in the open light of day. I am sure they are watching, and they are always suspicious of my actions."

After lunch, Scott took a nap on my couch as he watched a basketball game. It seemed March Madness was still alive and well after all these years. We had a couple cups of Alexi's herbal tea and talked about politics, weather, sports, and the normal stuff two guys would discuss while one was acting like a sneezing baby. Basically, killing the afternoon.

That evening, for dinner, we shared some of our leftover grilled fish, and Alexi fixed us some rice with broccoli and cheese to go along with the fish. Scott also got a second helping of chicken noodle soup. His color was coming back, the sneezing was less often, and I could see he was in full recovery.

We took a few hours to gather the food and amenities we would need for our camping trip. Scott said he would pack a bag in the boat and just bring it in the morning. He seemed a bit worried when I told him that we would not need a change of clothes, a tent, or any sleeping gear.

CHAPTER FOUR
CAMPING TRIP
13.19.17.17.16| TZLOK'IN DATE: 7 K'IB' | HAAB
DATE: 14 SEK | LORD OF THE NIGHT: G5
GREGORIAN: APRIL 1, 2405

At the morning's first light, Alexi made her announcement, *"Scott Hickman is approaching the back door. Scott Hickman is approaching the back door."*

I was up and enjoying my cup of coffee as I watched Scott make his way down the boat dock. I could see he was carrying a big blue duffle bag with the Navy insignia on it. I could also see he was limping a bit. I thought to myself that he might have hurt himself on the boat or dock last night. He hadn't seemed to be limping when I had last seen him at dinner.

I opened the door to help him in with his bag, and he greeted me with a, "Good morning, Poppy, sir."

"Good morning," I greeted back. "Come on in. We need a good breakfast in us before we start working on building that custom fishing rod."

He was sitting at the table, enjoying one of Alexi's fine breakfast meals with me when he reached into his pocket and pulled out a baggie.

I couldn't quite make out what it was, so I asked, "What's that? Fishing bait? Some new lure?"

He just smiled, didn't say a word, and shook his head.

Then it hit me. He had done it. He had cut that little bugger right off his left foot just like I had. However, I could not say anything more without risking Alexi eavesdropping on our conversation, but we would definitely have to resume the conversation in the shop.

Then Scott shocked me with the next thing he put on the table. It was another baggie that had a metallic capsule in it with a little blood. By the way he looked at me, I knew what it was. He had also cut the tracking device out of his arm. He then pointed to his arm, and I nodded to confirm that I understood. I snatched the baggie with the capsule off the table and put it in my pocket. I made a special mental note to leave it in the lab before we traversed the tunnel.

I then picked up all the gear that remained to be carried to the shop and signaled to Scott to do the same. "Let's get to work on making that rod. I'll show you how we used to do it."

Scott moved out of the house and started toward the shop as I followed.

The long count calendar read: *13.19.17.17.16 | 7 K'ib' | 14 Sek | G5*, and the atomic clock read: *0705 hours* (7:05 AM) as we entered the lab.

"Take note of the time and date," I told Scott, locking the door behind me after we entered. "Then plug the two ceramic manikins into the long extension cord."

Those manikins had been part of my anti-surveillance program for years. Normally, I just used one of them but, being that Scott needed to go off the radar with me today, we would plug them both in. They had a heating element that warmed them up to about 37°C (98.6°F), and the stools were on motorized wheels that were programmed to move up and down the bench every now and then in random patterns. All low-tech but enough to block satellite surveillance. They would see a few hot inferred (IR) signals that moved every so often if they were tracking me. Even if they used an IR surveillance gun or glasses from a closer range, all should look ordinary. There were no windows in the shop, so it wasn't like they could look in at will.

I took the baggie that contained the capsule from Scott's arm out of my pocket. "Do you want to be Tom or Jerry today?"

He pointed to Jerry, and I taped the baggie to Jerry's arm.

Wanting to complete the earlier conversation, now that we were in a secure environment, I said, "You had to try it. You just couldn't take my word for it, could ya? It hurt like shit, too, didn't it? And now you are stuck with that little toe for a long time."

"No, Poppy, sir. It grew back a little larger." He was excited about it. He had a big smile on that face that had me a little concerned about his reply.

"You better not get any bright ideas about cutting off some of your manly parts and expecting the same result. You just might be disappointed." It wasn't like I was willing to test it on every organ of mine. And who knew? Maybe not every organ or appendage would respond the same way.

"Now, come help me," I told Scott as I started to move one of the worktables. Then I pulled back the rubber floor mat to expose the trap door, asking, "Help me pull it open," so as to expose the ladder into the tunnel. I had constructed this tunnel many years ago. It was made of about two-foot-thick (61 cm) granite walls and ceiling. Good enough to keep out prying, surveilling eyes and capable of restricting electronic communications.

I turned on the lights in the tunnel. "Start climbing down," I directed, tossing down all our gear and supplies then moving to join him, pulling the access door closed behind me. As you looked down the tunnel, all you could see were lights mounted along the ceiling every ten feet (3 m) or so and the electrical conduit that fed it.

"Follow me," I told Scott.

It would take us up to the base of the cliffs that were partially on my property. I owned several hundred feet of them. Neighbors on both sides also owned a stretch of the cliffs, but they never seemed to bother visiting them. I didn't know if I had ever seen a neighbor walk the area. Being it was rather difficult to navigate the terrain along this line of fallen rocks and loose stones, I would think only the hardiest amongst us would even attempt it. I had eliminated the hazards with the construction of the tunnel that led me directly to the area we needed to get to.

As the tunnel came to an end, there was a door. It was made of heavy iron that had a skim of rust. It was laden with spider webs, and some cave crickets were dancing on the walls around the door. The hardware was difficult to operate, and I noted to Scott, "The lock and hinges could use some oil." Being this was all going to be his one day, I thought I should mention it. The last thing you would ever want was to get trapped in this tunnel or—even worse—have a problem getting into the tunnel to return to the shop building.

I pushed against the door and, with a squeak and groan, the old door swung open, revealing a chamber. The light only penetrated into the chamber a few feet (1 meter), but you could see it was dusty and had a somewhat musty smell like you would get in an antique shop.

I turned on the switch at the doorway, and it revealed that the chamber was actually the inside of a pyramid-shaped room. The pyramid was thirteen feet (3.9624 m) by thirteen (3.9624 m) feet with a ceiling whose four walls came together at a peak above us. This pyramid was much like the Sudan pyramids that had been built by the

Nubian Kushite people, and not like the Egyptian pyramids.

On the floor, there were two reclining chairs lined with leather cushions. There was a compartmented bookshelf where some paper money and coins were stacked, with each compartment dated for traveling backward in time. There was also a bin with a chip that contained WebDollars for traveling forward in time. Other compartments were filled with clothing that was vacuum bagged and labeled by size. These compartments were also dated. There was a battery-operated utility vehicle (ATV) and an air transport craft (ATC) that were both kept charged by the reactor and by the solar cells located on the outside of the pyramid. There was also a large, heavy iron garage door on one side of the pyramid to allow the ATV and ATC to be moved in and out.

A small nuclear reactor was built into the floor of the pyramid chamber. It was part of a thorium reactor development program that had once been going through development by the University of Maryland, but it been scratched back in the 2000s after funding had dried up. I had bought it as scrap from an online auction and had finished the project after I'd retired from the nuclear power plant. I had then used it in some of my early levitation experiments before repurposing it as a long-term power source. It was small and capable of generating the power I needed for thousands of years without having to be refueled often. Most of this reactor was underground and only the top could be seen in the chamber.

I turned to Scott and pointed toward the reactor. "The reactor is cooled with a molten salt system that uses a subterranean heat exchanger to maintain its required temperature."

Scott, having the nuclear background that he did, had a lot of questions about it and any exposure to a neutron flux that we might experience.

"Not to worry," I told him. "We'll be shielded well from neutron, gamma, and beta radiation. I even installed a system that permits refueling without any exposure. I already knew waste will be hazardous for about two hundred thousand years, but I figured there is only going to be about six pencils worth of waste ever generated by this reactor, and that it will be well worth it."

"What's a pencil?" he asked.

I could not believe it. I had to take the time to explain all about pencils and about how big they were, how to hold them, and what they were used for. "You're killing me," I exclaimed then pointed to the service manuals at the small control center. "Everything you need to know about operating the small reactor and refueling it can be found in those manuals. And that is what a book looks like, Scott. It is written in English, so don't forget how to read English."

Getting back on track, I continued, "I just refueled the reactor last year, so you should be good for hundreds of years or more. I always bring the system down slowly after each use, and it usually fires up without any problems." I walked over to the reactor control center and threw the main switch. "If a yellow light goes on, the reactor will need refueling in the next year, and if the red light goes on, it will require refueling before it operates. You just don't want to go too far for too long if the light is yellow. But no need to worry about the details now. You have a hundred years to get yourself familiar with the system before you need to do anything with it. The nuclear power procedure manuals make good bedtime reading."

Scott looked around. "What is this place, and what are we doing here? What do you mean, *too far for too long*? I thought we were going on a real camping trip or something."

"We're about to embark on a journey. You just need to pick a reclining chair and make yourself comfortable. And please, be patient. Now, take note of the calendar and clock on the wall." They were over the doorway where we had entered. The calendar had the same date as the one in the shop: 13.19.17.17.16-| 7 K'ib' | 14 Sek | G5, and the atomic clock now showed: 0745 hours (7:45 AM).

I walked over to the heavy iron door, closed it, and threw the large iron bolt, locking us in.

Scott was still walking around, taking in everything he could see. The money was of particular interest to him. Then he spotted the tray of gold nuggets in one of the compartments. He grabbed a handful and kind of weighed them. "You must be rich."

"What is mine will be yours. But that's not what this is about."

He noticed the acoustic speakers that were mounted in the corners of the pyramid at a height of about six feet (1.823 m), off the floor and one at the top peak, looking down on us.

I turned on some of the sound-generating equipment. "The sound level will be that of a very loud concert, but you won't be able to hear it because it is at a frequency that is inaudible to humans." The sound-generating equipment had been replaced many times over the years. Even so, it was now considered old for being an electronic device. It smelled a little like dust burning when I turned it on, and the lights were blinking and fading in and out. I knew we would be okay because I always had a couple of spares in the chamber, just in case.

"What's going on?" Scott asked a bit impatiently.

"Trust me; in a few minutes, you'll understand the true implications of all this."

When Scott finally took his place in one of the chairs, I said, "No matter what, do not get up and move around until I tell you it is safe."

He looked scared now. One more sneeze came out of him, and this time, it was from the dust.

I took my place in the main reclining chair with the controller next to it. I selected "*13.0.7.12.13 | 8 | 16 | G1, time 0813 hours (8:13 AM), July 25, 2020*" on the dials, pushed the green "*Go*" button, and we were off.

You could feel the nuclear power plant humming at full capacity, the lights were blinking, and the entire room seemed to be vibrating. All the dust in the place went airborne, and our skin tingled. I couldn't explain the total feeling, except to say that it was like riding your bike through the DDT mosquito spray clouds back in the 1970s. The tingle on our skin was a chemical burning tingle, and the ionic cloud obscured our vision and made it hard to breathe. This all lasted for about five minutes, and then the tingling stopped, the cloud cleared, and the reactor could be heard winding down.

I gave it a few more minutes then told Scott, "It's safe to get up now. Welcome to the past."

13.0.7.12.13 TZLOK'IN DATE: 8 B'EN | HAAB DATE: 16 XUL | LORD OF THE NIGHT: G1 GREGORIAN: JULY 25, 2020

Scott looked around, not seeing anything that he could detect had changed. He just stood there in disbelief.

"Look at the calendar," I told him.

The clock now read 0813 hours.

I took a pad of paper and a pencil, jotting down our arrival date and time.

Scott was not impressed. "Poppy, sir, I don't really think we did anything. You're just making this crap up, aren't you? Funning with me."

"No," I responded. "Now, we need to get out of this chamber and back to the shop. We can leave the food and everything else in here. Figure on sleeping in here every night we stay, but we are free to walk around. The most important thing is to not get picked up by the authorities, being we don't really have any valid identification." I turned on one last switch in the chamber. It was the switch to notify my 2020 me, and my 2020 wife, that I was there. It turned on a red light over the dining room.

Yes, I had to let me, living in my home with my wife, know that I was time traveling and in the same time zone. That way, the 2020 me, and the 2020 wife, could help if needed, and they could make themselves available in case we needed to discuss anything.

I grabbed some money out of the compartment marked "*2020*" and some clothes from the clothing compartment marked "*2020*," as well. These items would be vital to survival. Then I unlocked the big iron door and swung it open. I turned on the lights, and we proceeded back the way we had come in—up the ladder, and then I pushed open the trap door. Luckily, I (2020 me) had not blocked the trap door with furniture or anything and only a rubber mat restricted egress.

After we both crawled through the opening and back into my shop, I proceeded to the door where the light switches were located. I turned them on to reveal old Tom and Jerry, still sitting at their places. The shop looked different, being it was quite new at the time. Much different than the one Scott and I had departed from. The shop had been built over some twenty times. This one looked more like a true laboratory and not like some old woodworking shop.

Now Scott needed to find out if everything I was telling him was true. I had told him that we traveled back in time, and yes, the shop now looked a little different. He had felt the tingle, he'd seen the lights blink, but was it real? How would he really know?

I sat Scott down. "Before I go into proving anything, you need some vital information. First, don't forget what the date and time was when you started your travel. This is very important so your soul won't be split between two bodies when you return. Best to write it down before you take off and keep it next to the controls of the time machine. Next, in order to know one's actual age, you have to track the time duration in these other time periods. Best to write down the date of arrival, and then write down the date when you leave. Yes, all this writing should be done with a pencil, in a log. It actually works better than a pen, and computers won't hold information as they pass through time. This could be especially important if you are to stay any length of time in a different time period or if you jump from one time period to another.

"Next, do all you can to avoid changing history unless it is imperative to do so to save our country or mankind. This means not fathering children, not hurting or killing anyone, not running for political office, or taking advantage of others. Some things may not be avoidable, such as accidents. But, if possible, jump back to time before the accident and tell yourself what will happen so you can avoid it.

"This brings up one last issue that I almost forgot to mention. You can exist in one time period multiple times, but this can be very confusing, and you will be spending your living life twice as fast. If necessary, keep the periods of double living brief."

I then warned him, "This world is very different than anything you have ever known. There are trees, and we are in the mountains with freshwater streams. There are bears, wolves, coyotes, snakes, and all types of animals outside that door. You could be hurt or killed if you do not respect the environment and the creatures that are around. The biggest danger is the other humans, especially up in the mountains during hunting season. Now, go change your clothes if you expect to survive."

"Why?"

"Synthetic pants aren't really popular in this time period," I answered.

"But they are climate controlled, non-rip, and puncture resistant," he argued.

"Scott, those silky-looking, tight nylon pants might get you shot here in West Virginia. If you don't change them, you will have so many holes in them that you will leak out of them."

"Fine," he huffed. He did not understand, but he did change clothes after my vivid description of his possible demise. Then Scott asked, "Is there anything else I need to know?"

"Yes, don't tie a white bandana on your head and skip through the woods." I got a good chuckle out of that one. I cracked myself up, but he did not have a clue that I was referring to getting shot as a white-tailed deer.

Now we were ready for Scott's first outing into 2020. I couldn't wait to see his face as the door swung open. Like a child's first Christmas, or like seeing the ocean for the first time, I knew it was a once in a lifetime event, something I had experienced myself when I'd visited the Jurassic time period. But that's a different story.

Light beamed into the relatively dark room as the door swung open and the fresh air came in a gush. I had forgotten that sweet smell of morning mountain air. You could still smell the dew. And all one could see from the doorway were tall, standing trees and greenery.

Scott took one step out of the door and dropped to his knees with marvel. Time travel had been confirmed, signed, sealed, and delivered to Scott. He was experiencing the big secret, and there was no doubt his expectations had been met. There was no turning back now.

We could hear the birds as they called and chirped to each other, dancing from branch to branch in search of their daily bread. The mountain brook, Dillan's Run, babbled along with trout rising every now and then to snatch an insect from the surface. Deer were on the edge of the woods, near the fields, returning from their nightly grazing.

"This is God's country, wild and wonderful," I declared.

This was why I had built my cabin here. I had never expected that this valley and stream would become a saltwater ocean harbor. But after having traveled into the future and back into the past, I had found that these mountains were one of the oldest in the world and highly stable. The rising waters would never cover this location, and it made the perfect base camp.

Scott followed me as we traveled down the path to the cabin. I knocked on the door, even though it was my house, so as not to intrude on myself and my wife. The door slowly opened, and there she was, the love of my life, more beautiful than I had even remembered or any photograph I was able to duplicate.

In her warm, soft voice, she said, "Good morning, Max. And, who do we have here?"

"This is our forty-fifth great-great-grandchild, Scott Hickman," I introduced him to Terri.

Scott stepped up. "Good morning, ma'am."

Like me, she didn't like the formalities and gave him a hearty squeeze and a peck on the cheek. "Please, just call me Nana," she said. "Come on in and join us for breakfast."

There "I" was, sitting at the table, eating again. Didn't even bother getting up to answer the door for my own self.

"I have been expecting you," 2020 Max addressed me.

I smiled then turned to Terri. "We already had breakfast before traveling, but a cup of coffee would be great."

"I could go for a cup, as well," Scott said.

So, we joined myself, 2020 Max, and my wife, Terri, at the table.

2020 Max asked Scott about himself, and as Scott went into listing his accomplishments and life story, I found myself phasing out of the conversation and just staring at Terri as she ate her breakfast and moved around the table.

Later that day, I thought I would show Scott around and let him enjoy the world a little differently than anything he had ever experienced before. We drove the pickup truck to town. Watched as people walked from store to store. I even bought Scott an ice cream cone with paper money. He had never seen such a thing and found the whole experience amazing. I thought he found the birds and squirrels the most mesmerizing. You could see he could not get enough of watching the birds hop from branch to branch or the squirrels running up and down the trees, collecting acorns.

We stopped by a Mexican restaurant and had some wonderful burritos and tacos with fresh lettuce, tomatoes, onions, beans, and rice, all seasoned to perfection and smothered in cheese. Scott had never tasted such wonderful foods. I could tell he might not want to go back, and I would not blame him if he decided to stay for a lifetime or two. It would be his choice.

After an afternoon out, we returned to the cabin. I thanked my wife and myself (2020 Max) then led Scott to the lab.

"Take a seat and make yourself comfortable," I told Scott. Then I got him a drink and some popcorn and said, "I want to tell you the story from the beginning. It's going to take me some time, but I think it's important so you understand what you will need to do in the future and why I brought you here. Now, let me start from the beginning."

Scott kicked back on the couch as I started telling him everything.

CHAPTER FIVE

TERRI & MAX

13.0.7.9.2| TZLOK'IN DATE: 2 IK' | HAAB DATE: 5
SIP | LORD OF THE NIGHT: G2
GREGORIAN: MAY 15, 2020

Terri and I had gotten married right out of high school, at the young age of seventeen, on 12.18.6.15.0 | 11 Ajaw | 3 Pop | G3, April 13, 1980. We had two children together; one girl and one boy, who in turn each had two children—a boy and a girl. Unfortunately, once the children had started their own families, they moved away and had little contact with us. We would spend time with the grandchildren when we could, but even that was limited due to everyone's schedules and the distances that separated us. Terri was the love of my life, and we were married for ... let me think, forty years this past April 13, 2020.

She had been a smart, honest, loyal woman and, right from the start, she had known what she wanted and was willing to work for it. Terri had also been a woman who had demanded respect. She had run a tight ship and had insisted on everything being orderly. You could not move anything in the house without her knowledge, and if you did move something, and she did not approve, it would be returned to its proper position within a day. Each thing had a purpose and a place, and that was the way she had kept it. I loved her for all those things. She had kept my life in order, being I was the exact opposite when it came to organization and detail.

Terri had also been a great cook, and she could turn chicken shit into chicken salad. Maybe not that good, but she could give one of those televised chefs a run for their money, for sure.

Terri had also been the driving force in my life that had inspired me to attend college and get my degree in bioengineering. Then, later, she had encouraged me to attend school in nuclear physics. I could tell you, without her strong support, I would not have been able to complete any of those things, and I might have led my life working some remedial job. Who knew?

Having just retired with an education in Bioengineering and Nuclear Physics, I thought I would make some great discoveries one day. I had taken a job that had paid the bills, like many other people did, but it had left me empty because I could not just chase my dreams, theories, and hypothesis. So, after working more than thirty years at the nuclear power plant as an equipment maintenance engineer, I had decided to retire.

I had acquired a great arsenal of unstable and undependable equipment that the utility companies could no longer rely on. With a burning desire to research all my theories, I repaired the equipment I needed to carry out my own research.

I had always theorized that anti-gravity matter existed, but one was not going to find it on Earth. Why? It repelled matter, and it had been my theory that this anti-gravity matter was actually above and below and all around the plain of our universe, kind of like two positives repelling each other with our negative universe planets sandwiched in a neutral field between the anti-gravity forces. In layman terms, a large bowl of gelatin with a pineapple circle suspended in the middle and a cherry in the middle of that, topped with another layer of gelatin.- This was why I had theorized most universes stayed in a plane and only a universe that had been impacted by another force would break from this structure because its anti-gravity matter was out of balance with the matter sandwiched between. Otherwise, the matter of the universe stayed in a plane. The same forces seemed to keep our solar system in alignment, and surrounding solar systems, as well. I was sure, with the billions and billions of variations in the universe, there might have been planets that orbited their sun in random, unaligned orbits, and universes that did the same, but I thought they were the exception and not the rule. I didn't believe that would be the case if anti-gravity was not forcing them into a plane.

To research my theories, I had acquired the scrap thorium reactor and had installed it in the lab. I got it up and running then used a rabbit system and subjected samples into a neutron flux for various amounts of time in hopes that I would stumble on the right combination that would render anti-matter. This experiment proved to be dangerous and generated a lot more radioactive waste than I had initially anticipated.

After a short time, I changed paths and started building my experiments to use acoustic energy to alter the behavior of matter by having the interaction of various frequencies act upon various isotopes. I set the lab up to experiment with acoustic levitation where several automated acoustic experiments were going on at the same time. Each experiment was a set of acoustic speakers mounted in a bowl configuration that pointed upward and was in its own soundproof chamber.

As most people experimenting with acoustic levitation at the time, I was messing around in the 22 kilohertz frequency range. I used a laser setup to detect the movement of various types of matter as the computer cycled through the various frequencies that were being generated by high-powered frequency generators. The computer kept track of the time and the frequencies that were being generated then set up an algorithm being managed by artificial intelligence (AI) to pick the most probable combination to try next. Unlike anyone else, I decided to move forward using three frequencies at a time and not limiting my research to two frequencies.

The number three signified unity, perfection, and creation. The three rings were the Tripod of Life, and those rings made the foundation of the Seed of Life. This was the underlying strength of the Flower of Life, believed to contain all the patterns of creation. The Flower of Life was considered the physical representation of space and time. When three overlapping rings in the Tripod of Life were in three-dimensional form, energy was generated and emitted. Other symbols, hidden within the Flower of Life, included the six pointed star, the Merkaba, time itself (twelve even points), and the Tree of Life. The Latin principle *"Omne trium perfctum,"* where everything that came in threes was perfect and complete. Besides, Nikola Tesla liked threes, as well.

Tripod of Life   Seed of Life   Flower of Life

I was just looking for that right combination, capable of lifting one hundred grams of anything, and because history had proven the power of three. I concentrated my experiments on combinations of three separate frequencies, each focused on a target.

All the frequencies that I experimented with were out of the audible range for most animals, with the exception of maybe bats, whales, and dogs. I kept them operating inside soundproof chambers to limit their impact on each other and nature. The speakers produced so much sound that if a person were to enter the sound chambers and could hear it, it would be like sitting next to the speakers at a major rock concert, times two or three. I mean brain damaging loud but, to us humans, it was quiet, and outside of the sound chambers, I didn't think it would even bother a dog.

CHAPTER SIX

THE ACCIDENT

13.0.7.9.3| TZLOK'IN DATE: 3 AK'B'AL | HAAB
DATE: 6 SIP | LORD OF THE NIGHT: G3
GREGORIAN: MAY 16, 2020

It was Terri who had caused the accident that had discovered time travel. Being the ultimate neat and orderly clean freak, she had decided she was going to help me out by cleaning my shop/lab up while I was out hiking a section of Appalachian Trail with my good, longtime friend, Robert Smith. It was just as the Covid Pandemic was unofficially winding down and, like everyone else, I had felt the need to get out of the house.

As Terri went through the lab, dusting, cleaning, and straightening everything out, she accidentally unplugged all three sets of sound generators leading into one of the sound chambers. Not really sure where the loose ends had come from, she had spied three input ports and plugged them in. These ports were actually part of a separate experiment in a separate sound booth. There had already been three frequencies in use in this second chamber, and now Terri had added an additional three frequencies. There was now twice the power, two sets of three energies, with a total of six frequencies working on the mass that was to be moved. All this was unknown to her, and so she went about her dusting and cleaning. Then, when done, she turned off the lights.

In the meantime, the computer was not aware of the additional frequencies, so both sets of computers were running through various combinations.

At some point, the steel ball on the setup that Terri had added the additional three frequencies to just disappeared. The laser system registered it as a liftoff, printed the data in red with a time and date stamp, and stopped cycling because it had completely lost the mass sample, but the other experiment was not registering a liftoff and just kept cycling through various combinations. I had not programmed the unit that lost its mass to actually shut down, just to stop cycling. Therefore, it continued to broadcast the three frequencies that had been broadcasting when the mass had disappeared. Fortunately, both systems used the same atomic clock to track the frequencies and the computers kept a record of each. Then something strange happened—the mass reappeared.

When I returned from my hiking trip with my friend, Robert, Terri told me that she had taken the initiative to dust and clean the shop. I was sure I turned pale with the thought that she had messed up everything. She told me that if I had taken care of it myself, she would not have to do it. So, if there was anything messed up, it was on me.

Way too tired from the hike to argue or deal with anything at that moment, I walked out of the house and went to the lab. I just shut down the experiments, figuring I could study the results the next day after I'd had a good meal and a good night's sleep.

13.0.7.9.4 | TZLOK'IN DATE: 4 K'AN | HAAB DATE: 7 SIP | LORD OF THE NIGHT: G4 GREGORIAN: MAY 17, 2020

The next morning, I returned to the lab to find that the matter in both test labs were still in place. I pulled the reports from both computers and started analyzing them. To my surprise, one of the test labs had shown that the matter had lifted off. In an attempt to duplicate the liftoff, I set the three frequencies to those in the report that corresponded to the liftoff. With that done, I turned on the unit and found that the matter did not elevate, or levitate in any manner. I was somewhat confused by these findings.

It was only after closer examination of the test booths that I discovered that there were six wires hooked up to the test booth where the liftoff had occurred, and no wires were hooked up to the second booth. Once I noticed this, I had an idea who was behind the issue.

I checked the report to find out what frequencies were being produced by the second set of frequency generators at the time the mass had lifted off. I then set up the second set of sound generators to reproduce those frequencies and turned them on at the same time as the first set. What happened next was mind blowing.

The 100-gram steel ball did not rise up off of the bowl of acoustic speakers as I had thought the experiment had documented. Instead, the 100-gram ball just disappeared.

I tried it over and over just to make sure, each time with a new ball, thinking it was shooting through the roof so fast that I could not see it, or maybe vaporizing it. But no, no burning or levitation at all. It just disappeared.

I had to wonder how it could have disappeared, being the 100-gram mass had still been there when I had returned to the lab after my hike. So, that was when I figured out that if the first set of three frequencies was maintained, the second set of three had to be a set of three different frequencies that followed after the time of the mass disappearance.

Systematically, I had the computer replicate the experiment from the time of the recorded disappearance to the time that I had shut down the experiment. This time, the laser switch was set to stop the experiment when the object appeared.

I watched for hours, afraid that if I blinked, I would miss the moment it happened. Then, suddenly, after about four hours, six steel 100-gram balls clunked to the place that I had set each of the steel balls before. Each rolled off the other, and they all hit the table then each fell to the floor. They were back. From where, I didn't know, but they had gone and returned, and I had the priceless data.

I had real questions now, and a real project to work on. I worked endlessly every day and discovered many combinations that would cause the mass to disappear and corresponding combinations that caused the mass to reappear. These combinations seemed to be related to each other, and the AI computer I was using quickly identified correlation.

After some time, I was able to send and receive the mass quickly and precisely, and I found a whole set of frequency ranges that worked. However, I still did not know where the mass was going.

13.0.7.9.11 | TZLOK'IN DATE: 11 CHUWEN | HAAB DATE: 14 SIP | LORD OF THE NIGHT: G2 GREGORIAN: MAY 24, 2020

In order to find out where the mass was going, I built a new, larger acoustic test

PERPETUUM

chamber. This setup was exactly the same as the original set; however, the bowl formation was now upside down in the booth so that the speakers hung from various locations around the soundproof booth ceiling and pointed downward. I figured that, being the mass was not lifting off, there was no reason to point them upward. I was no longer counteracting gravity but something extremely different. The whole setup was larger, and I thought the best way to see where the mass was going was to send a camera hooked to a video monitor.

I plugged in one of the frequencies that I had found worked and hit the button. In a flash, the camera disappeared, but nothing was showing up on the monitor. It was obvious the cable had been cut or, let's say, no longer connected to the camera that I had sent. I entered the corresponding frequencies that made the mass return, and yes, the camera was back, but the cable was severed from the end running into the monitor. That was not going to work.

Then I tried a video camera with a SD card. I turned on the camera to record, plugged in the frequency combination, and the camera disappeared as I had predicted it would. After a few moments, I entered the corresponding frequencies that should make it return, and yes, it returned. I removed the SD chip and plugged it into my computer to see what had been recorded. I was so excited. Was I going to be the first to see a new dimension? Where was it going?

To my disappointment, the SD card only rendered a pixelated mess. Yes, there were some images, but I couldn't make anything out. Apparently, the file had been corrupted in the process.

I put my low-tech brain into action. What could I use to get an image of this place? I thought about using one of those instant film cameras, but it would have been a miracle to find one working with film that was still good. Then I would have to jerry rig the camera to actually take the photograph.

As the days went by, I finally rigged up a digital camera that would print out the images on a small, battery-operated printer. I set it all up and tested it to make sure it would automatically take photos and print them. I figured anywhere from three to ten photos would give me what I needed. Then I set the camera up on a tripod and rigged it to rotate slowly. All looked good, so I sent it off like the others and called it back as before. This time, I struck gold.

The photographs were there, all stacked up nicely on the printer. They revealed trees, rocks, and cliffs, just like the ones outside my lab. I could see the concrete pad that the tripod was mounted to, the legs of the tripod.

I walked outside of my lab and, sure enough, it was the same cliffs, yet the trees were different. Most of the larger rocks were in the same place, but some of the smaller rocks had changed positions. Being the camera was taking photographs, and both my cabin and lab were not in any of the photographs, I figured it might have been from a time before my cabin and lab had been built.

I tried this experiment several times, and then I reversed the order of the frequencies; first, sending the retrieval set then the sending set. The tripod, camera, and printer disappeared all the same, and then returned. However, this time, the photos were of the inside of my lab's acoustic test chamber, with obvious signs of disrepair.

I had discovered time travel.

I was able to send the camera to the future, and then bring it back. Or, should I say, Terri had accidentally discovered time travel, and I had perfected it.

I could hardly wait to tell Terri about my research and everything that I had discovered.

I took the printed photos that had returned from the future and showed them to her. I sat her down and explained everything over lunch. I might have mentioned a few times that we were going to be rich, that we had discovered time travel and the world would be our oyster. We were both so happy and went out to dinner that evening to celebrate over a few glasses of champagne. It was a high point of our lives together. An incredible discovery and the promise of having all we needed in our senior years. But it was Terri who cautioned me that I should tell no one until we thought this through.

Terri knew how excited I was, and that, in my current state of mind, I would go tell everybody, and then we could risk losing this great discovery. She cautioned me over and over, and I was glad she did.

As we got past the initial endorphin rush, common sense started working again on a normal level. It became obvious that if this research was as it seemed, then there was unlimited power associated with it. Every government in the world would want to control something like this if they knew about it. We were not safe if word got out.

CHAPTER SEVEN

HALF-LIFE

13.0.7.9.19 | TZLOK'IN DATE: 6 KAWAK | HAAB
DATE: 2 SOTZ' | LORD OF THE NIGHT: G1
GREGORIAN: JUNE 1, 2020

Now the hard work had to be done—trying to find out what frequencies took the objects to what date.

I could not just send a watch or clock and photograph it, because the items sent did not age. A watch sent to a new time period would still read at the same time as it would have in the lab. I thought about this, and the only solution I could come up with was to use more of my old nuclear power equipment and lab training. Knowing that radioactive sources of every isotope decay at a known rate, this rate of decay -is known as a half-life. A half-life is the time it takes for any isotope to lose half its energy. My thinking was that I could place several radioactive sources, such as Americium-241 with a half-life of 432.2 years, Radium-226 with a half-life of 226 years, and a Carbon-14 with a half-life of 5,730 years, just outside of the control booth and locate the detector just inside, inches away. Then I would take a reading before I sent the detector forward through time. I would then have the detector take a second reading after traveling to the new time period. By comparing the two readings, I could determine the loss of energy and calculate the time difference.

To make this work for traveling back through time, I would send the isotope sources back in time and use the mass spectrometer to take readings inside the acoustic test booth at my present time, comparing the two readings to determine how much each source had decayed.

I set the acoustic test chambers up to carry out these tests. It took me about two weeks to get all my data plugged into the computer so I could see how far each set of frequencies were moving the objects through time.

The real surprising discovery was that the computer running the AI software had identified that the Maya calendar was directly related to the various frequencies and basically a simple math equation was all I needed to figure out what frequency was needed to travel forward or backward. I did not believe that this association was a coincidence and hoped that I could possibly prove it one day. Neither Mayan history nor calendars were my expertise so, hopefully, I could bring in some experts to help me identify whether the association was intentional or just coincidence. Who knew? This might be the reason the Mayan people seemed to have disappeared. Maybe they had just time traveled to a different time period and still continue to exist. Interesting thought.

Actually, there had been many groups of people who seemed to have disappeared without a trace. I might really be on to something here. They were not abducted by aliens but, rather, they might be moving through time undetected.

Getting back to it, test after test was producing data that eventually made it easy to predict what frequency would send and return the mass to a predictable point, both forward and backward in time. I was able to lock in a simple system to send and receive inanimate items both forward and backward into time to predictable dates. This was a major accomplishment, but could I send a living organism?

I started off with what I had—bugs, lots of bugs. They had remained unchanged for millions of years, so I figured they were safe to send. Heck, they must have bugs in the future, and if not, they could thank me later. A simple cricket—I called him Peepers—was the first time-traveler. He went backward about a hundred years then returned apparently unscathed by the trip. Although I did not see any issues with Peepers, I didn't know if he was still thinking clearly.

Next, I acquired a trained rat, Nibbles. Nibbles could run a maze in about two minutes. I caged Nibbles up, sent him one thousand years back in time, then retrieved him. I tested Nibbles after his return, and he finished the maze without an issue. Lastly, I sent Nibbles forward one thousand years. When Nibbles returned, he was dead. He had a twig going through him. Poor Nibbles. I gave him a proper burial and said a prayer for him. Yes, I prayed over a dead rat.

A new issue—what happened as the landscape changed? Then I started to think about all the other things that could happen. What if the air did not have the right oxygen content? What if this location was under water, on fire, or there was a large predator standing there when you popped into their time period? Radiation exposure could be an issue. This took me some time to figure out. Back to the drawing board.

It occurred to me that, at every monolithic site, there was a location that was theorized to be a portal. That it had always been built into a mountain, cave, rock archway, or in a secure place where trees would not grow, and it was unlikely that anything else would impact the location. But how to do all this testing and secure a safe transport location?

My solution was to build a pyramid with thick granite walls and send it back as far as I could in time. The acoustic speakers would be on the outside of the pyramid to do this. Then I would move the acoustic speakers inside and transport myself back to my current time, leaving the pyramid in place. I would bring test equipment with me and enough bottled air to keep me alive for an hour. This would give me time to test for radiation and the atmosphere. If necessary, I would have time to change time periods if the atmosphere was toxic, returning if necessary.

I did some research on various types of pyramids and found that the Sudan pyramids were not as old as the Egyptian pyramids, yet they were much easier to build than the Egyptian pyramids. They were not as large, either, which would work better for my purpose. I didn't believe I had the resources to build a large Egyptian pyramid, but I was sure I could pull off building a smaller Sudan-style pyramid.

Being that I was not an architect, I chose an important masonic size—thirteen feet (3.9624 m) by thirteen feet (3.9624 m) feet, with a ceiling whose four walls came together at a peak. I carved an all-seeing eye on one side, making it look like the Egyptian Eye of Horus.

I retired the thorium reactor from the isotope, making source tasks that I had been using it for. I had accumulated quite a few radioactive sources and was sure I would not need any additional material for some time. The thorium reactor was to be repurposed and installed under the pyramid with just the controls and access port in the pyramid. It was set up to generate about 40 kilowatts of electricity. This was more than enough to power the acoustic equipment and meet my basic needs.

I spent the next year building my pyramid upon the flat surface of a large stone next to the cliffs on my property, connecting it to my shop/lab via tunnel that was constructed to be airtight and earthquake proof. I also worked on perfecting the time transport system.

Scott was on his feet at this point, kind of wandering around the lab, looking at everything, as I continued.

"I felt I was at the point where I was ready for my first trip in time—"

"I need a bathroom break," he interrupted me, stretching.

So, I put my story on hold. We took a couple of folding chairs and placed them just outside the lab in the woods. I could see that Scott was still completely amazed by all the sights and sounds, and yet we were not really doing anything.

After about a half-hour break, I asked, "Do you want to hear the rest of the story?"

He nodded his head, and we went back into the lab. Scott took his position on the couch, and I continued with my story.

"It's hell getting old. Where was I? Yes, It was 13.0.8.10.18 | 8 Etz'Nab | 16 Sotz' | G2, June 15, 2021." Terri was totally against my trying to time travel by myself, but I was determined to proceed. I felt that I would gain the most by traveling forward in time. However, I needed to put the pyramid in place as far back as possible to secure a safe transport location for all time periods that followed. But, how far back did I dare go? I felt that the Jurassic period would be adequate for anything I had interest in and could not imagine I needed to visit any time period prior to two hundred million years. I also knew that caution had to be taken around any time periods of mass extinction.

The Triassic period ended with a mass extinction, and the Cretaceous period ended with the extinction of the dinosaurs. I didn't want to be there those days, for sure. Therefore, much caution was needed when placing the pyramid.

I thought I would go back and place the pyramid at -380,200.0.0.0.0. What a risk. I was going to go back in time 149,996,504 years, some 54,748,723,960 rotations of the Earth, move the acoustic equipment to the interior of the pyramid, and then return to this current time period, and with the expectation of being deposited into the old pyramid. The pyramid would have to withstand the test of time and, hopefully, it would still be together and not a pile of crushed granite rocks when I returned. If it was destroyed, I would surely perish upon my arrival under the weight of the granite stones. Maybe I should stop every million years or so on the way back to check how it was holding up and do any maintenance that might be required. I mean, what were the chances that a pyramid could last that long? 149,000,000 years was a long time. Maybe I should check it every couple of thousand years? That would take me too long.

I gave up on the idea of traveling that far back on the first trip. I needed to keep within a reasonable range that I thought my pyramid could last. I knew the pyramids of Egypt had stood more than four thousand years, but the Sudan pyramids had not been proven to last that long. So, I decided to go back just one thousand years initially, and then return to see how the pyramid was holding up. If all was okay, I would return to the thousand-year point and take it back to 4000 BCE. This was a time slightly before the Mayan's claimed they were created. But, according to the Masonic calendar, it would be at the creation of Adam and Eve. That would be far enough for now. I would stop every thousand years on the way back to the starting point and do any maintenance required to ensure the pyramid would be stable for my ultimate return. Once this was done one time, I would never have to do it again, because the maintenance would stand in that time period no matter how many times I visited the time period or passed it by. Later, I could spend time going back further.

The first trip was planned to leave at 13.0.8.10.18 | 8 Etz'nab |16 Sotz' | G2, this Tuesday, June 15, 2021, at 1200 hours (noon). I had stocked the pyramid with survival food, a lighter, clothing, water, and a few weapons. I had watched many survival shows on television, so I had an idea of what I would need. I might have been afraid, but I was not going down cold, skinny, and naked. I added a book on survival to the mix of items I was taking with me. Who knew who or what I was going to run into on this spot a thousand years ago? I also brought along extra acoustic speakers and acoustic generators. I added some batteries to the mix, a solar panel, and an electrical inverter just in case the reactor did not operate as we traveled through time.

Lastly, I installed my first reclining chair into the pyramid. Might as well be comfortable while traveling. To me, getting there was only half the job; returning, if I got there, was more important.

Terri came to the lab and asked, "Is there anything I can do?"

"No, but know that I love you." We both knew that if this did not work, I would never see her again. "Expect the pyramid to change in appearance once I travel back. It's probably going to look old and dirty because, you know, it will be a thousand years old. Just don't stand or put anything in the place of the pyramid if I should disappear for a while." Then I handed her a copy of the door key, just in case she needed to get the door to the pyramid open. One last kiss and hug, and I entered the pyramid, just as the first astronauts had done on 12.17.15.16.16 | 13 K'ib' | 14 Sek | G3, July 16, 1969, to go to the moon.

I entered my pyramid through a doorway that was much like the one Edward Leedskalnin had built for his Coral Castle back in 1923. It was just a little different in that this door made an airtight seal that could be locked into place but, when unlocked, it could be opened with a simple push of the finger. It could be opened from the interior or exterior, provided one had the key.

I brought the reactor up and got it working to produce the energy I needed. Next, I entered the target date into the frequency generator: 10.9.14.1.1 | 6 Imix' | 4 Sak' | G3, June 15, 1021, and chose the hour of 1200 hours (noon). I wrote down the current date and time: 13.0.8.10.18 | 8 Etz'nab | 16 Sotz' | G2, this Tuesday, June 15, 2021, at 1200 hours (noon). Then I put my finger on the green button, closed my eyes, and pressed it.

My heart was beating so fast and hard that I could hear it in my ears. Then the fog set in, and the tingling of my skin and nose. I thought I might have even farted a few times, like I was going to crap myself, but a later check revealed that I was stable. Then I remembered I had not packed any toilet paper. Well, hopefully, that wouldn't be an issue.

Within a few minutes, the smoke cleared, and the tingling stopped. I could feel the reactor coming down. I waited a few more moments before I figured it was safe to move around. To the door, I inserted the key and unlocked it. With a simple push, the door pivoted open and revealed the old world to me. Guess what? It looked almost the same. I found myself along the same cliffs, in the same woods, with different trees but basically the same.

I walked around, not wanting to stray too far from the pyramid, and all seemed much like the same place, with the exception that there were no cabins or any signs of human life in view. Then I realized that there would be an issue with future travel—getting around. My interaction with the future and past would be limited if I must walk to every place. It would also leave me vulnerable. This was something that I would need to address before any future trips.

To work, I went, removing the exterior acoustic speakers, and then I installed them on the interior of the pyramid. Once this was complete, I took photographs and printed them. I took air samples and, lastly, I left the set of radioactive sources on the outside wall at the entrance of the pyramid so that I could check the decay upon my return to verify that I had indeed traveled a thousand years back in time.

With my tasks done, I entered the pyramid again, closed the door, locked it with the key, and then went back to the reclining chair. I wrote down the date and time on the pyramid time tracker: 10.9.14.1.1 | 6 Imix | 4 Sak' | G3, June 15, 1021, time 1400 hours (2:00 PM). Then I entered the time I wished to return to, but thinking I needed to give myself about an hour so as not to overlap myself: 13.0.8.10.18 | 8 Etz'nab | 16 Sotz' | G2, June 15, 2021, 1300 hours (1:00 PM). If this worked the way I thought it should, Terri would have only missed me for an hour, even though I had been gone for two hours.

I placed my finger on the green button and pushed it once again. The reactor fired up to full capacity, the chamber filled with smoke once again, and the tingle ensued upon me once more. As before, the air cleared, and the reactor could be heard winding down. I could hardly wait to see if everything was as I had expected and was hoping for. The key was inserted into the door lock and, with a finger push, the door swung open as it was designed to do.

There, standing in the open doorway with a video camera, was Terri, waiting for me. She ran to me as we made eye contact and seized me with a hug like I had never had before.

When I broke free from her grip, she told me, "That was the longest hour of my life. I filmed the whole thing so you can see what happened."

As I turned my head, I could see that the pyramid had weathered some with time, without any evidence of damage. Only some dirt had accumulated on the exterior walls, and some moss had grown in the soil that had accumulated at the base.

We had done it—traveled back in time and had installed the pyramid as a safe transport chamber. All the actual components that made it work were still new and had traveled with me to and from.

Next, I was planning on moving the pyramid back further into time, to -3.-5.-20.-11.-19 | -4 Imix" | -15 Sak' | G-7, June 1, 4000 BCE. Why had I chosen June? I expected it to be warmer than it was in January.

CHAPTER NINE

BACK AGAIN

13.0.8.11.5 | TZLOK'IN DATE: 2 CHIKCHAN | HAAB
DATE: 3 SEK | LORD OF THE NIGHT: G9
GREGORIAN: JUNE 22, 2021

A week had passed, and I had spent the days writing notes and entering data into my log. I had taken measurements of the radioactive sources that I had deposited outside the doorway to the pyramid and was able to confirm that I had, indeed, traveled back in time a thousand years. As far as I could tell, I had only aged two hours. I also spent a little time camouflaging the pyramid so it would not be too obvious if satellites were photographing the land and to keep prying eyes from detecting what I was doing.

I packed up the pyramid once again and made it ready for a new trip. This time, I did not forget the toilet paper. Additionally, I had added an electric ATV (All-Terrain Vehicle) to my arsenal of tools. I did not plan on riding around or anything else on this trip, but it was nice to know I could get around if I needed to.

The itinerary was to travel back to the previous trip, just after I'd left the last time, then install the acoustic speakers on the outside of the pyramid, as before. I would reenter the pyramid and travel back to 4000 BCE, move the acoustic speakers to the inside, and then travel to my original time period. This would leave me with a transport location with a 6,021-year window back in time. Far from the 150 million years I would love to see, but it was good enough for now.

Terri and I were both feeling a little better about this trip, now that the time travel system had been proven. A lot less fear about being lost in time. With that said, it was still all relatively new, and anything could happen.

I plugged in the destination date into the control panel—10.9.14.1.1 |6 Imix' | 4 Sak' | G3, June 15, 1021—and chose the hour of 1430 hours (2:30 PM). I took my position in the reclining chair and wrote down the numbers of the calendar on the wall over the doorway—13.0.8.11.5 | 2 Chikchan | 3 Sek | G9, June 22, 2021, at 0800 hours (8:00 AM)—and hit the green "*Go*" button. The reactor came to life again, the air filled with a haze, and my skin tingled as before. Within a few minutes, the reactor was winding down, the fog clearing, and the tingling ceased. I was still in the pyramid, alive and well. All looked good.

Taking the key, I opened the door once again and cautiously walked outside. Nothing around. Not a popular place, but perfect for time travel.

Before I went to work moving the acoustic speakers to the outside of the pyramid, I loaded my handgun and holstered it. During this process, I had realized just how vulnerable I would be and never knew if a mountain lion, bear, or native would identify me as prey or foe. If I could not complete this task because I was wounded or attacked, I would be stuck with some of the acoustic speakers inside and some outside. That could potentially make the system inoperable.

With haste, I went right to work, completing the task of moving the speakers again. I collected the radioactive sources that were at the door and brought them into the pyramid. I took a reading and found that they had not decayed by any detectable amounts. Then I closed the door, locked it with the key, and took my position on the reclining chair. I logged the date and time: 13.0.8.10.18 | 8 Etz'nab | 16 Sotz' | G2, June 15, 2021, at 1125 hours (11:25 AM). I had aged three hours and twenty-five minutes. I logged my ageing and set the new destination date into the control panel: -3.-5.-20.-11.-19 | -4 Imix" | -15 Sak' | G-7, June 1, 4000 BCE, at 1000 hours (10:00 AM).

This time, it was a little different. I was not starting at the same point in time as before, so I hoped that the system would calculate everything properly. Being the Maya calendar began at the creation of the Mayan people on August 11, 3114 BCE, the calendar date was negative for any dates prior.

I was seated in my reclining chair, wondering if the pyramid would be my tomb. If ever opened by my wife, would she only find the dust of what was left of me or my face longing to see her?

I wrote a small note just in case I did not make it. It read,

> *You never know what the day is going to bring into your life, or*
> *the life of a loved one. At any given moment, we may need to jump*
> *between celebration and sorrow. To laugh and rejoice with our loved*

one's success or mourn with them a loss they must endure. In those moments, disagreements and opinions no longer matter. We come together with love, provide support, and stay present. With grace and peace, my love, shall my spirit always be with you.

I rolled up the piece of paper, placed it in my teeth like I was smoking a cigar, and then hit the green button once again. As before, the reactor came to life, a molecular haze formed, and the tingling ensued. Within moments, the haze cleared, the tingling ceased, and the reactor was winding down.

I took the note out of my teeth and placed it on the control console next to me. I thought to myself, *You made it.* Then I checked the oxygen and radiation levels. All were well within a range of Earth still being habitable.

I grabbed my firearm once again and holstered it. Then I took the key in hand and proceeded to the door. I pushed it open slowly and spied through the crack to see if anything was moving. All seemed to be clear once again. I stepped outside and took in a good lungful of fresh six-thousand-year younger air, untainted by the Industrial Revolution. I could feel the difference compared to the air I normally breathed. Wonderful and wholesome, the sky was a different blue, and the trees around me were many times the size of the trees that grew in my time period.

I picked up the radioactive sources I used to document the years of travel and placed them just outside the entrance door. Then I went right to work, taking down the acoustic speakers from the exterior of the pyramid. Within a few hours, I had completed the task. I now needed to take a much-needed lunch break.

Lunch. -3.-5.-20.-11.-19 | -4 Imix" | -15 Sak' | G-7, June 1, 4000 BCE, 1300 hours (1:00 PM). I had packed all types of survival food to last me for months, should I become stranded, but I never really gave something as simple as a lunch thought. What should I have for this first lunch at the beginning of time? Surely, not an apple, not today. *I know*! Peanut butter on crackers. That would work.

I quickly opened a sealed can of peanut butter and a can of crackers from my collection of survival food. Hmm ... "*Good until Aug 17, 2050*" was imprinted on the cans, but it didn't say anything about how far back it could go. I chuckled to myself. And if I left it outside of the pyramid, would it still be good until 2050? *Surely not*, I thought as I laughed again at my own humor.

Now that I had my belly full and was just sitting there, enjoying a bottled water, I thought it would be really cool to take a few minutes and head up to the top of the cliff to just take a look around. So, I moved the ATV out of the door and checked to make sure I had a full charge on it. All looked good, so I proceeded to navigate the spaces between the trees as I headed up the hill toward the top of the cliffs. When I got to the peak, I thought I would see a beautiful view of the untainted Appalachian Mountains. Not quite.

It was the old, "you can't see the forest through the trees" scenario, and this old growth forest was most definitely impeding my view. I could barely see the area where the pyramid was located. One could almost get lost in the middle of the day in these woods, being it was so dense. I thought it would be best to return to the pyramid and not let my curiosity get the best of me. I had come too far to lose it all now.

I returned and parked the ATV back in its designated space within the pyramid. I then started installing the acoustic speakers on the interior so I could make my return home. It crossed my mind that instead of just heading right back to 2021, it might be wise to take it in a thousand or two thousand year steps. I mean, this pyramid was going to be more than six thousand years old when I arrived back in my own time period. That was a long time for nothing to go wrong. Who knew how many earthquakes would pass, or if someone would remove the stones, or break down the door? Tree roots or ice could have invaded the cracks and caused the stones to come apart.

It wasn't that anything was inside the pyramid itself that anyone or anything could hurt. All the contents, including the reactor, moved with me, so it would be an empty space. I just needed to make sure the stones didn't fall in or that a tree had not grown through the floor, causing me to suffer the same death as poor Nibbles.

The interior acoustic speakers were installed, and it was midafternoon. "*1500 hours*" (3:00 PM) was displayed on the atomic clock. I had a long journey back and needed to get underway.

I closed the door, leaving the radiation sources on the outside of the pyramid so I could gather it later and take measurements. I locked the door and returned to the control panel. The new destination date was entered: 0.5.15.7.2 | 11 Ik' | 0 Muwan | G7, June 1, 3000 BCE, 1500 hours (3:00 PM). I then logged the current date and time: -3.-5.-20.-11.-19 | -4 Imix" | -15 Sak' | G-7, June 1, 4000 BCE, 1500 hours (3:00

PM). I put the note that I had written earlier into my shirt pocket then hit the green button. Off to 3000 BCE.

I experienced the same sequence of events with each trip through time—the reactor engaging and running at full capacity, the mystic haze, the tingling of the skin and senses, and then the clearing of the haze with the reactor winding down. Within moments, I had traveled one thousand years forward.

I stepped out of the pyramid again, inspected it for damage, and before closing the door and locking it again, I would take readings of the radiation sources on the outside by the entrance. So far, all looked good. No damage or signs of intrusion.

Another one thousand years. The new destination date was entered: 2.16.9.17.17 | 5 kab'an | 10 Ch'en | G6, June 1, 2000 BCE, 1500 hours (3:00 PM). The current date and time was logged: 0.5.15.7.2 | 11 Ik' | 0 Muwan | G7, June 1, 3000 BCE, 1610 hours (4:10 PM). I followed the same procedure as before, performing an inspection of the pyramid each time and taking a reading of the radiation sources outside the entry door.

Again and again, new destination date entered:

5.7.4.10.2 | 2 Ik' | 10 Sip | G4, June 1, 1000 BCE;

7.17.19.2.12 | 4 Eb' | 0 Pax | G7, June 1, 0001 AC;

10.8.12.12.17 | 5 kab'an | 5 Yax | G5, June 1, 1000 AC;

Lastly, I entered the final destination to my own time period: 13.0.8.11.5 | 2 Chikchan | 3 Sek | G9, June 22, 2021, at 0900 hours (9:00 AM). This was an hour after I had departed. Then I logged the calendar date and time that was over the door so I could compute the actual amount of time I had lived: 10.8.12.12.17 | 5 kab'an | 5 Yax | G5, , June 1, 1000 AC, at 1612 hours (4:12 PM).

Up until now, I had only had to shovel off debris from the pyramid surface and clear debris from the doorway. Over six thousand years of clean travel. I had done well in picking a stable location for the pyramid. One last trip, and I would be back. I had done this trip before and, therefore, it should go without any problems.

As the haze clear, the tingling subsided and the reactor shut down. I took the key and placed it into the lock, unlocking the door. As the door swung open, my wife entered with a big smile on her face.

"How do you feel?"

"Tired," I admitted. "It's been a long day."

I didn't think she understood. To her, I had been gone for about an hour, but I had been traveling since 0800 hours (8:00 AM), and now it was 0900 hours (9:00 AM). However, I had lived twelve hours and fifty-two minutes, whereas she had only lived one hour.

I then realized that I would age at a much faster rate than everyone else if I always returned shortly after I had departed. I could have actually spent a year or two traveling and returned within that hour without anyone knowing but me, except I would be years older. Most likely, that type of absence would go undetected for trips lasting a year or two. But, eventually, this could really add up. Duly noted and added to my log.

The next task was to go as far into the future as I dared.

I spent the next couple of weeks on general maintenance of the reactor and making sure the pyramid was in good shape, being it was now old. The oldest documented pyramid on Earth, and it was mine.

I started to think about that. If anyone were to have looked into it before today, it would appear empty, and no one would know what it was for. Just a stone housekeeping pad and a hole where the reactor fit. Otherwise, it was empty. Maybe this was why the Egyptian pyramids and Mayan temples stood empty when we searched them.

On July 3, 2021 at 1400 hours (2:00 PM), I experienced a strange event. At the time, I had not known this was the first of many that would come.

I saw myself walk out of the pyramid and hop into the pickup truck. I then waved to me and drove off. Later, I saw the truck back in the driveway and figured this might become a new normal—seeing myself jump in and out of my everyday life. It was starting to get a little freaky, but I had to go with it. There had to be good reason for it, or it would not have happened.

After being startled by seeing myself jumping through time, I set up a system to let myself know when I was jumping into my present-day life—I added a light switch to the time-jumping board. I would turn on the switch that would light a red light in the cabin's dining area. This was a small bulb and not overly suspicious but enough to provide myself and Terri warning for any future encounters.

CHAPTER TEN

FORWARD MARCH

13.0.8.11.18 | TZLOK'IN DATE: 2 ETZ'NAB' | HAAB
DATE: 16 SEK | LORD OF THE NIGHT: G4
GREGORIAN: JULY 5, 2021

"You see," I started to explain to Scott, "the real value of time traveling is not going back in time. Yes, one can go back and study past events in real time, play the stock market, knowing they will succeed, or play the lottery and become rich many times. But, in my opinion, knowledge of future technology, geopolitical events, and discovering how our actions affect the future are invaluable."

I continued my story.

This trip would be my first attempt to go into the future. The goal of this trip was to gather as much advanced intelligence and technology as possible and to keep the integrity of the pyramid by tending to its maintenance so it could serve as a stable location for future travel forward. I told myself that a trip like this could really help humanity and the world become a better place. Or, at least, I was trying to convince myself at the time that was what the trip was about.

I thought that I would just leap forward a thousand years. Maybe just push it a few extra years, just to test the precision. Unlike my travel into the past, where there were no established civilizations in place to check the true accuracy of my travel, I was sure that my travel into the future would yield the information easily. Just for the fun of it, I planned to travel one thousand fifteen years into the future. If all went well, I would open the pyramid door to 15.11.18.7.19 | 2 Kawak | 2 kumk'u | G6, July 5, 3036.

At this point, time travel seemed quite routine to me. However, Terri still wanted to be present and to record everything. Even though I had made several trips, from one time period to another, to another, and so on, she had only experienced me taking two trips total, and all she saw was my pyramid looking worse than it had when I'd started. Nothing really to show for the trips other than some readings off of some radioactive sources. This time, I was going to come back with something real—proof of my travel, some new advancement, and information about the future.

"Do you want to go?" I asked her.

"No," she replied. "If it fails, someone needs to be able to tell the story."

I had everything ready to go by 1000 hours (10:00 AM). I gave her a nice long hug, a kiss on the cheek, and said, "I'll be back by lunch."

The pyramid was loaded, this time with toilet paper and a cooler with a couple of sandwiches and sodas. I was really starting to get the knack of this.

The door was closed, locked, and I took my position in the reclining chair. I entered the new destination date and time: 15.11.18.7.19 | 2 Kawak | 2 kumk'u | G6, July 5, 3036, with an arrival time of 0900 hours (9:00 AM). I jotted down the time over the doorway: 13.0.8.11.18 | 2 Etz'nab | 16 Sek | G4, July 5, 2021, 1000 hours (10:00 AM).

15.11.18.7.19 | TZLOK'IN DATE: 2 KAWAK | HAAB DATE: 2 KUMK'U | LORD OF THE NIGHT: G6 GREGORIAN: JULY 5, 3036

I was thinking this was going to be a breeze, a short jump in time, nothing like my long jump into the past. The pyramid was all cleaned up and looked as good as ever. I hit the green button, and the reactor fired up, the ionic cloud formed, and the tingling was kind of pleasant this time, almost like a time massage. Within moments, the reactor was winding down, the haze clearing. Then, without notice, the radiation alarm started going off. I was not sure if my reactor had sprung a leak or what.

I leaped to my feet and inspected the control panel, looking for any sign of malfunction. None. I picked up the Geiger-Muller (GM) meter and walked toward the door. The meter was screaming. I flipped the meter to the next higher range. It was now reading 5. That was 5,000 millirem, or 5 REM. All right, not a killer dose. I could withstand this for some time without any ill effects, but this was inside the pyramid, with thick granite walls shielding some of my exposure. Who knew what the reading was outside of the pyramid?

I then felt the ground shaking and heard the loud sounds of explosions going off in the distance. It suddenly became obvious that I had traveled into a war zone.

America was under attack. A nuclear attack, at that.

Then, without warning, the oxygen sensor started going off.

I sprang to the box with my SCBA equipment and donned my respirator. Apparently, the oxygen levels had dropped below 19.5%. This was bad. High radiation, lack of oxygen, and bombs going off in America. I had to abort the mission.

I quickly plugged in my return destination date and time: 13.0.8.11.18 | 2 Etz'nab | 16 Sek | G4, July 5, 2021, at 1100 hours (11:00 AM). Then I hit the green button, and I was out of there.

Terri was there as I unlocked the door and pushed it open, still in my respirator. She ran to me and helped me out of my gear, asking, "What happened?"

"The travel was fine but, apparently, there was something really wrong. Bombs were going off in the distance, radiation levels were elevated, and oxygen levels were depleted." I sat down on the bench near the entrance to the pyramid, and I could only speculate that some force, whether it be man or alien, was ending life as we knew it on Earth.

"What did it look like?" she asked.

"I didn't even open the door, but I do know humans can't live with oxygen levels below 19.5% for long."

I wrapped up my trip for the day, totally disheartened that man most likely did not exist just one thousand fifteen years into the future.

Additionally, I figured out that I had only lived about ten minutes traveling to and from, yet Terri had aged one hour during my trip. This was a twist I had not expected. I could travel to some other time period, spend a few minutes there, and then return years later, only minutes older, yet everyone else in my time period would have aged from the time of my departure to my return. I could be young as they grew old. Noted in my logs for future analysis.

That evening, after dinner, I sat with my wife in the living room. She was surfing the internet and sending messages to our grandchildren as I wrote in my travel journal. I was still awestruck at the realization that life had been eliminated not all too far into the future. I was thinking about it, and from what the researchers had discovered at Göbekli Tepe, man had been living in organized communities for more than 10,000 years. Even in Australia, there had been the Aborigines who could trace their ancestries back to about 75,000 years. They were more tribal, but yes, organized communities. But we, modern man, had somehow ended it all in less than 3,036 years.

I knew at that moment, as though God had whispered it in my ear, that I had been given a holy mission. I could hear the old *Mission Impossible* TV series from the 1960s and early 1970s theme tune, written by Lalo Shifrin, playing in my head. No, it was not some churchy music of angels singing; it was the *Mission Impossible* theme song. My whole reason for being had just been presented to me. God had awakened me, given me the tools, and had made me aware. Me, simple old me, Max, with my only support being my wife, Terri. I had a holy mission.

These were big shoes to fill, much like Moses or Noah. I asked myself if I was worthy of such a calling. I would have to do what I had to do, at all costs, to complete the tasks necessary. If not, man would surely vanish and become just dust on Earth.

That next morning, I discussed this realization with Terri. We prayed together, and we both agreed that we could not turn our cheek and ignore the calling.

CHAPTER ELEVEN
MEGA-MILLIONS

13.0.8.11.19 | TZLOK'IN DATE: 3 KAWAK | HAAB
DATE: 17 SEK | LORD OF THE NIGHT: G5
GREGORIAN: JULY 6, 2021

First things first, I had to deal with funding this new mission. I handled this by checking the national Mega Millions lottery numbers. No winners for months now, perfect. The jackpot was standing at eighty-two million dollars. This would work well for me. I would not be stealing from anyone, or at least anyone who would know, and humanity was indirectly funding me to save the world.

I thought to myself, *Humanity will surely forgive me if they find out I'm saving the world.* Plus, the government got to tax the money.

The numbers drawn last night had been 18, 47, 63, 68, 69, and Mega Ball 14.

I went into the pyramid, locked the door, and set the travel time to three days earlier: 13.0.8.11.16 | 13 K'ib' | 14 Sek | G2, July 3, 2021, at 1400 hours (2:00 PM).

Upon arrival, I flipped on the red light then went to the driveway and hopped into the pickup truck. Seeing myself, 2021 Max, looking at me, I waved as I drove off to the local liquor store to buy a six pack of beer and my lottery ticket.

Returning half an hour later, I quickly walked back to the pyramid, locked the door, and set the six pack on the floor. I turned off the red light and plugged in the travel time back a few minutes from my departure: 13.0.8.11.19 | 3 Kawak | 17 Sek | G5, July 6, 2021, at 1200 hours (noon). All good, Terri was not even aware of my time jump and in my pocket was the winning lottery ticket.

I checked the internet to make sure the winning numbers were still the same. Yes, they were. I was now the winner of the eighty-two-million-dollar lottery. But instead of being happy and rejoicing, I felt like a scum bucket for having won it the way I had. No matter. I needed to fund this project long term. I had a holy mission, and this would make it possible.

Terri and I took the lottery winnings and set up a trust. The Hickman Holy Time Trust (THHTT). This trust was set up as a dynasty trust that would be capable of funding the time travel mission. Additionally, this trust ensured that my wife and descendants would always have what they needed. We then assigned all of our properties to the trust so that THHTT could establish the Hickman Nature Preservation Park. My goal was to keep the general population from messing with the pyramid for generations, if possible.

Additionally, I had the attorneys who managed the trust set up a cash-out system where they would put a large sum of cash into a safe deposit box. This would amount to no less than two years' salary for a well-to-do person. The trustees would pay for the box every year out of the trust account. This cash would be brought up to the minimum amount and rotated in and out of the box every year. That was, the amount would be adjusted and the old bills would be purged every year if paper money still existed, with new bills placed in the box to reach two years' salary. If cash was no longer used and only digital currency existed, a chip, phone, or whatever media currently in use would be placed in the safe deposit box, and it was to be switched out and updated every year.

The second thing I had the trustee group do was to provide Terri and myself with an ID that reflected our credentials. A valid ID for each that could not be disputed and contained all of our biometric information. We needed to be able to prove who we were and be able to become a part of society anytime we jumped into a future time period.

The trustees went right to work and set everything up, including the security ID cards. Our biometric information was recorded—fingerprints, eye scans, and DNA. We should be set, provided this organization did its job.

For future travel, I figured I needed to be able to see outside of the pyramid when I arrived at a new time-period, and I needed to be able to use both my radiation detection equipment and atmosphere monitoring equipment from the inside of the pyramid. I could not risk my life wondering what I was opening the door to.

I thought about it and came up with the idea of installing a lens in the all-seeing Eye of Horus engraved on the pyramid, and then I would have the actual camera and monitor travel with me so that it would not age. I would just need to clean the outside of the lens occasionally.

I also installed two thick gold tubes through the granite blocks to allow me to install an ion tube radiation detector and atmosphere detector. These tubes would be capped, and I would have to hook up the equipment that traveled with me, but this would help me see what the true hazard levels were without leaving the pyramid, should I run into a problem again.

I thought about it for some time and figured that I would have to travel forward in small increments until I found the cause of the radiation and oxygen depletion. I would then do all I could to make changes to avoid the extinction of man.

It was now time to travel forward. The pyramid was loaded. The new equipment was in place, and this time, the respiratory equipment was kept close at hand. I had also included a few lead blankets to serve as gamma ray shielding. I figured I would place them over me during my leap forward in time just in case. They were just some used dental x-ray blankets I had purchased online. They were not heavy or thick enough to provide complete protection but thick enough to buy me some time if I needed it.

Unfortunately, if I arrived during a neutron flux caused by the detonation of a neutron bomb, I would surely die, and my reactor would surely go critical. To counter this possibility, I put in a thick poly low-Z shield around my lounge chair and another over the reactor head. I didn't know if it would be enough shielding, but it was worth the try. I knew in my head that I was taking some big chances now, but I did not discuss the risk with Terri.

The door was closed and locked after my goodbyes to Terri. I took my place in the reclining chair and plugged in my new destination date just twenty-four years out: 13.1.13.0.6 | 2 Kimi | 9 Pax | G4, July 7, 2045, with an arrival time of 0900 hours (9:00 AM). I logged my current date and time: 13.0.8.12.0 | 4 Ajaw | 18 Sek | G6, July 7, 2021, at 1000 hours (10:00 AM). Off on my new mission.

I thought to myself, *Right, me, Max. I am going to save Earth and mankind. What a joke. I am all that stands to defend Earth.*

Poor Earth, having such an unworthy soldier, but I had the most powerful weapon ever, and I was going to use it.

I repeated the Lord's prayer then pushed the green button and launched into the future as before.

CHAPTER TWELVE
CONFIRMATION
13.1.13.0.6 | TZLOK'IN DATE: 2 KIMI | HAAB DATE: 9 PAX | LORD OF THE NIGHT: G4 GREGORIAN: JULY 7, 2045

As before, the travel to the future went well. As the mist cleared, the tingling stopped and the reactor wound down. I flipped the red light on just in case Terri and I were still living in the cabin. Then I unlocked the door, pushed it open, and who was standing there as I opened the door? It was Terri. She was still alive but twenty-four years older, standing there at the entrance of the pyramid with a big smile on her face. Now, I had not been expecting that. I was sure my mouth was slung open for a moment.

And then she asked, "Did you miss me?"

I laughed. "No, it's only been a minute or two, but apparently, you missed me."

"No, you return home every day," she said. "I just needed to see if time travel was real, and now that there are two of you—a 2021 Max and a 2045 Max—I have all the confirmation I need." She laughed then asked, "You need anything to eat or drink? Anything else?"

"No, I'm all good," I answered. "Anything I need to know about any geopolitical events, planetary events, wars—anything like that?"

2045 Max walked up and joined the conversation. "Biden won a second presidential term in 2024. He didn't live long enough to complete his second term, though. His eighty-fifth year of life, midway through his third year, he passed away. A huge national loss." He shook his head. "The entire country shut down for three days while funeral services were held. Then Kamala Harris was appointed as the first woman President of the United States. That drove the country to the brink of civil war. Fortunately, the country hung on long enough to get through another election in 2028, being the primaries were already well underway."

"Wow," was all I could say.

"Yeah," 2045 Max said. "When November came along, the election was held, and Adam Schiff became President. Most people ended up liking President Schiff, but there was still that underlying group of crazies who made the country miserable. Schiff was President for two terms and, in 2036, a republican, Tom Cotton, won the election. He was a good President, as well, and served two terms until 2044.

"However, during his time as President, our relationship with the Russians, Chinese, and Iranians slipped to new lows, and we ended up in a war that is still raging on. Most of the battles are being fought on the Chinese and Russia doorsteps, but Japan, Taiwan, South Korea, and the Philippines are in the center of the battle. Occasionally, a skirmish is fought at sea in American waters but, so far, nothing has happened in any of the fifty states. Everyone has a finger on an ICBM with nuclear warheads. It's just a matter of time," 2045 Max concluded, with Terri nodding her head.

I thought to myself that maybe this was the cause of the end of the world.

"Can you take me to town so I can withdraw some money and buy some modern clothing to stock in the pyramid?" I asked 2045 Max.

"No need. I can transfer several thousand WebDollars to you immediately. We don't use paper money any longer. WebDollar, a cryptocurrency, is the only currency used. It's universal. There are no exchange rates anymore. Trade's made easier with one standard currency used throughout the world."

He then beckoned for me to follow him. "Come on. You can select any clothing you need from my closet." Being we were the same size and person, that worked out. "I'll try to keep the balance in my WebDollar account up as long as I live to save you the trip to the safe deposit box."

"Thank you." I shook my hand with a smile.

Once I got the clothes and confirmed the WebDollars were in my account, I said my goodbyes and reentered the pyramid. Locking the door behind me, I turned off the red light and made ready for the next jump forward. I figured I would try one hundred years this time.

13.6.14.8.8 | TZLOK'IN DATE: 13 LAMAT | HAAB DATE: 6 YAXK'IN | LORD OF THE NIGHT: G6 GREGORIAN: JULY 5, 2145

I made the jump as before, now under a Plexi-glass low-Z shield and lead blankets. New destination date: 13.6.14.8.8 | 13 Lamat | 6 Yaxk'in | G6, July 5, 2145, with an arrival date of 0900 hours (9:00 AM). I logged my current date and time to track my ageing: 13.1.13.0.6 | 2 Kimi | 9 Pax | G4, July 7, 2045, 1230 hours (12:30 PM). Pressing the green button, I was on my way once again.

Upon arrival, I hooked up the camera to the glass eye, looked out, and could see my cabin was still standing. There appeared to be walking trails, and the area around the pyramid seemed to be cleared with benches all around. I hooked up the radiation monitors and the oxygen sensing equipment. All readings were well within a normal range. There seemed to be no issues.

I then took the key and unlocked the pyramid door. I pushed it open and walked out. Everything seemed fine. I loaded up my backpack and moved the ATV to the exterior of the pyramid, closed the door, and locked it.

I drove down to the local town, Capon Bridge, went into the bank, and opened my safe deposit box that was supposed to contain an ID and two years' cash. On the way, all I saw were multiple drone-like vehicles zipping to and fro.

I found a chip in the box with instructions that would allow purchases to be made without cash. The instructions directed me to load the funds into my phone, and I could use my phone for purchases. It seemed the personal phone lived on.

I then checked the balance of the THHTT account. The account seemed to have grown exponentially. Apparently, the trust I had set up in 2021 lived on and had been properly managed. Imagine that, trustworthy attorneys. I didn't know how I had lucked out with that pick.

The ninety-million-dollar lottery winnings had grown to 1.5 billion WebDollars. This was good. It had kept up with inflation. This should provide me with the resources I would need.

I visited the county courthouse and made sure the taxes on the land were up to date. All was being taken care of by the trustees. Everything was in order. I just could not believe it. They had actually done everything I had contracted them to do. Let's hope it lived on.

I then proceeded to the clothing store and purchased a few pairs of pants and shirts in various sizes for the pyramid and to update my appearance. My 2021 denim jeans and tee were a little dated. Apparently, I had been quite fortunate to have even found a clothing store still in existence. Fortunately for me, the small town of Capon Bridge was one of those small, slow-to-change type of places.

I selected the clothing from a viewing screen in the store, and it was printed as I waited. The new norm was to do this online while at home. When I asked about the care instructions for washing and drying, I became the joke of the store. I was told to just throw them in the recycler when soiled and replace with new. Really, no washing, drying, folding, or even storing them in dressers or closets. Just order, print, wear, and recycle.

After getting changed in the dressing room, I went in search of basic information. I found that the world had changed a lot. Everything was interconnected on what we called the internet, or web in the 2020s. There were no printed information type materials to purchase. No newspapers or magazines were in the stores. When I asked the teller robot where I could buy a newspaper, the other store patrons started to laugh. The bot clerk said they did not sell newspapers and suggested that I log into the "DS" (DataStream) and do a search. I was a fish out of water, for sure. I had no choice but to buy a device to access the DS. The mobile phone was still in existence with a screen, and it could be projected onto a wall, but you had to talk to it to make it work or use a projected image of a keyboard on a table to type anything in.

I must have spent an hour in the store getting the robot working the technology counter to help me. He kept asking what century I was from, being I didn't know anything about how to work the damn thing. The whole phone thing was a little awkward, especially if you did not want to have anyone listening in, but when in Rome, do as the Romans.

I purchased a disposable phone so that I could purchase additional service hours on it as needed. Then I returned to the pyramid without incident, transferred the WebDollars on the phone, and placed the clothing in the segregated rack.

I went to work searching the DS for all the information I could. I was surprised to find there was a regular shuttle to the moon and another to Mars. Apparently, there had been major advancements in propulsion and space travel. I also found that most vehicles were more of an aircraft when it came to getting around. It seemed that wheeled vehicles were limited to heavy trucks and construction. Passenger vehicles were buzzing around like mosquitoes with little regard of any roads. Electricity was now being generated using fusion reactors, and all burning of hydrocarbons had been banned.

I was at a point in history where I could pick up some real technology to help myself and mankind. I didn't know the range of the air transport craft (ATC) vehicles, but one of the big negatives about having placed my pyramid in such a remote location was the isolation when I time traveled. I mean, how would I ever see Egypt, or Rome, or even Washington DC, for that matter, stuck in the dense woodland of West Virginia? One of these ATCs would be a game changer if they had a decent range or a way to refuel.

Apparently, they ran on electricity with some type of advanced battery. I had plenty of power with my small reactor; therefore, I figured I could use one of these ATCs to get around.

I searched on the DS for the longest-range ATC I could find. I selected an average-sized one that had a range of 3,218 km (2000 miles). That was the other thing; the US was now on the metric system. What a pain in the butt for an old-school guy like myself.

I ordered it from the on line retailer, Ama-Zing–, and they said it would be delivered tomorrow. Perfect. Now, how did you learn how to drive an ATC? There it was, on the DS. ATC virtual driver's license courses. I signed up and figured I might be able to take a short crash course. Excuse the pun. The class ran for four days, so it looked like I would be camping here for some time.

Lunchtime, 1200 hours (noon).

It was getting warm in the pyramid. I needed to make some modifications to it and install a climate control system and an entertainment system. While I was at it, I needed to install better lighting and a toilet with a shower. I could do this now, being they would deliver everything right to the door. So, I set up an Ama-Zing account and placed an ordered for a bio-toilet, a camping shower, lights, extension cords, and an air conditioner/heater that was a portable unit. I also ordered a water cooler/heater unit, a microwave, small table, and a chair. Then I sat back with one of my sandwiches and had lunch.

Everything would work out. I would take delivery on the ATC and attend a class for about a week to learn how to use it. Then I figured I could really see how everything was changing in the world. This was exciting. Not just jumping time but mingling with the people of the period.

All that afternoon, I sat out on the bench in front of the pyramid and surfed the DS, bringing myself up to speed on the geopolitical climate. It seemed the war with China and Russia had fizzled out with some agreement that had left Taiwan as a China-run communist state. Russia had had their ass handed to them, and now both countries were poor because they had been cut off from trade with all NATO nations. Russia was piling up oil that no one wanted, and China had no one to buy their goods. As with all wars, everyone lost.

There was a lot of chatter about the ocean levels rising so much that many island countries were going underwater. It also seemed that low-lying areas of larger mainland countries were starting to succumb to the rising sea levels. Cities and towns along the coasts of all nations were being lost to the sea.

I then ran across some educational opportunities. College classes were no longer taken in person. All virtually. This was the answer. I would sign up for classes, buy the books, and have access to almost any cutting-edge information I needed.

That evening, I enrolled in Bio-Mechanics Institute of Technology's (B-MIT) online classes. They had both engineering programs and a bioengineering/biomedical program. I signed up for a semester. If you had the crypto, you could attend, so there were no restrictions on my taking the classes or working in the laboratories. I would have to travel to Bethesda, Maryland, to work in the laboratories, but that was fine. I figured, by the time I needed to do any lab work, I would be ATC licensed.

I made sure no one was looking, unlocked the pyramid, and entered and locked the door behind me. It was time for a good night's sleep.

CHAPTER THIRTEEN
DRIVER'S LICENSE
13.6.14.8.9 | TZLOK'IN DATE: 1 MULUK | HAAB
DATE: 7 YAXK'IN | LORD OF THE NIGHT: G7
GREGORIAN: JULY 6, 2145

I awakened early in the morning and made my way outside again. This time, in search of breakfast. I did unexpectedly find a decent little diner in town. Everyone was eyeing my ATV, standing around it and asking me questions. I told them it was an old antique that I had restored and was just giving it a spin. That seemed to go over well. They all seemed to buy that story, so I figured I would stick with it until I had an ATC and a license in my hand.

I sat on a bench in the Hickman Nature Preservation Park for most of the day, waiting for my Ama-Zing deliveries. It would have been nice to get the deliveries to the cabin or my old laboratory, but I found the cabin was being occupied by the park service and the laboratory had completely crumbled.

That day, I had also received a message from Bio-Mechanics Institute of Technology, accepting my enrollment. Being I paid them twenty thousand WebDollars for the semester, I should think so. This was the part I had been waiting for. I got my key to the laboratory and a passcode so I could download the required literature. I wasted no time downloading everything.

A new issue had to be addressed. I could not keep the information on the phone and bring it back to the year 2021. I would have to print these books and all the references in order to take them back in time. Back to Ama-Zing, placing my order for a printer and paper. Seemed these were special order items but still obtainable. Delivery today. Couldn't beat that.

Midday came, and my Ama-Zing orders arrived, by ATC. They delivered my new ATC, lights, bio-toilet, portable air conditioner/heater, table, chair, microwave, paper, and printer. I spent a few hours setting up everything and charging my ATC.

When it was time for my ATC class, I found out that I was the oldest guy who had ever taken the class given by this online group. These classes were generally attended by twelve-year-olds.

It seemed these ATCs just about drove themselves, but you had some navigation rules to learn, and there were restrictions about going over public buildings. It was actually a fun class, and it didn't take me long to master the basics of controlling the unit. Anyone could do this stuff. You paired with the craft, and then named the craft—I named mine Hal. Then you learned to control it. *Hal, up. Hal, down. Hal, take me to ... Hal, faster. Hal, slower.* Okay, I was not kidding; the thing flew itself.

I got this list of fifty or so commands that I had to learn for the test that would be given on the fourth day. Completely doable.

This ATC fit nicely inside the pyramid, too, so I parked it inside and shut the door. It was starting to get crowded in the pyramid, to the point that I was having to walk around each item like a rat maze, but I used the 15.7 m² (169 square feet) to its fullest.

I made a trip to the diner for just about every meal those first couple of days. I tried to keep to myself, but the ATV drew a lot of attention, and there seemed to be at least one enthusiast at every meal who wanted to question me about it. Then I found that I could order food online, and they would bring it to me. Good old home delivery was still alive and kicking. This was great; home delivery to a pyramid in the park. I just played I was picnicking and asked them to meet me at the pyramid in the park. That did not seem to cause any alarm, and everything came as expected.

13.6.14.8.12 | TZLOK'IN DATE: 4 EB' | HAAB DATE: 10 YAXK'IN | LORD OF THE NIGHT: G1 GREGORIAN: JULY 9, 2145

My big ATC test date had arrived. It was Friday, and I was going to take my test and obtain my ATC license. I was as excited as a sixteen-year-old. I understood that the robot came to you and followed you around as you drove solo. It wasn't like I had to parallel park or anything, I just had to give all the proper commands, and they would hand me my license.

When the robot arrived, I was ready to go, and it told me not to enter the ATC until I had passed my examination. It started asking me questions that I had to answer, and they were not multiple-choice questions, either. There were like fifty questions, not just a few, and many off the cuff about wind speeds, power lines, and all kinds of stuff. I thought I did all right on that part of the test, but I was not sure. Then the bot had me look into a box and proceeded to test my vision. A few moments later, the robot announced that I had passed my test and that I now needed to enter my ATC and follow.

I got in, checked my mirrors and, you know, adjusted the seats and everything you did when you drove a car. Then I signaled my liftoff and followed the bot, calling out orders as we buzzed along—*Hall, up. Hal, down. Hal, left. Hal, stop. Hal, Hal, Hal.*

After about thirty minutes, the bot stopped at the pyramid. I parked and got out, and the bot handed me my fresh new license. Wow, I was a legal ATC operator, and I now existed in 2145. This was a good day. I now had my wings.

I buzzed all over the place throughout the day. I could get to Washington DC in just over fifteen minutes. I visited my old hometown of Annapolis, Maryland, and could see that the majority of the city was underwater with only the state house and church circle above water. The city docks and Ego Alley were gone, and poor East Port had been swallowed up by the intruding waters. That brought a tear to my eye.

I proceeded south, past Edgewater that was now underwater, down to where Deale and Shadyside, Maryland, were supposed to be, but all were completely submerged. Lastly, I headed to Chesapeake Beach. There, the water had intruded into the low-lying areas and only the peaks of the hills were visible. I could see that the environment had changed, and much of what I had known of the area had been lost to the rising sea. As the afternoon went on, I decided to head up toward Bethesda to the research labs. This took less than fifteen minutes, a far cry from the two hours it used to take me to commute back in 2021.

The DC Beltway was now just a wide, grass-covered strip that everyone followed, so as not to fly over any public buildings. It was so busy and complex that if the ATC had not been flying itself, I would surely have crashed within a few minutes. Autonomous flying was what I called it.

I had plugged in the lab address and told Hal to take me there. Hal was like a god, always knowing and able. I was delivered to the doorstep of the biolaboratories that was located in the area of the old National Naval Medical Center.

With my education in Bioengineering and Nuclear Physics, I knew my way around a laboratory. I put on the laboratory personal protective equipment (PPE) and entered the research and development area. There, I found what I had been looking for—a gene splicer. A crisper, as they called it, with a huge library of genetic code. Even better, I ran into two students who were working on their PhDs.

"Hey," I greeted them as I walked in. "What are you up to today?"

"Hello. We're just working on some new experiment. Todd here is trying to blast through his doctorate as quickly as he can. I am Ed, by the way." The guy held out his hand for me to shake.

"Yeah," the other guy, Todd, said, "We're also on the brink of a breakthrough with our research."

"That sounds exciting. What exactly are you working on?" I asked.

"We've been experimenting with gene editing, and it's been really promising so far." Ed looked really excited. It was infectious.

"We're hoping to make some significant contributions to the field. The potential applications could be groundbreaking," Todd added.

"Wow, that's impressive," I told them. "You guys seem really enthusiastic about your work."

"Absolutely," Ed said. "We're thrilled about the potential impact of our research. It's great to see our hard work paying off, and I am thankful to have a partner like Todd to bounce ideas off of."

"It's been a great collaboration," Todd agreed. "We're pushing each other to explore new possibilities."

"Well, I can't wait to see where this research takes you. Keep up the great work, guys." I then told them, "My name is Max. I graduated a while back, but I signed up for these bioengineering classes to brush up on my skills."

"No worries, Max. It'd be cool to have you hang out with us."

"Yeah, man, it's all good."

"Great. I look forward to seeing how far gene splicing and the sequencing of the human genome has come since I was last in a bio-lab."

"We are moving fast." Todd laughed.

"The advancements in bioengineering have been incredible. It's amazing how far we've come," Ed said, looking back at the computer in front of him.

"Come take a look at this," Todd added, also returning to the project at hand.

The older of the two, Ed Carney, was definitely a cool, seasoned lab nerd who really knew his way around the biolab. The second guy, Todd Woerner, was a sharp guy. Unlike Ed, Todd was looking to get in and out, but these guys had teamed up and were really working on some cutting-edge, breakthrough stuff. You could see they were excited with their work and fed off each other as they worked in the lab.

"You guys wanna grab a few drinks and continue this conversation at the local watering hole?" I asked hours later.

"Sounds like a plan to me," Ed agreed.

"I'm in." Todd quickly took off his lab coat. "Let's head out."

At the watering hole, I held up my drink. "Cheers, guys. Here's to the marvels of bioengineering and the future of science."

Todd raised his glass. "Cheers! It's awesome to have you in the mix, Max."

"Absolutely," Ed said, raising his own glass. "Here's to lifelong learning and good company."

Todd said, "Did we tell you that we've been working on bringing back extinct animals, too? Our latest success was a woolly rhinoceros."

"No way!" I exclaimed. "That's incredible! How did you manage to do that?" And whoever heard of a woolly rhinoceros?

"It's a long process," Ed explained, "involving extracting DNA from well-preserved specimens and then manipulating it to match the genetic code of living animals."

"And with gene splicing, we can modify the genetic code of viruses to make them more effective in combating various diseases," Todd tacked on.

"I'd love to see all the research you've been doing."

"We'd be happy to show you. Besides, Todd loves showing off his work to others."

Both the guys laughed.

"We can meet up at the lab tomorrow and show you some of our lab toys," Todd promised.

"Awesome."

I fed them a few more drinks. -Everyone liked to talk about themselves as long as you spoke their language, and I did.

The best part of the ATCs was that you could drive them totally impaired. "Hal, please take me home," and in less than thirty minutes, I was landing at the pyramid, safe and sound.

13.6.14.8.13 | TZLOK'IN DATE: 5 B'EN | HAAB DATE: 11 YAXK'IN | LORD OF THE NIGHT: G2 GREGORIAN: JULY 10, 2145

This was my sixth day in the year 2145, and I was starting to really miss Terri. However, I knew she would not miss me. I would be back in her life an hour after I had departed.

I was living the 2145 life now out of the Hickman Nature Preservation Park pyramid. I did the diner for breakfast, this time in my ATC. Nice that I did not have to talk to everyone about my old ATV. I sipped my coffee then headed back to the pyramid to start printing books. Around 1000 hours (10:00 AM), I grabbed a notebook, which I was sure was not commonplace, a pencil, and jumped into the ATC. Off to the lab again to meet my new friends, Ed and Todd.

I used my code and entered the university's laboratory again, finding Todd working with the crisper already.

"Hey," I greeted him. "Where's Ed?"

"Ed never comes in early, but he should be here soon."

"What are you working on?" I asked.

"We took a common virus and manipulated the genetic code to target individual persons, families, or races of people." He enthusiastically showed me, and I took some notes and noted the library reference name that he was working with.

Then he went into explaining, "You can cut genetic code from one animal and splice it into the virus to have it implanted into another." Todd went through how to use the equipment.

"Could I try to splice some code into a virus that would only impact me or my descendants?" I asked.

Todd quickly replied, "Yes," and took a swab out, collecting a DNA sample from me. Within minutes, he had my genetic code up on the screen. "What do you want to change?"

"I want to add in some naked mole rat, blind mole rat, elephant, and bowhead whale genetic material. I want to make modifications that would give my genes the ability to reproduce without causing cancer. Then I want to mix in some genetic code from starfish, an axolotl, and some exoskeleton sea creatures that would give me the ability to regrow almost any organ."

He laughed and brought up the code from the library, targeted the sequence that was known to control the regenerations, and added it to the mix.

Then, as a finishing touch, I told Todd, "Now I want to splice in some *Hydrozoa turritopsis dohrnii* (eternal jellyfish) to the mitochondria DNA." We were having a good time messing around as we made a special DNA soup.

When we finished splicing the code, he loaded it into the carrier virus, had it multiply until there was a substantial quantity, and then had it reduced to a powder. I took this fun little project and saved it in a library for me to mess with at a later date.

Ed came into the lab, asking, "What are you up to?"

We showed him our project, and he looked a little scared.

"You know this virus could kill you and only you, right?" It was a virus that was designed to only attack me and make all these changes.

I laughed and told Ed, "It would most likely just cause me to grow two heads, eight starfish arms, and a penis the size of a whale's."

Looking relieved, Ed, said, "Come on; I want to show you all the other equipment." He took hours giving me the grand tour of the laboratory. It was helpful.

"Well, guys, thank you for taking the time to show me all this. Let's do the bar again later tonight."

"Sure," they both agreed with grins.

With that, I logged out of the laboratory and went back to the pyramid with my notes. It was now 1400 hours (2:00 PM), and I continued to print my course books so I would be able to take them back with me to 2021.

My classes were scheduled to start on Monday, so I started to dig into the course work as I lounged around the park. These courses were important so I could work with cutting-edge technology in the bioengineering field. I planned on attending the entirety of the classes for six weeks then pack up and return to 2021, an hour from my departure. I would age more than my wife doing this, but I might now be able to thwart ageing by infecting myself with the newly designed virus.

Before I just exposed myself, though, I wanted to go through the code to make sure I knew exactly what was going to be altered and what the possible results would be. I needed to attend these classes and mess around in the bio lab by myself.

CHAPTER FOURTEEN
THE VIRUS
13.6.14.8.14 | TZLOK'IN DATE: 6 IX | HAAB DATE:
12 YAXK'IN | LORD OF THE NIGHT: G3
GREGORIAN: JULY 11, 2145.

I attended my bioengineering classes with a lust to learn, like I had never done before. I needed to really get the most out of this technology. In addition to bioengineering, I had taken several mechanical engineering courses in hopes of obtaining as much knowledge as possible about interstellar travel and nuclear fission. It wasn't like there hadn't been some major breakthroughs in propulsion, but nothing close to traveling at the speed of light or anything like that. The major advancement was just that there were now civilizations on both the moon and Mars.

Travel to the moon took about three days, and an affordable roundtrip ticket could be purchased without a passport. The Mars trip travel time varied, depending on when you departed and planned to return. The trip was about thirty to sixty days each way. I actually thought the price for the ticket was a great value, considering you could actually stay at either place for as long as you liked, provided you worked. I mean, you could not go outside and sit in a park, like the Hickman Nature Preservation Park or anything, but to an Earthling, I was sure the landscape was awesome, at least for a while.

I did well in keeping up with my classes, and in my spare time, when not studying, I would hang with Todd and Ed at the local bar and talk trash about all the lab work we had messed up over the years. I also worked every weekend diligently in the laboratory to refine the virus that Todd and Ed had engineered to work with my DNA.

I was able to engineer the virus to only work on males that carried my DNA in their "Y" chromosome and then, once that condition was met, it would infect the body and implant the changes to the "X" chromosome that gave cancer resistance, the ability to regenerate lost or damaged organs and appendages, and lastly, extend life for many years. I might not have been able to extend the longevity of my existence forever, yet I was able to identify the proper code to accomplish nine hundred years. I felt that nine hundred was more than adequate, so that was what I stuck with.

Once I had finalized this designer virus, I replicated enough of it to make about ten doses. That should be more than enough. I packaged it and kept it in the pyramid. Then I cleared most of the records from the laboratory files with the exception of leaving the original concoction that Todd and I had put together, minus the eternal jellyfish DNA and all my manipulation that allowed the virus to only work on my bloodline. I figured they would probably never even visit this information again, but just in case they did, I would not want to leave someone a complete record of my work.

13.6.14.10.16 | TZLOK'IN DATE: 9 K'IB' | HAAB DATE: 14 CH'EN | LORD OF THE NIGHT: G9 GREGORIAN: AUGUST 21, 2145

It had been six weeks of intense bioengineering and mechanical engineering classes. Although I could continue this education forever and keep feeding my hunger to learn, I knew in my soul that I could never learn everything. The sciences had advanced so far and fast that it would literally take ten lifetimes to master everything that I wanted to know. So, I decided it was time to take my printed books and the engineered virus back to 2021. Besides, I had been away from Terri for more than six weeks now, and I was really missing her. If I really wanted to continue this education, I could always return and pick up an hour from my departure time, continuing on with my education.

I packed up my pyramid and made ready for the leap back to 2021. Then I met with Todd and Ed one last time at the bar and told them I was cutting out and heading back to stay with family for a while. They seemed good with the story.

"I'll be graduating in another six weeks and heading to Mars where they are offering big WebDollars for people with my education," Todd told me. "Some bioengineering firm already made me an offer."

"I'm going to continue my education and just work locally for a while," Ed said.

It was hard to say goodbye, thinking I would never see those two guys again, but

I knew I had to return to my own time period and let them proceed on their own paths without ever telling them about my time travel.

I set the target date to: 13.0.8.12.0 | 4 Ajaw | 18 Sek | G6, July 7, 2021, at 1100 hours (11:00 AM). Then I logged the clock over the entrance doorway: 13.6.14.10.15 | 8 Men | 13 Ch'en | G8, August 21, 2145. I had aged forty-seven days and seven and a half hours while Terri would have only aged one hour.

I sat back in the reclining chair and, without any worry of shielding, hit the green button. I was off and heading back to my own time period with a slew of engineering and bioengineering advancements. I intended to spend a few days at home then try advancing further into the future.

As the ionic fog cleared, I walked to the door and unlocked it. Yes, she was there. The love of my life was back to the way I had left her at about sixty years old. I gave her a big hug.

"Are you okay?" she asked. I guessed she could see that I had changed somehow.

"Yes, of course. Just missed you."

All that afternoon, I spent time telling her about my trip and about new advancements in technology. I showed her the books I had printed, and I could only wish that there was a way I could electronically save all the data and bring it back with me. The paper printing was laborious and limited the volume of information I could bring back. It also made it much harder to search for information.

Then came the subject of the virus.

That evening, I told her, "I developed, with the aid of my friends, Ed Carney and Todd Woerner. It's an engineered virus that will extend my life to about nine hundred years."

She didn't say anything.

"I plan on returning with a sample of your DNA so I can engineer a virus specifically for you, so you, too, can live nine hundred years with me."

Surprisingly, she said, "I want no part of it. If you want to live nine hundred years, then that's your decision, but I intend to live the life God gave me, and I have no intention of doing anything to change that." She was upset that I had even bothered to create something like an engineered virus or to think that she would consider extending her life in such a way.

I did not understand but thought it would be best to drop the subject for now and pick it up again later. I did know that the virus couldn't take you back to your youth. It could only maintain your current age and appearance for nine hundred years, less your actual age. The last thing anyone would want to do was wait until they had some debilitating disease and then subject themselves to the virus. This might have played a role in my wife's comments and attitude, as she had quite a few aches and pains, arthritis, heart problems, and some mobility issues that were not easy to live with. I, on the other hand, did not suffer from any advanced signs of ageing, other than the loss of some hair, wrinkles, and the usual old man look.

The virus did have limitations. It could not stop death from any outside force, such as an automobile accident or gunshot. Yes, if you could live through the initial blow, you would be able to regenerate and repair the damaged organs and limbs, but if you were to be shot in the heart or head, dead was dead.

13.0.8.12.1 | TZLOK'IN DATE: 5 IMIX' | HAAB DATE: 19 SEK | LORD OF THE NIGHT: G7 GREGORIAN: JULY 8, 2021

I started the day with a great home-cooked breakfast that included eggs, sausage, and pancakes. Why would I ever want to leave this time period again? Yes, the mission. To save humanity. I couldn't take my eye off the ball. I still needed to find out what had wiped out humanity, and then figure out a way to stop it from happening.

My thoughts quickly turned back to the virus issue, and I told myself I could always cut my life short if I did extend my life and the results were undesirable. Additionally, I thought about how Terri did not want any part of it, that her decision might have been what it was because of her current ailments. Maybe she would reconsider if I went back in time to when we were younger and subjected ourselves to the virus then. We would basically lock in our youth. I wanted to offer her this option to see if it would change her opinion on the subject.

As we were working together to clean up the breakfast mess, I asked, "If I were to go forward in time, engineer the virus to give you nine hundred years of life, then go back to when you were twenty years old and subject you to the virus to lock in your youth to about twenty years old, would you then be open to the idea?"

80

Within three seconds, I knew I should not have asked her.

She gave me the most cross face I had ever seen and said, "Absolutely not." She then asked, "What part of this subject do you not understand? I am going to live my life the way God intended, and there's not going to be any wavering in my conviction. If you want to do it, then go for it. But I will have no part of extending my life by using some engineered virus that you concocted."

After an hour or two of her chewing on me, I said, "I won't bring up the subject again." But I knew that life would not be as sweet after she had passed. "No matter, I made up my mind. I'm going to do it. I am going back to the early 1980s and subject myself to the virus so that I have the option."

Later that day, I made ready for the trip. I figured I would plug in 1984, when I had been a twenty-two-year-old man, living in Annapolis, Maryland. I had felt my best back then, with no physical ailments, and I had been strong.

Once I did this, I was not sure how I would actually age in appearance, but I figured I would still age, but about ten times slower. So, every ten years, I would age about one year in appearance. When I returned from this trip, I should be able to look in the mirror and see myself as I had looked when I had been about twenty-six years old. I didn't know how Terri was going to handle that, but before I went off and saved the world, I was going to take care of this.

I figured the best way to do this was not to talk to myself and have to explain everything to Max 1984, but to rather just contaminate something I would eat or drink then let the virus do its thing. How was I going to do that? Yes, I smoked back then. I would just walk by Max 1984 and ask to bum a smoke. When Max 1984 opened the box to offer me a cigarette, as I had always done if someone had asked to bum a smoke, I would reach for one of the cigarettes with a contaminated hand and basically contaminate the entire box of cigarettes. I knew, for sure, I would expose myself—Max 1984—within an hour of that contamination.

Without further ado, I put a capsule filled with the dried virus powder in the pyramid. Then I locked the door to the pyramid and entered the destination date: 12.18.11.3.15 | 13 Men | 18 Xul | G3, August 5, 1984, 1000 hours (10:00 AM). I then logged the time over the pyramid door to track my own ageing: 13.0.8.12.1 | 5 Imix' | 19 Sek | G7, July 8, 2021, at 1000 hours (10:00 AM). I sat down in the reclining chair and hit the green button. All went as planned as the ionic fog cleared and the reactor wound down.

I quickly unlocked the door and peered outside to make sure the coast was clear. All was as I had hoped. I pulled out the ATC and quickly sped to Annapolis.

There was an old derelict field located in the neighborhood, Annapolis Roads. I grew up in this neighborhood and knew it well. It had tall grass and was in a somewhat remote area, only visited by teenagers hanging out and smoking weed. It was also located on the Chesapeake Bay, so I would have easy access in and out without being seen. From there, I could walk to the Forest Hills Apartments, where I would find myself (Max 1984) living. It would take me about an hour to walk each way, but I knew all the back trails and shortcuts between the neighborhoods.

I quickly zipped to the field and landed the ATC. I was having to navigate Hal manually. Apparently, the GPS guidance systems that Hal relied on were not in place. Poor Hal had no way of knowing where to go. That was okay. I did, and we made good time, and without being shot out of the sky.

People didn't have cellular telephones with cameras and stuff like that in this time period so, even if they had seen me, they would not have known what they had seen. Maybe I would be reported as a UFO or something. I would never know.

From the abandoned field in Annapolis Roads, I walked to the Annapolis Roads Apartments, cut through over to Edgewood Road, and then through Fairwinds over to Victor Parkway. I crossed Bay Ridge Avenue and walked over to Forest Hills Avenue. From there, I could see the apartment I had once lived in. Now it was a matter of waiting for myself to emerge from the building.

My 1984 Chevy Chevette was parked in the parking lot. I was home. I would just kind of hang out along the edge of the woods and just try to keep an eye out.

A couple of hours later, I saw the apartment door open and my 1984 self emerged. This was my opportunity.

I broke open the virus capsule in my pocket and put my fingers into the white dust as I approached my 1984 self. As I approached the sidewalk, I could see that I (Max 1984) was smoking a cigarette.

"Hey, man," I said. "Can I bum a smoke? I thought I had mine with me and would really appreciate it if you could spare one."

Max 1984 pulled his pack of boxed cigarettes from his top shirt pocket, flipped open the top, and offered me one.

As I extracted a cigarette, I made sure I touched the rest of the smokes and made sure some of the virus-carrying powder fell into the cigarette box.

"Thanks," I said to Max 1984 and offered him some money for the smoke.

"I don't want the money. It's cool," he replied.

So, I continued to walk down the sidewalk and around the building as I lit the cigarette. It was the first cigarette I had smoked in more than twenty years.

I worried about what this virus would do to poor young Max 1984 as I made my way back to the ATC the same way I had come. I could almost picture the virus running through my 1984 veins, invading each of my cells and splicing in genetic patches that Todd and I had almost playfully concocted. I thought to myself, *This could actually kill me. I might not even exist when I get back to my own time period.*

I must have been a complete idiot for doing something like that with an unproven virus, but there was no turning back now. I was all-in, even if it didn't work on Max 1984.

I had now contaminated my 2021 self.

The thought of what I had done played havoc with my emotions for the rest of that day. I wanted to get back to my own time period and tell Terri what I had done, but I was afraid to have her scorn me. No, best to just be a man and keep my mouth shut. I was sure it would pass or kill me, and either of those two options would work out fine.

That day was one of the longest in my life. I was scared, alone, and everything just kept playing over and over in my head. I had just added naked mole rat, blind mole rat, elephant, bowhead whale, starfish, an axolotl, and some exoskeleton sea creature's genetic material in, as well as topped it all off with *Hydrozoa turritopsis dohrnii*. I mean, what the hell had I done to myself? If I was alive when I got back, I might be as blind as a mole, have grown as large as a whale, or formed some type of gills. One slip by either Todd or myself, and I could have spliced-in eyes that grew on top of my head or a blow hole in my back.

Once back at the field, I looked around to make sure no one was in sight then took my seat at the controls. Again, I had to give Hal all the manual commands to return to the West Virginia pyramid site.

I landed, moved the ATC into the pyramid, locked the door behind me, and noted the time over the doorway. It was now reading 1430 hours (2:30 PM). I set the new destination date and time: 13.0.8.12.1 | 5 Imix' | 19 Sek | G7, July 8, 2021, at 1030 hours (10:30 AM). I took my position in the recliner and hit the green button. As the tingling stopped, the cloud cleared, and the reactor wound down. I got up and walked to the bathroom section of the pyramid. I had aged four and a half hours and had returned just thirty minutes after my departure. But was my mission successful?

I took a gander in the mirror that I used to brush my hair and almost fell over in shock. I looked much younger. About thirty years old and not twenty-five, as I had thought. Still, I was much younger than the sixty years of my age. It had worked, but how would Terri take this? I was afraid to even show myself.

I got past that soon enough. I was hungry and needed to get out of this pyramid to get something to eat.

I unlocked the door and, as it swung open, Terri was there. She was looking at me with her arms open for a hug. Apparently, she had never known how I looked as my real sixty-year-old self. She was not aware that I had changed at all. To her, I had always looked like this. I was just ageing gracefully and always looked good for my age.

We went back to the house for a late lunch, and I noticed that all of our family photos around the house included myself looking young. Even the most recent photos taken. My son and I both looked young in the photos. I had pulled it off. I had changed history, and those changes were unknown to anyone who had not traveled with me through time.

I stored the balance of the virus media and started digging into some of the engineering literature that I had brought back with me from 2145. I took the fusion reactor information and sent it to an old friend of mine, Doug DeLeo, who was working on the experimental fusion reactor at the Larry Livermore National Laboratory (LLNL) in California.

CHAPTER FIFTEEN
TRANSPLANT
13.0.8.12.2 | TZLOK'IN DATE: 6 IK' | HAAB DATE: 0
XUL | LORD OF THE NIGHT: G8
GREGORIAN: JULY 9, 2021

I was glad to see the sun greet me that new morning. I had done some real shady stuff yesterday, and I needed to not take any more chances like that again. I could not help but wonder if I now had the ability to grow organs and my appendages back. That thought rested in my mind as I enjoyed my cup of coffee, watching the sun come up over the neighboring mountain.

I sat in that chair and continued to pour over the information contained in the printed pages that I had brough back from 2145 all day. I also thought about the possibility of burning DVDs with the data I needed to transport through time. It would be a digital hard copy. Chips could not hold the data, but burning a copy into a digital media like a CD or DVD might actually work. It was not a magnetic recording, and it was not a chip with gates and transistors, but an actual digital imprint burned with a laser into the media. I would add a CD/DVD burner to my travel arsenal in the future and, with that, a laptop computer that could boot off of a CD/DVD and a CD/DVD with COMOS code that could be loaded to make the laptop work. This might be the answer to information transportation through time.

I was starting to accumulate quite a few items in the pyramid in order to sustain myself in the other time periods. I needed to add even more items, like a freezer stocked with food, dehydrated food, bottled water, and a few more cooking appliances with utensils. I decided to work on reorganizing the pyramid and figured that it would be best if I equipped the pyramid with multiple reclining chairs so that more than one person could make the trip, if necessary. Of course, that would also require multiple shields.

The interior of the pyramid was now starting to look like a man cave. In a sense, that was what it was. Fully equipped with tools, a nuclear reactor, refrigerator, freezer, barbeque, and lounge chairs, all I needed was a pool table, and it would be complete. But there was no room for that.

Evening was approaching, and as I was enjoying a couple of Negroni cocktails, I decided I just had to know. I could not stop the question from echoing in my head over and over. Yes, I had to know: could I cut off a toe or finger and have it grow back? If so, how long would it take, and what would it feel like?

I put my hand on my shop table. I took out a large knife and lit my lighter. I heated the blade until it was really hot. Then I went to cut off my own pinky finger. However, I stopped and asked myself, *Are you crazy or what?* I had just told myself this morning that I was not going to take any more dumb chances, and there I was, about to lop off a finger with a hot knife in my shop. Not even a bandage within sight.

I chickened out.

Then I gathered some clean rags from the lab area of the shop, some duct tape, and a bottle of vodka. I rubbed the knife down with the vodka and wet my foot with a splash, as well. I was going to chance my left little toe. I had to know, and it wasn't like I could find out any other way. I had been drinking, and I was not feeling any real pain. I was most definitely making poor decisions, but I did it.

I stuck the point of the knife into the board between my little toe and the one next to it. It cut the skin on my little toe, and it started to bleed. I then pushed the handle to the board.

Shit! It hurt like hell as the knife went through the bone and the toe separated from my foot. I screamed out in pain. I was bleeding like a stuck pig. I was getting dizzy and sick just looking at the remaining nub of my little toe as it spat out blood.

I grabbed my foot where my toe had been cut off and put the vodka-soaked rag on it, wrapping it with duct tape to stop the bleeding. The pain was running up to the stem of my brain. I took a few hard panting breaths and watched the rag start to turn red from the blood.

After about two minutes, it started to feel a little better. I was not feeling any significant pain at that point, so I took the rag away from the wound and peeked. I could see that the nub where my little toe had been had completely stopped bleeding and a new toe was already developing.

I sat back and had another Negroni as I watched my little toe grow back. Then I put my sock back on, slipped on my shoe, and walked back to the house from my shop.

I was almost feeling invincible now. The engineered genome splicing had worked. Hopefully, I would never really need to find out if my organs could replace themselves.

CHAPTER SIXTEEN

JUMP PASS

I took some time to introduce Terri to Hal, the ATC, and to go over some of the information on technical advancements that I had been able to acquire during my last jump forward in time. Even the ATC's batteries were highly advanced compared to anything we had in 2021.

By the way she looked at the ATC, I got the impression she really liked it. I could tell she wanted to take Hal for a spin, but that was a big no-no in this time period.

I then sat down with Terri and asked, "Do you want to travel forward in time with me on the next up and coming time jump?"

Her first question was to ask, "Can I bring my cats?"

I shook my head. "It's really not possible. If one got out of the pyramid or needed special care, we could lose them forever. They would be safer just staying here. Besides, they won't miss you being gone for just one hour in their lives. We will be back before it's time to even feed them."

"It's not that I will worry for the cats; I'll miss them if we stay for more than a day. What if something were to happen to us where we couldn't return? The cats will die in the cabin before anyone knew we were missing." After that, she made the decision that she would rather just stay behind. That she would rather just wait for me to return in an hour.

That was the end of that discussion.

My thoughts quickly turned to the mission. I was going to try the year 3035 or maybe January 3036, to arrive just before the events had escalated to the point of no return. I figured I would focus on what needed to be done and make the jump in a few weeks.

Of course, the ATC would be about eight hundred ninety years old when I got there, and the ATV (All-Terrain Vehicle) would be more than a thousand years old. Keeping up with the Joneses so as not to draw attention had not been an issue that I had anticipated. The transportation from the pyramid to town was a challenge, and linking into what I called the internet would be increasingly difficult as I traveled further and further into the future. Each jump where I wanted to review the current world events would require that I obtain access to the internet, and possibly transportation, as well. I did not think that advancing in smaller jumps would help me much, as technology seemed to advance at a fast pace. So, even a ten-year jump would possibly require the same effort as a hundred-year jump.

Later in the day, I got a call from Doug DeLeo.

"This fusion reactor specs are amazing!" he exclaimed. It seemed really excited about the information that I had sent. "The LLNL (Larry Livermore National Laboratory) team is spending a lot of time pouring over these documents. However, we are all curious where the designs come from. Please don't tell me Russia."

We both had a good laugh at that.

"Anyway, we're so impressed that we're looking into incorporating many of the changes by December of 2022."

I thought to myself, *How awesome is this?* Man would be able to stop burning fossil fuels to generate electrical power maybe fifty to a hundred years sooner than if I had not given Doug this information. At least some good would come from this time machine, no matter what else happened.

13.0.8.13.9 | TZLOK'IN DATE: 7 MULUK | HAAB DATE: 7 YAXK'IN | LORD OF THE NIGHT: G8 GREGORIAN: AUGUST 5, 2021

It was Terri's birthday, and we had planned a full day together. It included a movie, dinner, and her favorite thing in the world—birthday cake! She was now fifty-nine years old and still looking quite good for a woman of that age. Not nearly as youthful-looking as myself, but still a good-looking woman who would catch the attention of every man in a room when she entered, no matter their age.

"Do you want to go buzz around in the ATC? You know, as kind of a special birthday gift? I asked.

She gave me an absolute no. "I do not want to spend my birthday in jail or being chased by F-16 fighter planes."

She got dressed, and we caught one of those *riveting, action packed* movies that was showing at the local theater. I wasn't sure if she even liked it, and I suspected she had chosen the movie for me, being she didn't want to put me through the pink, girlie doll movie that had been the hit at the time. No matter, the popcorn was great, and just being out with my girl made the day special for me, too.

We did a fine Italian dinner, and after, we went to a club in Winchester, had a few drinks, and danced. She loved to dance but not the slow kind of dancing you would think. She was from the disco era and liked to do her own thing. I was from the same era but born with two left feet and a rock-n-roll soul, not a dancer at all, but I did my best to keep up with her so she did not have to be on the dance floor by herself. After all, it was her birthday.

Then the special time of the day—the cake with the cats sitting around at the kitchen table, watching her as I sang "Happy Birthday."

As the day ended, we both knew I needed to jump forward again soon. The clock was ticking, and something needed to be done. We both agreed to put the rescue of humanity in motion and ahead of our own aspirations.

A toast to another birthday and the continuation of a journey to save the world.

13.0.8.13.9 | TZLOK'IN DATE: 8 OK | HAAB DATE: 8 YAXK'IN | LORD OF THE NIGHT: G9 GREGORIAN: AUGUST 6, 2021

I started loading up the pyramid for the next jump. This time, I loaded food, water, hundreds of blank CDs & DVDs, a laptop, and a Boot CD that contained a self-loading BIOS. I didn't know if it would work, but I was going to try to find a way to bring any data I could get my hands on back to my own time period. I should also try to find a recording system from the more advanced time period to accomplish this task, as well. The answer might not be available in my current time period, or past, but one might exist in the future that would allow me to successfully transport more data through time. I needed to find that solution.

After making the pyramid ready for any emergency that I could anticipate, I said my goodbye to Terri, locked the door, and took my position in the main lounge chair. I put the gamma ray and low-Z poly shield in place and entered the new destination date and time: 13.12.1.1.10 | 6 OK | 3 Yax | G3, January 15, 3036, at 0900 hours (9:00 AM). I logged the current date and time from over the doorway: 13.0.8.13.10 | 8 Ok | 8 Yaxk'in | G9, August 6, 2021, at 0900 hours (9:00 AM). Then I hit the green button, and I was off again. The reactor fired up, the ionic cloud filled the pyramid, and the tingling burned a little this time. I could even feel it in my lungs. After a few minutes, the cloud cleared, the tingling stopped, and the reactor wound down.

15.11.17.17.7 | TZLOK'IN DATE: 12 MANIK' | HAAB DATE: 10 CH'EN | LORD OF THE NIGHT: G5 GREGORIAN: JANUARY 15, 3036

I sat in the reclining chair for a few minutes, waiting to hear if the radiation detectors or atmosphere alarms would sound. Then I removed the shields and made my way to the viewing port and inserted the camera. I looked around and saw that there had apparently been some event that had taken place that had caused all the trees to die off. There were only stumps and remnants of downed trees. The quantity of green vegetation that I could see was minimal. Some grasses and small shrubs, but that seemed to be it. Quite barren.

I attached the atmosphere collection tube to the gold pipe that penetrated the pyramid and turned it on. It read 19.5% oxygen. The carbon dioxide level was reading 4,900 ppm. This indicated unusual air conditions. Apparently, something had gone wrong. This air was borderline breathable, at best.

I unlocked the door of the pyramid and stepped outside. The air smelled laden with smoke and felt heavy to breathe. I had to find out what was going on.

I brought out the ATC and closed up the pyramid. I figured I would go to the town of Capon Bridge and get to the bank safe deposit box.

The trip to town was as interesting as ever. People were traveling around in what appeared to be Plexi-glass crafts. No fan blades or propellers were visible. Apparently, someone had finally mastered levitation and some electromagnetic propulsion system. I would need to find out how it worked. Levitation was what my research had been about before I'd stumbled upon time travel or, should I say, my wife stumbled upon it. It was all inspiring to see it in action, and I found it unbelievable that it had taken so long to be discovered and become common place.

Hal got me to town without any issues. Upon arrival, it became apparent that clothing styles had changed. Everyone was wearing sheer, almost see-through clothing. Not just the young folks but even the old group was sporting this see-through attire. Men and women alike. Now, it was just my opinion, but when you get to a certain age, you needed to cover your junk up. There was nothing to make one more conscientious about oneself than to realize that you were dressed inappropriately after it was too late. In this case, I was fine being the odd man out.

I made my way to the bank counter, produced my safe box key, and got quite the look, dressed like something out of a history book. I had not dressed in the 2145 clothing but still had on my 2021 clothing—cotton denim jeans and a tee-shirt—and no, you could not see through any of it.

I just smiled and said, "I'm on my way to work my tour job at the museum." Then I pointed to my ATC, Hal. "Keeping it all authentic today."

The teller smiled. "Follow me to the boxes."

I followed the teller, whose hairy ass was visible, into a bank vault. This was not my time period, for sure, but I had no choice and just let the chill run up my spine and did what I had to do.

Once in the back, I withdrew my safe deposit box and took it to the private room. Within it was a phone and a paper written note. The note gave me my phone number and told me that my eye scan was my passkey to gain access to my account that The Hickman Holy Time Trust kept funded. There was supposed to be two years' salary in the account.

I turned on the phone, and it scanned my eye. Then it responded with a, "*Hello, Max. What can I do for you?*"

"The balance for my cash account?"

The phone responded, "*You have one million two hundred seventy-six WebDollars.*" That meant that the average income for a person was about five hundred thousand WebDollars a year. Nice.

I closed up the box, placed it in the vault, locked it in with my key, and exited the bank. Then I figured I would look around town to see what was going on. There were no actual stores or anything, other than restaurants. The place looked rundown and unkempt. I knew the only way I was going to find out what was really going on was to hook into the data stream (DS) and spend some time surfing.

Back at the pyramid, I was able to get the DS up and logged in. The phone projected everything as three-dimensional images, and I had to figure out how to move through the pages and pages of information. Believe it or not, my old account from 2145 was still there. That really took me by surprise. All the research data I had saved and photos of Todd and Ed were all there. It was good to see that the cloud storage was working. Anything that had been stored on the DS seemed to live on, but not my stuff from 2021.

I then shifted my attention to current world affairs. I was not surprised to find out that China and India were now taking on the world for natural resources. Clean water, timber, and food were in short supply in their nations due to the number of people and the years of ignorant neglect for the environment. It seemed the West, along with many European nations, were using satellite-mounted photon beam cannons to defend their borders while China and India had used nuclear weapons on their neighbors to eradicate them. Russia, not siding with the West or Europe, had also used its nuclear weapons to fend off China, and both China and India had unleashed a large-scale attack on Russia. Russia seemed to be lost as to why the European countries and the US had refused to join them in defending their lands. I thought to myself, *Imagine that.*

The oceans had risen approximately one hundred feet (30 meters) to new levels, wiping out most island nations that did not have mountains or volcanoes. The Caribbean Islands were gone, and the barrier islands in most countries around the world, along with a vast majority of Malaysia, were just shallows in the sea.

Most wealthy individuals in the US and the other NATO nations were boarding flights to the moon and Mars. According to the information on the DS, only personnel from NATO nations were being permitted to travel to Mars, and any other crafts were being shot down before getting anywhere near NATO assets of Mars. Both China and Russia had assets on the moon, but NATO has taken the position that China, India, and Russia would be denied access to Mars until the war was settled. As a direct result of the war, the Earth's atmosphere was declining; the ozone had been damaged and was no longer offering much protection as the Earth's atmosphere was quickly drifting away into space.

I continued to look for the exact start of the war and to identify the people and events that had caused it. My goal was to alter anything I could to stop this war.

I downloaded the names of presidents, generals, events, and anything I could to study the history of events leading up to the war. Fortunately for me, I had not tried to reach out for even a few months further in time. That, apparently, would have been a complete fail.

What I needed was someone with training in political sciences or social sciences to help me out. With all this information, I needed someone who could analyze the current affairs and, with some precision, identify what could be done to possibly alter the outcome. But who and how could I find someone competent in the field? Maybe I should travel back to 2145 and see if there was a professor or a government person whom I could discuss the matter with? Maybe the US government's Office of Foreign Affairs?

I was at a loss but knew I needed to be able to reach up high enough in the government to get the powers-that-be to listen so changes could be made. How did one go about telling the government what would happen almost a thousand years into the future then have them act in a manner that would prevent disaster? No, this would not work.

Then I realized I had to either go back to my own time period or travel to Mars then work with officials to reconcile the events for a more favorable outcome. At least, if I went forward in time, they might understand the time travel technology and be better equipped to fix things than someone in the year 2021.

My concern was now that if I traveled to Mars and spent the time traveling there, Earth might not be habitable long enough for me to return so that I could return to my own time period again. If I went to Mars, I might have to live out my life on Mars—all nine hundred years of it.

As a last-ditch effort to save humanity and Earth, I would have to take the chance, but I would pack up my backup frequency generators and acoustic speakers. Those items and a list of what frequencies were associated with travel both forward and back in time would give me the basic tools necessary to move through time on Mars. If necessary, I could always travel back in time on Mars then return back to Earth in an earlier year.

CHAPTER SEVENTEEN

MARS

15.11.17.17.8 | TZLOK'IN DATE: 13 LAMAT | HAAB
DATE: 11 CH'EN | LORD OF THE NIGHT: G6
GREGORIAN: JANUARY 16, 3036

I made ready to travel to Mars. All the assets I had, including all the funds managed by the trust, were loaded into digital currency and onto a chip, then implanted into my left hand, between my thumb and index finger. Billions of WebDollars, and all of it was with me. I hoped I didn't lose my left hand somehow. If I did, I would have to go win another lottery to make it all work. It seemed WebDollars continued to reign supreme both on Earth and on Mars, so at least that was one thing that I wouldn't have to worry about.

I noticed that the vast majority of life moving around was that of robots. They looked like some type of cloned humans, all handsome men and beautiful women, but most looked the same, or at least like brothers and sisters with different hair color. As a human, one could only admire the physiques of these robots. Perfection without flaws, and everything was in proportion. Nothing to complain about and easy on the eyes.

I had all my equipment packed up and my identification credentials in order. My credentials, they, too, were in the left-hand chip. So, as long as my eye scan and chip biometrics matched, there was no question as to who I was. The last thing I did at the pyramid was to hide the key under a large rock about a hundred meters from the pyramid door. I could not take any chances that I might lose the key.

I took a shuttle from Capon Bridge to the launch facility, located outside of Richmond, Virginia. That was about a fifteen-minute ride. From there, we boarded the Mars transport and awaited liftoff. Everyone was nervous except the robotic stewards, who gave directions and helped people find their proper place on the transport shuttle.

Apparently, this trip to Mars was going to take approximately three Earth days to complete, so small rooms, or pods, were assigned, complete with bathrooms and showers. The craft looked much like a plane from the 2000s but about the size of a cruise ship. The wings were thicker and proportionately shorter than a plane. The craft had multiple levels and, after leaving Earth's atmosphere, we would be able to move around to the various areas of the ship. There were several bars, food courts, and dining areas. There were stages with entertainers and a gym. I mean, this was like a luxury cruise ship if I ever saw one, and it was going to fly and get me to Mars in just three days!

I asked if we would have gravity once in space. I was told by the robot steward that I should not notice any changes in gravity from what I would normally experience. However, there had been some instances where the crafts artificial gravity had failed and everyone had to strap in. Hopefully, that wouldn't be the case.

As scary as the situation was, I could not help but feel like I was going on a vacation or something. I was really detached from the major events that were happening here on Earth as I sat in my launch chair. The need to resolve the issues was going to be on hold for a few days as I traveled to Mars and, in the meantime, the planet was being bombed with nuclear weapons. It was only a matter of time before the Earth's atmosphere would just be completely blown into space, leaving life with nothing to even cling to.

Liftoff came, and everyone was seated for the event, apart from the robot stewards. As we took off, I could not help but wonder why we were strapped in—it was so smooth that you could have threaded a needle during the event. Then I started to understand why when the craft started to accelerate and the G-forces became serious. I mean, old folks were in a panic and blacking out as the craft continued to accelerate for almost thirty minutes. It was unlike a typical aircraft takeoff, where you accelerated for a few minutes, and then everything seemed to level off. No, this thing just kept you in your seat for the full thirty-minute duration. You could not even lean your head forward and would have had to work to reach your hands out straight in front of you. We were really moving and had left Earth's atmosphere within a few minutes, but the G-forces kept coming. I was not sure how the physics for that worked.

Then, all at once, everything was calm. The craft stopped shaking and was flying as smooth as glass. The G-forces that had been holding everyone in their seats just vanished.

"Thank you for your patience. We are now traveling at Mach 8 and should have smooth travels. Although asteroids can be an issue, we are not expecting to encounter any on this trip. You may now proceed to your room. Enjoy our trip," the robot pilot said from over the speakers.

Great, we could walk around and enjoy the cruise, devoid of the fresh ocean air, but the craft did have large viewing ports so we could enjoy the view of distant stars, Earth, the moon, and the sun as we proceeded to our Mars destination.

I spent some time just exploring the shops. That was to say, I was seated in the shops in front of various three-dimensional color projections, trying to figure out if they had a conservative selection of clothing that I would feel comfortable in. They had a laser measuring system that did a complete analysis as you entered the shop, so there was no need to enter sizes, gender, or anything.

The see-through clothing stuff that was in style was not working for my psyche. I did not even want to be cool, hip, or whatever they called it these days, but I also didn't want stand out, obvious that I did not belong.

I finally found a few choice pieces. They were robe-like, and they had a semi-transparent look to them, but I figured I could wear my regular clothes under them, and it would not be too obvious. Within moments of ordering them, they were printed out, and I was able to take them to my room. There, I tried them on, and I felt I could get away with the look. It felt a little like dressing up for one of those 1977 space movies, but even they did not have to subject themselves to see-through versions. This was what they had that I could work with, so it would have to do.

Next on the list were the bars and clubs. I felt I might be able to talk to people and get a lot more information about current events from actual people rather than from the DS. What was strange, however, was that people did not seem to talk often. Not even to order drinks. To order drinks, you just scanned a photo that was printed along the bar, and the drink was delivered to you by a bar robot, all paid for and everything through the phone.

The folks in the bars and clubs were automatically added and removed from a chat room as they entered and left the establishments. Almost all communication was by talking to your phone, smiling in the camera, and selfies. I mean, these people had lost the art of talking face-to-face! They were in the same place, talking to the phone, waving, smiling, and sending messages even as they sat just one or two seats away from each other. These holographic mini-images of the person they were communicating with were dancing and doing elicit acts on the bars and tables, only six inches (15 cm) tall, but everyone had one going in front of them. I guessed you could have your hologram do whatever you wished without it being offensive. Then, if they decided to hook up, they made arrangements to do so at some mutually agreeable place and never even communicate face-to-face in the establishment. It was amazing that they even had the drive to connect face-to-face long enough to reproduce.

From what I could see on the DS, there did not seem to be marriage as I knew it any longer. People lived by themselves, and yes, they did have children where both parties contributed financially, but the robots raised the children. Child-rearing seemed to be quite hands-off compared to anything that was happening back in the 2000s. Quite different, indeed.

How was I going to communicate with any of these strangers on a level like this? I mean, there was no interaction for talking about politics or social events of any kind in public. I didn't know if they even knew how to talk face-to-face with someone about these issues. I guessed the DS was the only way they aired their views and discussed social subjects. I could be sitting anywhere and connect to one of these chat rooms to discuss my views on almost any subject I wished, but to pull up a chair and have a beer with a stranger, talking politics, was not going to happen in 3036.

I decided to drop the bar and club angle. Besides, I was the only guy in the place who did not have a hologram dancing in front of me, performing illicit acts. I guessed my robe was not working for me. Church was out, as religion was strictly DS delivered. So, I sat in one of the quieter bars and sipped on a drink as I pondered my next move while the ship slipped through space at eight times the speed of sound (2,744 meters/second).

Then, what started as a little spark of suspicion in the back of my mind grew into an overwhelming realization. All these people had been raised by robots. The DS provided them with their information, and the people seemed to only communicate directly with the robots and through the DS, and not with each other. That might be the case when it came to geopolitical subjects, as well.

What was really going on? Did people of one country actually talk to the other country, or was there a robot that operated between the two parties that was manipulating the outcome of the negotiations? Had I just identified the source of war and the destruction of Earth's living beings? Maybe the poorer countries, who were not privy to robot interaction every day, were fighting the wealthy who were letting the robots run everything?

The robots were gladly helping the group who would follow them. They were moving the followers who could be controlled, like sheep, to other uninhabitable celestial bodies—the Moon and Mars—as the robots had no need for the atmosphere. The robots might be the architects of a plan to destroy Earth and have Earth left in a state that only robots and artificial intelligence could survive. Ship after ship of humans, who were willing to surrender authority to the robots, were carted off to base camps on other planets, leaving those unwilling to cooperate behind to die at each other's hands.

I had found myself a victim, having been blindly led to this ship traveling to Mars, as a sheep would to the slaughterhouse.

Being the DS could easily be monitored, it would not be wise to just start suggesting there was an issue out there in some chat room. That would surely be the end of my life. I had to find a way to communicate with all humans without the robots knowing.

This called for a second drink as I pondered the possibilities and a way to get around the robots. I scanned in another margarita, on the rocks, no salt, and waited for the robot server to bring it. I wondered if I could insert a computer virus that would cause the computers to go blind in some way. Figuratively speaking, that was. Blind to a code or blind to a message. Blind to something we humans could hear, but they did not or could not monitor. Maybe I could make a computer virus that caused the computers and robots to not be able to hear just one frequency. I could communicate with everyone through the DS, and it would leave the robots unknowing.

When my margarita arrived, I thanked the robot server and offered a tip.

"No tip is necessary. It's my pleasure to serve you," the robot assured me kind of suggestively, but let's stay focused here.

"Do you mind if I ask you a couple of questions about yourself?" I quickly asked.

"Sure," the female robot said.

99

"Is your vision in full color or just black and white?"

"I can see up to ten million colors and in the infrared spectrum, as well as the ultraviolet spectrum," she answered.

"What about your hearing?"

"My hearing is tuned to 85 Hz to 3 kHz," she responded, which was the human audible range. "I also communicate on several digital frequencies with the other robots and servers simultaneously."

I gave her the, "Wow, that's impressive," feedback that the robot seemed to be looking for, and then she went on her way.

15.11.17.17.9 | TZLOK'IN DATE: 1 MULUK | HAAB DATE: 12 CH'EN | LORD OF THE NIGHT: G7 GREGORIAN: JANUARY 17, 3036

I awoke after an uneasy rest, hurling on a trajectory toward Mars at an ever-increasing speed. A sheep being thrown down the path of no return, along with the entire flock, as we displayed smiles on our faces, with dancing holograms and fancy mixed drinks.

The rest of the day, I tried to casually look for weaknesses in the robots' operations. I studied what I knew about them and did a little more research, trying not to be too obvious as I did so. A question or two here and there. A search on the DS about this and that. Looking for that one weakness that I could exploit.

I did find that the robots were communicating with each other, and the mother server on frequencies 462 MHz and 467 MHz These were the old Family Radio System (FRS) and General Mobile Radio System (GMRS) frequencies used back in the 2020s. All digital and scrambled, I was sure, but still not too hard to access and low enough power that they might be easily blocked.

I found myself wondering what the Mars' facilities were like and what I was heading into. I was going there and probably didn't have a real choice but to what?

I went into one of those Mars chatrooms where I could ask questions. I was told I would be assigned a room, or pod as they called them, and that everyone was grouped by age. However, gender was random. That it was like living in the desert where you had to live indoors due to the heat. There were pools and recreation facilities, depending on what package you could afford to buy and what you liked to do. None of the folks on Mars were poor or would be considered lower-class, or lower-middle-class, for that matter. Each pod was assigned a bot that kept the place clean and made sure you had everything you needed. They were there to keep an eye on you, should you ever need help.

Was that it? Was each person actually being monitored, one on one, by a robot?

The robots lived with you and took care of your needs throughout your entire life. You grew up trusting them. They even monitored the DS so they knew who and what you were discussing. These poor people had no idea! They had handed over their freedoms a long time ago, and artificial intelligence (AI) had exploited mankind's weaknesses and had set up its own agenda. This was getting scary. I might be dealing with an AI being, leaving me no way to anticipate its next move. Additionally, AI was connected to every part of Earth, Mars, and the moon, and it had almost everyone streaming it live data.

As I strolled around the ship, it was surreal knowing I was traveling in paradise as man's demise grew ever closer. The spas, the food, the view of our solar system as I could never have imagined. Tiny dancing holograms on tables, a buzz for almost all day from kalua and cream coffee, or mojitos for breakfast to margaritas at night. All you had to do was ask your bot, and most reasonable requests were met. To be walking with gravity in space as we sailed forward on a ship, powered by element 115 (moscovium), at almost the speed of light, on a trajectory toward Mars. It felt like a true dream. Or, should I say, a nightmare in the making. I was going to just keep this buzz for the day, and maybe some answers would come in my sleep.

15.11.17.17.10 | TZLOK'IN DATE: 2 OK | HAAB DATE: 13 CH'EN | LORD OF THE NIGHT: G8 GREGORIAN: JANUARY 18, 3036

Usually, after a day of drinking, I would be hungover and in the mood to do nothing. Today was different. I woke up with some ideas on how to test for weaknesses. This ship was the perfect place to try everything out, as it was a small sample of the robotic network. I really only had a theory as to what was going on, and the last thing one should do was to assume that some far-fetched theory was fact, especially when it might affect so many people. I was not going to be able to prove that the robots were, in fact, plotting and working to eliminate humans on Earth, but I could explore the idea of communication with other humans without the robots knowing. This way, I could actually try to connect with someone of power without the bots shutting me down.

I had my bot fix me a nice breakfast and requested that we skip the liquor this morning. Just eggs, bacon, toast, and jelly, please. Then I opened my gear with frequency generators and acoustic speakers, setting a few up. Just a couple. According to the one bot in the bar, the bots had a hearing range of 85 Hz to 3 kHz. That would make sense being that was the range humans made most vocal sounds. However, we humans could hear in a range of 20 Hz to 85 kHz. There was a range from 20 Hz to 84 Hz, and from 4 kHz to 85 kHz, that were outside of our speaking range, but we were capable of hearing within these ranges.

As the robot watched, it asked, "What are you doing? May I assist you?"

I set up two of the acoustic speakers and told the bot, "I'm just messing around with my own music sound system. It's a hobby. I enjoy altering old music to make new sounds."

That gave it something to ponder and, of course, there was a barrage of questions, but I thought I had gotten past the red flags.

I then played some music that the bot could hear and asked, "How does that sound?"

Lying its teeth off, it said, "The music is great, but is that not the point of this exercise?"

Then I let a message play at 80 Hz that asked the bot, *"Please get me a drink."*

Over and over, it played, and the bot did not respond.

I kept working through the frequency ranges until I got a response. Right on que, at 85 Hz, the bot asked, "What type of drink do you want?"

"Never mind," I told it then jumped up to 4 kHz.

Again, no response.

I ran the message all the way through to 85 kHz, and I could honestly say I couldn't hear all the way up the full range myself, but there was enough range there that I could play the message over the DS or announcement system, and it should go undetected by the bots. Only humans would be able to hear it.

As I sat back, listening to some nice jazz music, mid-morning, under the surveillance of the pod robot, I inconspicuously rigged up a transmitter that could broadcast on frequencies 462 MHz and 467 MHz Just white noise and enough power that it could basically make the frequencies useless for communication on this spaceship.

How long would I be able to mess up the robot communication system before they found a workaround? I was not sure, but I figured the next thing they would try to use to connect with each other would be the DS.

Most of the routers used 2.4 GHz and 5 GHz. However, I was aware there were also Wi-Fis operating on 6 GHz and 60 GHz. I would need to build a transmitter that could block out those frequencies and all cell phone frequencies that were currently in use. I could do this by programming an existing router to broadcast a single message on those frequencies. This would have to be done using a virus that would spread throughout the DS. Additionally, a virus would have to be planted into the personal phone network to block any possibility of the robots turning to the human's communication system to coordinate a defense.

I knew I could not do all this on the trip to Mars, and I really did not have the programming skills to hack and plant such viruses, but I also knew where I could find someone. I would have to travel back in time to get that developed, but that was a possibility I would not rule out. Later, I would just try scrambling their 462 MHz and 467 MHz frequencies, just to see how they chose to respond. I also needed to make sure that severing the system would not lead to the loss of the ship's controls. I would have to plant this transmitter up in the craft's communication chase. Someplace they couldn't find it. I would just have it power up for five or ten minutes and see how my robot dealt with the inconvenience of being isolated from that communication network. Let's see if the ship ended up in trouble for the blackout time or if it could continue to operate normally. I suspected the robots would have to keep some type of communication going to fly this ship right.

It was getting close to lunch, and so I asked my robot, "Please fix me some ramen noodles with sliced up tomato and avocado. Add in some sardines and, if possible, some marinated artichokes."

"Would you like anything else?" the robot asked.

"Mix it up with some virgin olive oil, sea salt, and white pepper," I answered.

"Do you want to eat at the food gallery or in your pod?"

"Please bring it to the pod. I don't want to eat in the gallery today," I told the bot.

It didn't take long before the robot was placing my order and making a place on my little table ready.

After about thirty minutes, the bot announced, "I am going down to the food court to pick up your lunch. I will be back in ten minutes."

I thanked the bot, even though it wasn't human. Then, as soon as it left the pod, I went to work removing the ceiling tiles for access into the hallway chase. As quickly as I could, I placed the transmitter in the communication chase and strung out a long wire as an antenna across the adjacent hallway. I plugged it in and set the timer to start transmitting in about thirty minutes, for a five-minute duration. That should be long enough to see how the bot reacted, and it should not interrupt my lunch.

Just about the time I got the last of the ceiling tiles replaced, the robot entered the pod with my lunch and presented it on my small pod table. Again, I thanked the bot and proceeded to eat.

The bot stood by patiently as I indulged myself with this strange mix of a meal. I took my time eating, still listening to the jazz music, tapping my foot and rolling up my ramens as though it was spaghetti. Then shit hit the fan.

The bot just collapsed on the floor.

I could hear them all collapsing throughout the ship, like hundreds of bots hitting the floor all within a few seconds. Apparently, these robots didn't have the ability to function on their own. They were unable to even stand or function in any way without the ship's main computer controlling them. They used cloud processing of some type through a high-speed communication network. They had no computing power of their own.

I walked over to my bot. "Hello? You okay down there?"

Nothing. It was dead. Not wiggling or anything.

I thought it would come back to life after a few minutes, using some other frequency or backup frequency, but no, nothing.

The five-minute duration for my transmitter was up, and then the lights came on in the bot's eyes. It was rebooting. I could see the spark come back.

I was standing over the bot when it got up off the floor and asked, "What happened?"

"I don't know. You just dropped to the floor. Are you all right? Should I do something?"

"No," it responded. "The ship passed through a high-frequency radio wave storm or solar flare. The cause is under investigation." The bot then took its place back next to the table to wait on me.

When I finished my lunch, the robot gathered all my dirty dishes and utensils, announcing, "I will take them back to the food lounge."

"Thank you," I told the bot.

As soon as my bot left the pod, I quickly removed my transmitter and replaced the ceiling tiles. This time, I packed the transmitter away.

When the robot returned, I turned off the jazz music and kind of nonchalantly packed up my toys. I thought to myself that I had found the Achilles' heel for this ship, but that might not cover robots everywhere. I needed to do a little more homework on the subject matter. If it was that easy to overcome these robots, both India and China would have already exploited this weakness.

Announcements started coming in over the pod speakers.

"*We will be docking at the Mars base in two hours. Please have all personal belongings packed and ready to depart. A one-hour warning will be given when all persons need to return to their designated seats and fasten restraints for entry into Mars' airspace.*"

Then another announcement came over the speakers. "*The unexpected disruption to the robots was due to a radio frequency burst associated with a solar flare. All robots are now functioning at one hundred percent.*"

Okay, we were almost to Mars, and I didn't think the robots—or, should I say, the ship's AI computer—had been able to detect what had really caused the interruption in the robots operations.

After an hour went by, the announcement came over the speakers. "*Everyone is to return to their assigned seats and secure their restraints to make ready for entry into Mars' airspace.*" This announcement was repeated over and over, as though we were daft or something.

When we got to the half-hour mark, the lights went out in most of the craft, with the exception of the walkways. Then the lights dimmed in the cabin with the chairs, like when a movie in the theater was about to begin. It looked like almost everyone was back in their chairs, but there was still an empty chair here and there. Those holdouts were obviously frequent flyers who knew they could wait until the last second, so as not to have to sit in the chair, strapped in for an hour. Duly noted for the return trip.

What a marvelous view, I thought as we approached Mars. The red planet had earned its nickname for a good reason. It was more a rusty red but red, indeed.

As we descended, the mountains and craters came into view. Then, slowly, the small outcropping of a city became visible and grew larger as we neared our landing location. This cruise-ship-sized craft was landing without a runway, on a big *X* next to a large building.

"*Please remain in your seats until your personal escort arrives to take you to immigration,*" another announcement told us.

A large tube extended up from the ground to the underside of our craft. It was an elevator of sorts. Then, row by row, the robots came in and escorted each passenger to the elevator. From there, to the immigration desks. Here, they checked you in and scanned in your identification data. They asked about plants, food stuff, and basically did a scan to make sure you were not bringing in any pests, bombs, or firearms. They wanted to know what your skill set was and if you had sufficient funds to sustain yourself on Mars. I was sweating throughout all this. However, I tried to not let it show on my face.

I did not know if my identification was real, or some type of phony ID just made up to bluff the locals. However, when they scanned my biochip in my hand and my eye, that seemed to check out. They saw I had a substantial amount of WebDollar cryptocurrency, and when they asked about my skill set, I told them, "I'm a retired nuclear health physicist with an expertise in equipment maintenance and a geneticist."

The robot that was checking me in suggested, "You should come out of retirement and work while on Mars."

"I'll think about it. But, for now, I just plan on enjoying some rest and relaxation."

Apparently, it was uncommon to suggest such a thing, but I was waved on through the check-in.

Next, I needed to find out what was involved in acquiring the basics here on Mars—food, water, and shelter. I was directed to the counselor robot to help me with the acquisition. The counselor placed me in an area of Mars city for people of my age. I would be given a three-room pod overlooking Mount Sharp, equipped with a kitchen, living room, and one bedroom with a single bathroom, all for forty-thousand WebDollars per month. This included power, water, entertainment, and a female-identifying robot. What more could a guy ask for?

Next booth, they added my Martian identification data to my hand chip. I guessed I was officially a Martian now. I would have to check the mirror the next time I was in the restroom to see if I was now a little green man with an antenna growing out of my head.

This new identification would allow me to travel around Mars with the swipe of my hand, and I could also travel to and from Earth without having to go through immigration again.

I was told that, each Thursday, the President of NATO Mars, President Ron Kline, had a meet-and-greet with all new immigrants. "You will be expected to attend on August 21, 3036, at 1400 hours (2:00 PM), where you will have the opportunity to mingle with President Kline, his wife, and many of the congressional representatives. It's a semi-formal event, lasting for about four to six hours. It's considered an opportunity to present oneself for open government political positions. Most nominees for political positions are currently selected as a direct result of this initial meeting with the governing body."

I thought that was cool that you did not have to be born on Mars to hold a political position and you did not have to be from any one country, just a NATO country. I knew so little about this Martian government, and I was sure it would be best if I was not nominated or elected to any political positions, being I was not going to be around for long. I still had a mission. I needed to save Earth, and I needed the help of Earthlings, excluding the robots, to make that happen.

The Martian President might be the person who could help. If I could get a sit-down with him and other humans, without the robots listening in, I could air my suspicion and possibly have them help or intervene before it was too late for Earth. President Kline would have the political power to speak with NATO Earth countries' heads of state. What better way to get the message out to everyone?

That afternoon, I was transported to my pod that had a nice view of some mountains and a crater. I was told that I would have a great view of the rising sun coming up over the mountain chain.

My neighbors looked nice enough, though they failed to give me so much as hi. However, I was approached by two neighbors, Lydia and LeeAnn, who expressed their displeasure that I did not appear to be in the proper area due to my age. There was only one Italian guy, Joseph Blumeraitis, who lived a couple of pods away, who was even half-accepting of my presence. I could tell he would have been a great guy to know back in the day, but it was obvious, like with the others, that he did not have the social skills to communicate.

CHAPTER EIGHTEEN
HEAR ME NOW

I was having some trouble adjusting to the time change. Sleep was not coming easily, so I found my mind working overtime. My obsessive-compulsive disorder (OCD) was in high gear. I kept thinking about how to communicate with the President without the robots knowing, or the surrounding humans exposing me. I thought I might have to take some chances with the other humans in the area and just use the acoustic speakers to broadcast my message to them when I was face-to-face. Something like, "I need to talk with you in a secure room about a major security issue without any robots or listening devices." Something along those lines. But who knew how he would respond? If this didn't work, I could always travel back in time and try something else, as long as they didn't incarcerate me.

I rigged up my little transmitter with a small speaker clipped on my collar with a new message. No, I did not use the "please get me a drink" message. I figured that would not go over well if the President did hear it. I laughed out loud as I cracked myself up again, which put my robot on alert.

"What's so funny?" she asked.

"Just some childhood memories coming back to me." I smiled at her, and she went back to taking care of the pod.

This might be really tough. These robots were on high alert. Anything I did set them in motion. The rest of the humans didn't realize it because they had been raised by these bots and had lived with them all their lives, but it was like some type of hovering parent watching you all the time or something. You couldn't do or say anything without them getting involved.

I set up to broadcast my message at 80 Hz. That should make it detectable to most humans and undetectable to the robots. Or, so I hoped. Then I spent the day broadcasting on this frequency to various robots to see if they picked up on it. I went to the bars and food court, trying to order food and drinks, but the robots were unaware of the message I was broadcasting. Younger folks heard it easily, and some of the older folks could hear it, but others could not. I was careful not to say anything alarming or that might cause concern. I thought, after a full day of testing this transmitter out, I had a chance of making this work. Mars' President Kline was not that old, so I hoped he could hear my message as I transmitted it during our introduction on Thursday, January 21, 3036.

What should my broadcast say to Mars' President Kline was all I could think about. "Hi, I am Max Hickman. I am here to discuss with you a matter of utmost importance." Or maybe something like, "It is imperative that we have a private, unmonitored discussion." Or what? I kept thinking about how *I* would take such a message if some stranger were to say it to me.

I finally came up with, "This message cannot be heard by robots. It is imperative that we have a secure conversation as soon as possible. Humanity depends on it." He would know who I was because, when I introduced myself, I would give him my name, so there would be no need to repeat it. Besides, I was sure they would be logging in who the President spoke with by scanning our ID chips.

15.11.17.17.12 | TZLOK'IN DATE: 4 EB' | HAAB DATE: 15 CH'EN | LORD OF THE NIGHT: G1 GREGORIAN: JANUARY 20, 3036

I spent some real time in the restroom, recording my message. It was the only place that I could get away from the pod robot. Apparently, the robots were accustomed to only entering the restrooms if asked or to maintain and clean them. Once my recording was done, I played it back one last time to myself then made it ready for my meeting with President Kline.

The rest of the day, I investigated the various types of modern digital storage that was available. I was surprised to find that five-dimensional (5D) crystal quartz was the storage in use. That a see-through flexible chip, about the size of a credit card, was capable of storing all the words ever written since the beginning of time in every language. This type of storge claimed to be able to store information without corruption for 13.8 billion years! I also found that the readers and writers were commonplace, and that I could purchase a reader/writer and the media without any problem. Or so I thought.

I requested that my robot order a reader/writer and ten quartz storage cards. This request seemed to be a red flag.

"Why do you want so much storage?" this pod robot wanted to know.

"I want to keep various types of photos and documents on different cards, and I want to make backups just in case I misplace one," I explained.

The robot told me, "You can just keep your documents and photographs on the DS cloud. There is no need for a physical hard copy."

I was then forced to explain, "With everything happening on Earth, I just felt better creating hard copies. Will you please place the order?"

The robot actually took a moment, like it was stuck or something, and then replied, "The order has been made. The items will be delivered later today."

I figured that no matter what happened here, I needed to secure this superior storage media and hardware so I could take it back in time with me if necessary. I had an associate at South-Sampton University, Beverly Lord, who would love to get her hands on this technology. Think about what this could do for society back in 2021. All the lost data, all the CDs and DVDs that had gone bad. All the hard drives that had crashed. Just the sheer amount of data loss, and the money spent to keep it from being lost, could all be avoided by just having the data written using this stable quartz crystal storage media. I was sure it would take her a few years to perfect it, but this would be a great gift to bring back. I was almost positive that I could record anything I wanted to and bring it back with me on this media. I was no longer going to need to worry about electrical or magnetic charges holding the data and being corrupted as it was subjected to the various frequencies of time travel. This quartz technology was actually altering the polarization of the quartz in a permanent way using lasers, and this record was so stable that I thought it would surely be superior to anything else I could possibly use.

I also found on the DS that personal computers no longer existed. Not even an option. Apparently, all computers were just terminals that fed into the DS cloud. No processing power at all. You just had your phone, and you set it on the table, and you talked into it. Everything was processed over the DS, and all responses were cloud generated. All photos and written data were shown with a three-dimensional (3D) projection. So, my old laptop was an interesting piece of hardware, as far as the robot was concerned. It had a keyboard and was not operating on the DS.

Once I got my laptop operating using the DVD BIOS system, I did some finagling to figure out how to get the Wi-Fi to hook up directly with the new quartz reader/writer. I then burned the BIOS into one of the quartz storage cards. All the while, the robot was watching everything I did and kept after me about the laptop. I knew it was monitoring everything on the screen and anything being broadcasted to and from the computer. All this was surely feeding into the AI cloud system.

I thought to myself, *There is no way the DS AI doesn't already know about these systems, being they predated all current systems.* Apparently, the Mars AI system had never seen a personal computer used, or maybe it had not been provided information about this type of computing system, but it was surely studying my every move.

I took a few breaks and used the food court to just get away from my pod robot. I was starting to get paranoid by having it watch over me all day. I was mostly just doing research and really did not have anything else to do. I had no job, but I had all the WebDollars I would ever need.

I thought the robot would basically get bored with me and just move on, doing whatever pod robots did. But no, that did not happen. My pod robot had other robots come in and do the cleaning, stocking, and performing the normal day-to-day services as my main pod robot just watched me. Apparently, I was on the national Mars' watch list. At least, that was the way I felt.

I also had a concern about leaving my laptop in my pod. I did not know what I would do if the pod robot took my laptop when I was away. Tomorrow's meeting with President Kline could not come soon enough.

I asked my pod bot to please help me select the appropriate attire for tomorrow's meet-and-greet with the President. She was quick to select my wardrobe, have it printed, and set it aside. Then she set up my entire itinerary for the day, including breakfast, lunch, bathing, and transportation.

That night, I sat back, watching a movie.

"I won't need you any longer today," I told my pod robot. "I'm just going to finish my movie and go to bed."

"Enjoy your movie. I will see you in the morning," she responded then stood on her induction coil, recharging.

That was when I took the opportunity to stash my laptop under my mattress, knowing I would not be around tomorrow afternoon to guard it.

15.11.17.17.13 | TZLOK'IN DATE: 5 B'EN | HAAB DATE: 16 CH'EN | LORD OF THE NIGHT: G2 GREGORIAN: JANUARY 21, 3036

I awoke early, as this was now my new norm. Being Mars had a day of twenty-four hours, thirty-nine minutes, and thirty-five seconds, referred to as a sol, I was starting to get into sync with my inner clock again.

Today was my big day. My chance to meet the Mars President, Ronald Kline, and most of Congress, as well. This day could have far-reaching implications, as it could either be the saving day of Earth or the day Earth met her fate.

"Are there some glasses or something I could wear that will allow me to know the names and titles of each person as I'm introduced?" I asked my bot. "Or, is there some way, other than my memory, to find out who's who?"

She went to the small storage dresser in the pod and pulled out a contact lens. "This will provide you with the names and titles of each person within .6 meters (2 feet) of you and keep a record of your encounters for future review. The video of each encounter will be uploaded by the room surveillance system, onto the DS cloud, and the actual encounter will be time stamped so that you can always access who you meet and what they look like."

Imagine that. No camera on me, and this one eye contact lens was going to track me, tell me who was within my immediate space, and allow me to review the encounter at a later date. I imagined that each of the politicians were using the same system so they could go back and find anyone they cared to promote into their political regime. Made sense that they would have this type of system in place, but for just anyone to use it, I found that quite odd. I guessed, if they did not want you to use the information afterward, they could withhold the output and leave you with nothing. Besides, this gave them a tracker on your whereabouts and the knowledge of who you were talking with.

I had a good breakfast brought to me by my pod bot. As she went to retrieve my meal, I wired up my speaker and had it on my lapel. It looked like a standard lapel pin that all the politicians wore. It should not draw any attention.

The actual message was being played by a small integrated circuit (IC) that I had programmed. Much like the ones in greeting cards that had sung songs back in the 2020s. This was a small system, and if there were any real security, I was hoping it would pass muster even upon close scrutiny. I mean, it was a black dot under my lapel, no bigger than a small button. I then hung the suit back up so that it would be fresh for later that day.

As the pod bot brought back my breakfast, I sat down and started to eat.

Then the pod bot asked, "Where is your personal computer?"

"I put my toys away for another day. I'm not going to mess around with my hobbies today," I replied.

She did not press me as to where I had put it, and I had no intention of clarifying its actual location unless pressured into it.

I watched the broadcast news that morning in three-dimensional (3D). Some things seemed a bit too real—a lot of photos from Earth showing attacks that the countries were making on each other. These war reports were scary and, even though they were not anywhere near Mars, they were upsetting to watch. To see our mother planet, Earth, torn apart by the people who needed her to survive, like these remaining people were somehow going to be able to live on her after they had poisoned her with radioactive material and stripped her of her life-giving atmosphere. What the hell was man thinking to pursue such a war? But, believe it or not, they were going at it like never before, as the reporter showed hundreds of multi-megaton nuclear bombs being detonated each day. So sad. I guessed that each of the participants in the war figured that if they could not have the resources, they were taking them with them on the way out. The old, "if I can't have them, you can't either" mentality.

I strolled up and down the pod corridor a few times that morning, saying hi to all the nice old people that I passed who were my age but did not look nearly as young as I did. I was quite the stud muffin compared to most of these guys who were in their sixties and looked their age, while I only looked thirtyish. I was sure they were all upset over how I had gotten my pod in their area of Mars, as they were supposed to group everyone by age. I could tell by the stares they gave me whenever they looked up from their phones that I did not belong and would never be accepted.

On the rare occasion when one of them did speak, they would ask how old I was. I never lied to them. I replied that I was fifty-eight years this coming December. I had to stick with this because my ID chip was programmed with my age, and any deviation could cause me problems.

Lunchtime came, and my pod robot suggested I eat light because they usually had a nice selection of food at the meet-and-greet. I took her advice and just had a simple sandwich. Okay, not so simple, this was a get-what-you-want kind of place.

"A Reuben sandwich with sauerkraut and thousand island dressing, please."

The bot responded with, "I suggest you not do that. The sauerkraut may cause you embarrassment."

I then rethought the situation. "Okay, a simple chicken sandwich, then."

She smiled and went to retrieve my order, noting, "You don't have time to eat at the food court if you're going to make the meet-and-greet."

As I ate my lunch, I could hear the pod bot getting my things ready for my shower. This pod bot was on it. She was determined to make sure I made it to this meet-and-greet, being she had already arranged everything. I believed if I died that morning, she would have delivered me to the event dead and picked me up afterward to dispose of me. I was going dead or alive at this point.

After lunch, the pod robot cleaned up after me and suggested that I get dressed. I proceeded as she had suggested, taking a shower and thinking to myself that it might be my last, so I better enjoy it. Afterward, I dressed in the clothes she had set out. The lapel with my special button was still intact.

This suit was better looking than the robes I had been wearing since I had been on Mars, but it was still too revealing. Fortunately, they were a little more conservative than most people out there, walking around. It seemed the politicians were a trifle more traditional in their attire than the general population, or at least I was. Hopefully, I wouldn't have to show off too much skin to blend in with this crowd. Still, the shirt was see-through. I thought I could live with that, being my jacket was not. With any luck, my pod bot would have me dressed appropriately for the occasion.

I exited my pod at 1345 (1:45 PM), with my pod bot in attendance, and proceeded to the transport shuttle that served my section of pods. I said nothing but was quickly sealed in this see-through acrylic tube, and then the action started.

Like one of those delivery tubes that were used at the drive-thru banks, I was moving through a maze of tubes at mind-bending speeds. There had never been a rollercoaster on Earth that had as much action as this transporter. I was upside down at times, taking hard turns, and doing loops while moving at hundreds of kilometers per hour (km/h). Hard to say just how fast, but I figured 300 km/h or maybe 400 km/h (approximately 200 mph to 250 mph). What a ride! Then I came to a station with a smooth, deceleration gush, and the top opened.

A robot came over and said, "Please, follow me. I will be your escort to the meet-and-greet, and when the event concludes, I will escort you back to this transport."

I thought to myself, *How nice is that. This bot is going to help me get there and back. How considerate.* What I did not realize at the time was that I did not have the proper clearance to use the station. The robot was actually a secret service type of robot, assigned to protect Martian President Kline and the other congressional persons attending the event.

When I arrived at the entrance to the hall, I was stopped, and my hand was scanned. A spotlight was turned on and beamed on my head as I was announced.

"Maximilian Hickman," was called out, and then I was motioned to proceed forward.

I had not heard my birth name in years, so it took me a second or two to realize they had just called out my name. Everyone just called me Max, so it had taken me off guard. Yet, for some reason, my given name seemed appropriate for this event.

I smiled and did a right hand up hi wave. Then I proceeded down the red carpet like some type of movie star. From there, I was directed to a table with my name on a small digital screen. There were seven other chairs around the table. All but one was occupied by other newly naturalized Martian citizens. The open chair was for one of the Martian congressional people to sit. It seemed our table had been assigned a woman representative, Ms. Norma Baker.

Now, I must say that I was right about the dress for this event being much more conservative than the general population's daily attire but by no means conservative by 2020 standards. The women were showing full frontal ta-tas, and some lingerie-type panties could be seen on the bottom half under their sheer dresses, while the men were showing their chests. I was still living in the 2020 mindset and found it hard to look the women in the eye while talking with them. I had to consciously make myself act as though I could not see their bodies. I was a happily married man, and I was not out trying to look at other women, but I understood why there was no longer marriage.

While at the table, the occupants of the other five chairs just stared at their phone devices and totally ignored the others, each in their own world. Even when the spotlight turned on and someone's name was announced, they did not look up.

As the time came for Martian President Kline to speak, the chairs filled in, and Ms. Baker joined us at the table. I proceeded over to her chair and introduced myself. Then I went back to my assigned seat and waited for the event to begin. It seemed that the one-on-one introductions were no longer common. None of the others at the table bothered to do anything like what I had, but they might be doing it on the phone devices and I was just lost when it came to what was good etiquette. Regardless, they never said anything to me, and I did not see any greetings on my device, so I could only assume they just sat there and ignored each other.

Then I heard the announcement—President Ronald Kline.

I looked at the runway and got my first glimpse of the man. He resembled the robots in that he was a handsome guy but a little bit older. He walked and dressed like most politicians and did a lot of greetings with the other dignitaries on the way to the podium. It took him some time to get there, and when he took his place, I noticed that all the phone devices had been cut off and the occupants at the tables had stopped staring at them. They then looked up at Martian President Kline as he began his speech.

Now, this speech was well rehearsed. I was sure he gave the same speech each week, and all the dignitaries did the same thing week after week, as well. The only ones who did not have a written script were the newly naturalized Martian citizens, like myself.

President Kline had us stand up, raise our right hands, and repeat after him in what he called a swearing-in ceremony. I mean, it would have been nice to know that I was going to be sworn in and what I was swearing to before I actually said the words, but when in Mars, you did as the Martians. So, I went along with the program, as did everyone else.

Afterward, President Kline welcomed us and gave some long-winded speech about the history of the Martian civilization. "I encourage each of you to visit the

Martian Museum and to study the history. In fact, did you know that the building that houses the museum dates back to the first Martian settlement?"

When he concluded, we all clapped.

"Now, each of the dignitaries and I will be coming around to the tables as drinks are served." He pointed to the buffet table full of hors d'oeuvres. "Help yourselves, but please eat at your designated table so I can greet each one of you as I make my rounds."

This was going to be it. The time I had been waiting for. The only people who would be within earshot were the five other newly naturalized citizens, one dignitary—Ms. Baker—President Kline, and maybe a security guard or two. I was getting nervous now.

I quickly went to the buffet table and filled a plate of some really wonderful-looking finger foods. Each was perfectly presented, and being a foodie, I thought to myself that I would have to try one of each before leaving today. Maybe they would allow me to take some back to my pod. That might be pushing it, but if I knew what each was called, I could have my pod robot order them for me.

I was now back at my table, nibbling on a full plate of food, trying to eat as much as possible as quickly as possible, so as not to draw attention as to how full my plate was. The truth was that no one seemed to care. I drank champagne, smiled, and ate until the dignitaries came to the table and introduced themselves. I shook each of their hands as they transferred their contact info by coming into the range of my contact lens. Each of their names were written with a balloon text box as they approached me, and it seemed not everyone had contacts like mine. My pod bot had done well to give me this device.

Then I saw President Kline heading my way. He had two security robots by his side, and there were only five people remaining at our table, besides myself, because Ms. Baker, being a dignitary, was in the process of making her rounds.

President Kline started with the gentleman to my left before making his way around the table clockwise, having a little side conversation with each as he worked from one person to the next. Finally, it was my turn.

I hit the lapel button. I could hear it broadcasting my message, "*This message cannot be heard by robots. It is imperative that we have a secure conversation as soon as possible. Humanity depends on it,*" as I smiled and shook President Kline's hand. It played twice as I introduced myself and we had a quick conversation about me possibly joining his political party. It seemed this was why he had the meet-and-greets in the first place—to promote his political party and not really to be a nice guy.

I noticed that President Kline did not flinch or respond to the broadcast message that only humans could hear. But neither did the other humans at the table, as they had gone back to looking at their phone devices. I saw nothing that implied he could hear the message, and the security bots did not seem to hear anything, either. I also noticed that when I shook President Kline's hand, it was cold, not warm.

He looked human enough. He did not look like an obvious robot with portions of his neck as wires and metal structure, but something was alarming. Maybe it was his uncanny resemblance to the robots. Were the robots made in his image when he'd been younger? That would be understandable. Or, was his image what it was because he was one of them?

I did not know what to do next. Was President Kline able to hear it or not? He had the best poker face I had ever seen if he could hear it, and if he could not, it wouldn't mean that he was a robot but maybe a slightly hearing-impaired individual. How was I to know?

I watched President Kline closely as he cycled through the guests, table by table, person by person. I thought to myself that I would wait until he used the restroom, and then I would try to play the message with just myself and maybe a few robots around. Or, maybe at the buffet table.

I waited and waited, but the man never once approached the food table, drank anything, or used the restroom. Not once in four hours. I mean, it was completely acceptable for one to practice puritanical self-abnegation toward food, drink, and restroom breaks for four hours, but not the norm. I could only imagine the worst. The entire living Martian community might be led by a robot named President Kline. Unless that man contacted me within the next day, I would have no choice but to assume he was also a robot. If that was the case, I would quickly return to Earth then travel back in time to an earlier period to seek help or travel back to an earlier time here on Mars to muster a calvary and attempt to intervene before all was lost.

The event was starting to wind down, and I didn't think I would get that one additional chance to play the message to him, so I visited the buffet table one last time to fill a plate in hopes I could take it back to my pod.

I put as much food as I could on the plate then covered it with an additional plate. Then I took some plastic wrap off of a covered dish and wrapped it around my food plates to keep it all intact. Seemed to work. Now to get it back to my pod.

On the way out, I noticed everyone was lining up at the exit. Apparently, President Kline, and most of the political dignitaries, were shaking everyone's hand on the way out as they thanked them for attending. It was going to be a ballsy move, but I would try one more time while exiting and shaking President Kline's hand. This just might work.

I approached with my covered plate in my left hand, hit the lapel button with my right, then extended my hand for a firm exit handshake. I locked eyes with each politician, smiled, and kept my words to a simple "Very nice, thank you." Meanwhile, I could hear the message playing, "*This message cannot be heard by robots. It is imperative that we have a secure conversation as soon as possible. Humanity depends on it.*" I did this with each political dignitary as I found my way out of the conference hall. Then I exited the hall, where my escort robot greeted me.

I was promptly shown the way back to the transport station and directed to a transport shuttle that would take me back to my pod.

The robot asked, "What do you have?"

"I took more food than I could eat, so I figured I would take it back to my pod and eat it later rather than waste it," I explained.

I didn't think my explanation for taking the food was accepted because the robot asked, "Can I look at what you took from the buffet?"

I said, "Sure," pulled back the wrapping, and lifted the top plate.

He examined it and asked, "Why did you take so much?"

I shrugged. "I really liked it and just overestimated how much I could consume." I was sure this was all going on my record or something, but being I did not plan on hanging around long, I really didn't care.

I wrapped up the covered plate once again and took a seat on the shuttle. The robot hit a few buttons, and I was off like a rocket, heading toward my pod. I could barely keep my plate of food intact as we banked, climbed, and dropped. Then, with a sudden but smooth motion, it decelerated and the shuttle door opened.

As I stepped out of the shuttle, my pod bot was there to greet me and escort me back to my pod.

I had her carry my plate of food and told her, "I'll be eating the contents for dinner this evening."

It was now pushing 1800 hours (6:00 PM) as I arrived at my pod. I figured that even if Martian President Kline did not reach out and contact me, that maybe one of the other political dignitaries had heard the message. One of them could possibly try to contact me for a meeting. I did not know what to expect, but I thought I should be ready for anything.

Later that evening, I sat back in my pod lounger and watched the news with a plate full of yummy finger foods. I told my pod robot, "I won't need you for the rest of the day."

She then responded by saying, "Good night," as she stepped onto her induction unit charger.

CHAPTER NINETEEN
ESCAPE
15.11.17.17.14 | TZLOK'IN DATE: 6 IX | HAAB DATE: 17 CH'EN | LORD OF THE NIGHT: G3 GREGORIAN: JANUARY 22, 3036

I stood up and refilled Scott's drink and popcorn bucket as I continued with my story.

The next morning, I woke up and realized that if I did not hear anything, I might find myself needing to return to Earth as soon as possible.

"I'm feeling a little homesick, being on Mars," I mentioned to my pod robot. "I miss the trees, the wildlife, and the sound of the babbling brook that I'm accustomed to in the mountains of West Virginia."

"I don't understand," she said. "My data documenting the history of Earth's West Virginia states that there has not been any meaningful quantity of standing trees or wildlife for more than a hundred years. There are feral cats and wild dogs that rely on handouts to survive, but I am not sure what wildlife you are referring to. Feral pets are not considered indigenous wildlife."

"Never mind," I told her. "It must be wishful thinking of what life used to be like on Earth."

I had my breakfast then sat back, watching the news with a cup of coffee. Steller event news was being broadcasted as part of the morning report. It seemed that the war on Earth was escalating.

The newscaster then said, "*All indications are that planet Earth will be uninhabitable within seven days. Ambient radiation levels are spiking. The atmosphere is thinning quickly.*" Being a Friday, that would mean I would need to board a transport back to Earth by Tuesday, January 27, 3036, in order to return to Earth by Thursday, in time to get into my pyramid. These were only estimates and, obviously, it might happen even faster as the fighting escalated.

Then the newscaster stated, "*Transport back to Earth may be halted, starting early next week. The Secretary of Transportation will be making a decision later in the day, announcing his decision."*

Timing was becoming critical, as the entire planet of Mars was on high alert. It seemed many ships from non-NATO nations were trying to come to Mars as a last-ditch effort to survive. However, the Martian military was not allowing it, turning the ships around and sending them to Earth's moon. Only people from NATO nations were permitted access. The ships that did not willingly turn around were shot down long before they entered Martian airspace. Reports of thousands of refugees being destroyed on their way to Mars because they refused to turn around seemed to fill the broadcast news. The Martian government had a zero-tolerance policy on immigration from Earth. They wanted to avoid all fighting on Mars.

I continued to watch the news and await a sign that President Kline, or one of the political dignitaries, had heard my message. I was sure that one of them would reach out and contact me today. There was no way none of them had heard the message I had played.

As the day drew on, I became troubled by the thought that my message had not reached someone with political clout. I found myself overcome and bewildered by the thought that the entire planet, Mars, was being run by robots that were posing as humans. If there was no help to be had here on Mars at this time, I needed to come up with a plan to get back home. I figured that trying to get back to Earth this late in time was too risky. I needed to go back in time here on Mars then travel back to Earth.

Being they tracked everyone who came and went from Earth to Mars, it was going to be hard to explain how I had just happened to be on Mars and needed a ride back. That was going to be tricky, especially if I traveled back a hundred years or so and Mars was already being run by robots. Additionally, the structure I was in, and the surrounding structures, might not have existed a hundred years ago.

When I decided to make this jump back in time, here on Mars, I needed to make damn sure that I would be able to breathe and get inside of a building. Maybe I could use the old section of the city, where everything had started, as a place to jump back in time. As President Kline had stated, the original Martian settlement was now used as the museum. There must be a restroom, or janitor's closet, or someplace in the space that I could go to make a time jump without being detected and without the risk of some inanimate object spearing me as I arrived. I didn't want to end up like

Nibbles.

It was now afternoon. I had just finished my lunch when my personal phone rang. It was a Martian government line calling. I answered, and it was President Kline, in miniature three-dimensional (3D) hologram, on my kitchen table.

I answered, "Hello, sir. How can I help you?"

"Your name popped up more than once as a potential candidate for several of the Senate and House positions that are vacant, but you need to register with the proper political party before you can be taken seriously," President Kline said. "My party is the Rights Party, which represents the conservatives of Mars, and I am in opposition with the Freedom Party, which represents the liberals of Mars. I strongly encourage you to register with the Rights Party, and I look forward to you becoming a nominee for one of the open seats." With that, he thanked me for my time and wished me a good day.

After the telephone conversation, I asked my pod robot, "Please make the arrangements for me to tour the Martian Museum. I would prefer a personal tour guide versus a general tour guide."

"I can make the arrangements for later this afternoon and will accompany you as your personal guide," she said. "I have access to all the informational data associated with the museum and will be able to answer any questions you have during the tour."

I packed up my backpack and made ready for my visit to the museum. I packed my clothes from 2021, the quartz data storage cards, the quartz reader/writer along with the schematics, and included my equipment to make the time jump—three acoustic speakers, some wire, and the backup frequency generator I had brought with me.

As I packed, the pod robot told me, "Arrangements have been established for a 1500-hour (3:00 PM) departure from the pod. We will return by 1700 hours (5:00 PM)."

When 1500 hours arrived, my pod bot announced, "It's time to depart if you still want to tour the Martian Museum."

I picked up my backpack and said, "I'm ready." Then we proceeded out of my pod and down the hall to the transport station.

Within moments, the transport shuttle arrived, and we both climbed in. It was strange to see this small, female-looking pod robot climb into the transport shuttle and see the shuttle sink about 5 cm, (2 inches). It didn't move when I got in, and I was about 91 kg (200 lbs.), so this pod bot of mine must have weighed about 250 kg (about 550 lbs.) or more. A deceiving weight to body size, being she was so light on her feet; I would have never guessed. I guessed she would be considered big boned with thin wrists.

Within minutes, we were on our way. Like a bullet, we moved miles in just a few moments then came to a quick stop. I didn't know if I would ever get used to the breathtaking rides. I had never been a roller coaster fan back on Earth, and the Martian transport system was not made for sissies—all underground and dark so you could never brace yourself for what was coming. It just came, so you were forced to be reactive rather than proactive with each turn, rise, and drop.

My pod bot stepped out of the transport first, and the entire transport rose 5 cm (2 inches) with her departure. Then I joined her on the transport station platform.

We exited the station, and I found that we were actually in the museum. No need to walk anywhere to get to it. My pod robot then started to walk with me as we approached each exhibit.

The first exhibit included some Martian landers that I recognized. They had wrecked Soviet landers dating back to 1962 to 1973 on display. Basically, pieces and parts of wreckages. Then there were two US Viking probes that had been successful. And the list of landers and probes went on, with the US having success and the Soviet and Russian landers failing. China had finally had a successful landing in 2021.

We then moved to a section of the actual museum that was part of the original NATO Martian settlement. Mostly constructed of aluminum and Plexiglass, this part of the museum was still in the actual place where it had been built and was still habitable. My robot told me that it had originally been built in 2035, making it 1,001 years old. Due to the low exterior oxygen levels, and the lack of rain, the building had been holding up well, having to only survive the extreme temperatures and dust storms that frequented Mars.

Our tour continued, and I was shown the original oxygen-generating rooms, water recycling rooms, and the original greenhouses where all the food was grown.

"When did regular tourist trips to Mars start?" I asked my robot.

"In 2140, several tours were started by private companies. The trips took nine months each way and cost about two million WebDollars. A regularly scheduled shuttle from the US to Mars was started in 2145. The trip took thirty to sixty days, depending on where Earth and Mars were in their respective orbits at the time. Back then, one could purchase a one-way ticket and stay if they wished to reside on Mars."

I recalled my lab buddy, Todd Woerner, telling me that he had been going to Mars to work after graduation. That might work for me—a jump back in time to November 2145. I could look up my buddy, Todd, and he might be able to help me get back to Earth.

With that information, I decided it was now or never. I figured I would slip into a restroom and set up the three acoustic speakers in a restroom stall, hold the frequency generator in my lap, and go for it. The worst that could happen would be that the seat was up when I traveled back in time, or someone else was using the stall. I figured I would go back to an hour when it was less likely to be in use. Early in the morning.

"I need to use the restroom," I told my pod robot. "Just wait for me. I might be a few minutes." Off to the old restroom, I went.

It was indeed scary. It was a thousand-year-old restroom that recycled your waste. But it was supposedly still functioning, so I picked a stall away from the urinals. It was completely empty, and the setup was quick.

I plugged into the restroom receptacle, sat on the throne with the three acoustic speakers mounted over my head and the frequency generator in my lap, pants up and lid down on the toilet. Then I plugged in my new destination time: 13.6.14.14.7 | 2 Manik' | 5 Mak | G8, Monday, November 1, 2145, at 0600 hours (6:00 AM). I noted in my log the current date and time: 15.11.17.17.14 | 6 Ix | 17 Ch'en | G3, January 22, 3036, 1610 hours (4:10 PM). I hit the green button on the frequency generator, and the lights went dim, the ionic cloud formed, the tingling started, and I could hear someone entering the restroom. Then, in a split-second, the cloud was clearing and the tingling stopped.

I had made the time jump, and whoever had been walking into the bathroom as I took off had most likely not known what had happened. Maybe they thought the recycler had gotten me or something. Who knew or cared? I was out of their reach, and they had nothing but a cloud to remember me by. Now I had to make my way back to Earth. Let me see what it took to find my old friend, Todd Woerner.

13.6.14.14.7 | TZLOK'IN DATE: 2 MANIK' | HAAB
DATE: 5 MAK | LORD OF THE NIGHT: G8
GREGORIAN: NOVEMBER 1, 2145

I packed up my acoustic speakers and frequency generator, putting them back into my backpack. Then I changed my clothes from the standard see-through attire to my only 2021 selection and opened the stall door. I was in the same restroom, with basically the same fixtures and everything. Little had changed. They had apparently preserved the old museum better than I would have expected for having such minimal changes take place in a thousand years.

I washed my hands then walked out into the main room that had been a museum display when I had entered the restroom but was now a work area, full of computers and workstations.

I approached the first person whom I came to. "Is there was a directory that I can use to locate someone?"

The pretty young lady was really nice. "I can help you if you'd like."

I enthusiastically exclaimed, "Sure! Yes, please. I am looking for Todd Woerner, from the US."

She entered his name by speaking to the computer and, within seconds, stated, "I found him." She provided me with his phone number and some basic directions to his work area.

He was on the other side of the compound, but no matter. I was going to find him and see if he could help me get back to Earth.

I pulled out my phone and ... duh, no service. It seemed my advanced phone had no place in this old 2145 Martian world. *Nothing is easy about time travel*, was what I told myself then asked the nice lady, "Can I use your phone to contact him? It seems my phone's not working."

She smiled, dialed Todd's number, and handed me her phone.

Todd answered, "Hello?"

"Hey, Todd. It's me, Max, Remember me?"

He laughed. "Max! So good to hear from you. What's up?" He sounded excited to hear me on the other end.

"I'm on Mars and really need to meet with you. It's an emergency." Then I asked the nice lady, "What is this part of the compound known as?"

"It's the utility and services section."

I repeated it to Todd, and he said, "I know where that is. Just wait in the lobby, and I'll come by to get you."

I ended the call with Todd and handed the lady back her phone. "Thank you for all your help."

"No problem." She reached out her hand and shook mine. "I'm Elizabeth Holland."

"Oh, sorry," I replied. "Hi, Max Hickman."

"I have never seen a wardrobe like yours. It seems simple but functional."

I smiled. "Thank you for all your help. Can you point me to the lobby?" I did not comment on my clothes any further. I just let that one go.

She pointed toward a door, and I went on my way.

Now I was conscious of my clothes again, and I was apparently not blending in.

I found the lobby easily enough, and a bench. I took a seat and took off my backpack. The thing was heavy, and I had already been walking around for more than an hour with it. I was also ready for dinner, and a nap, and it was not even time for lunch in this time period.

I spied Todd as he entered the lobby.

He saw me, came over, and gave me a bro handshake and a bro hug. "What's up, and why are you dressed like that?"

"I need to speak with you in private. Can you help me get some clothes?" All I had were these rags, and I needed to blend in.

"Sure, dude, whatever you need," he replied. "I'll help you."

Great, Todd was going to be my key to getting through this, but I didn't want to reveal anything about time travel to him. Besides, he didn't have any power to change what was happening in 3036, anyway.

Todd told me to follow, and he took me to his living quarters. There, he let me have a pair of his shiny coveralls. This was the latest Martian fad.

Being a lot larger than Todd, I didn't look too good in his coveralls. They were so tight that they were going up my ass and giving me a man package camel toe thing. I found if I walked hunched over a bit, they didn't dig in so much, but standing up straight was an absolute no-no.

"I'm in trouble," I told Todd. "I can't give you all the details, but I need to get back to Earth as soon as possible."

"Calm down," Todd said. "You don't need to worry. I got this."

As I sat in his apartment, he offered me lunch. He ordered me a pizza and a soda. I needed that. Feeling calmer, secure, and somewhat refreshed, we sat and talked about our time back at the Bio-Mechanics Institute of Technology (B-MIT) laboratory in Bethesda, Maryland.

"I knew you were half crazy to sit there with me and make up some bioengineered concoction like you did." He laughed. "I knew we would never subject ourselves, or anyone else, to anything we made like that, so it was just fun to make the witches brew."

I looked him in the eyes and didn't say a thing.

"No, you didn't," he said, shocked.

"I did take it, and I haven't suffered from any ill effects so far. I even cut off my left little toe, and it grew back." I pulled off my shoe and sock, showing him my new toe.

He sat back, looking amazed that I had done it. "I may take this to the next level. You want to work with me to develop the processes so that it can be marketed?" This was something new, and maybe something that could change his life.

"Thank you, but it's all yours. You can do whatever you want with the bioengineering. I saved my work on the B-MIT cloud data bank, so it's all there ... provided you can help me get back to Earth."

"You're covered. Don't worry," he said.

As I sat there, a delivery came to the door that included a vacuum-sealed package with a pair of XL shiny coveralls with his company's logo on it and a new pair of shoes. He handed them to me. "You should probably change."

We laughed as I immediately changed into the new outfit.

"Don't worry. I'm working with a bioengineering firm that does nothing but cloning." It seemed cloning on Earth was banned, but they had a business that did nothing but clone rich people from Earth at the Mars facility then send the clones to Earth. He pointed to the outfit that he had provided me and said, "It's a clone outfit. You can have as many as you want. They dress the clones in them so they don't have to travel nude. Once on Earth, the clones are implanted with all the donor's memories and thoughts so each person is, in essence, reborn into a fresh new body. You can just ride back to Earth as a cloned person. You can even be delivered to your home address upon arrival."

That was unbelievable. I could not thank Todd enough.

"I need all the details to pull this off," I told him.

"Don't worry." He pulled a chair up to his computer, typed in a few things, and then looked at me with a smile. "All taken care of. You can board the transport tomorrow and, in thirty-five days, you should be back on Earth." Then he got a big grin on his face. "The regrowing of limbs is mine, right?"

"I will make no claim for the technology or try to patten the gene sequence," I promised. "It was discovered all in fun. Besides, I have what I need."

"You have a copy of the sequence in you," Todd pointed out. Then he stood up. "I got a few things to finish up at the lab, but you are welcome to crash here until your flight out tomorrow."

"Thank you," I told him as he handed me the remote.

"Feel free to nap-out and listen to music or watch television. Whatever you want to do to, just do it. If you need anything, just order it. I'll be back in a few hours." He gave me a fist-bump then exited, leaving me in his apartment by myself.

It was always a strange feeling to be in someone else's space when they were not around. It was like you were violating them if you did anything. At least, that was the way I always felt in that situation, but I needed this safe harbor, and Todd's offer to help me was comforting.

I got a drink of water, kicked back on his couch, and took a nap for an hour or two then watched the news. Nothing out of the ordinary seemed to be happening. However, being this was Mars, what would one consider normal? I would be the last guy on this planet to know what was or was not normal. All I could say for sure was that there appeared to be little bad happening.

I did see that Mars was being claimed and settled by NATO, and they intended to occupy it and control it as it was developed. It was hard to believe that man had actually planned the Mars' community to be an international NATO settlement and had resisted the temptation to put it under one nation's flag. The settlers did limit control to free democratic nations and excluded those that had a history of communism and authoritative government. Only active NATO nations on Earth were permitted to visit Mars or occupy any of the established community infrastructures, whereas other countries could just visit Mars, but they had not established any working communities on the planet.

I heard Todd as he entered his apartment. I sat up so as not to look too comfortable.

He entered and greeted me with a big smile. "How's it going? Do you need anything?"

Stretching, I told him, "I napped out and watched the news; all good."

"I'm going to get changed so we can go out, get a drink, some good food, and party like it's your last day on Mars." He laughed. "There's only one place to go on the entire planet for that."

"You think that's a good idea?" I asked.

"Well, let's see what I got here from my office." He opened his hand and showed me a new identification chip. Then he took out a tool that was used to remove and insert the implants. "Hold out your left hand."

I did so.

"You'll feel some pressure, but it won't last long," he told me.

I remembered what it had felt like to get the chip I had in me now inserted, so I knew he was full of crap. It was going to hurt like hell.

He jabbed me with the tool, and yes, it hurt like hell. Blood was all over my hand as Todd withdrew the tool that he had used to extract my identification chip. He handed it to me and said, "You need to keep it wrapped in foil and safe from damage. You should get it switched out once back on Earth, being it has all your biometrics and assets, which are huge. I implanted you with a clone identification chip."

I was now the clone of Mr. Maximilian Hickman, and I would be delivered to my house in West Virginia upon my return to Earth. If anyone stopped me on Mars, I was legal as long as I was with him.

"Are clones permitted to drink, eat, and party like it's their last day on Mars?" I asked.

He laughed. "Only if I'm escorting them and they're picking up the tab."

We both laughed, and then Todd continued to get cleaned up and ready to go out to the only club on Mars—The Red Nightcap.

Within an hour, we were sitting at a table in The Red Nightcap. Two bio-nerds, drinking, eating, and talking about the biogenetic concoction we had brewed up back on Earth. Anyone listening in would have thought we were stoners, talking about a dream.

I could almost read Todd's mind. He wanted me to cut off something so he could witness it growing back—anything. He was just so excited that our concoction had worked and he'd been given permission by me to market it without any restrictions. "It can benefit so many people who have lost limbs and need to have organs removed."

That was when I told him, "I don't think you can get cancer with this genetic infusion, either. I believe that one is totally cancer resistant once the gene infusion is complete."

At that point, he was totally ecstatic about getting his hands back on the genetic code we had made. He then came out and asked, "Will you cut off something so I can see it happen? I could take the removed appendage and sequence the gene code in my new Martian lab."

"No. It hurts when you cut something off, just like it would if it didn't regrow. I don't need that pain. Besides, I took the project further by limiting the ability of the virus to change anyone who is not a male and a direct descendant of mine. My gene sequence is very restricted, and I don't think it will help you much. It would be better to just take our work back at B-MIT and work with it rather than try to extract the additional work I put into it for my own use."

He seemed to take in my comments, mulling them through his smart, ingenious, genetic-altering brain then nodded. "You might be right, but I would still love to have the alterations you made, as well."

"That's not part of the deal," I told him. "Only the regeneration of organs and appendages with any cancer resistance that came with the mix is the deal. Not my work limiting the ability of the virus to affect only select groups of the population." What I really didn't want him to have was the genetic code for longevity. We did not need an entire population living nine hundred years. Besides, it would put his current employer—a cloning company—out of business. I could not tell him that, but that was really my only reason for not wanting to share my genetic code with him.

If I could just get on the shuttle without having to cut off my finger and without Todd extracting my genetic code, all would be okay. All I needed was about twelve hours.

It wasn't until about the third drink that Todd informed me, "I'll be accompanying you back to Earth next month."

I didn't catch the "next month" part right away.

"I'm sure you won't mind letting me stay at your place for a few days while we get back to B-MIT and collect the altered genetic code that you stored in your account."

"Yes, fine," I told him. "But you'll have to sleep in a recliner, and I kind of live in a garage with my vehicles."

He was taken back by that a little, but then he said, "I can make it anywhere for a few days.

I laughed, ordered a refill on my drink, and then asked, "Did I catch that right? Did you just say *next month*?"

He nodded. "Sorry, but the transport that was scheduled to leave tomorrow morning is full and, even though I assigned you a seat, apparently, someone else removed you and replaced you with a rush job. Plus, I won't be able to accompany you if you depart tomorrow, but you're now assigned a seat on the transport that leaves next month, and I'll be able put in leave to make the trip."

This was a big shock to me. Like, what had just happened? An hour ago, I thought I was on my way off of Mars. I had been ready to board a transport in the morning, and now I was on hold until *next month*. Todd had known this when he had gotten home and before we had gone out.

"How am I supposed to make it a month without being detected?" I asked.

"Don't worry. You have your new identification chip implant, plenty of clothing, and you'll have food, shelter, and a friend to talk to. There's no problem; just a slight delay." He then smiled and said, "Plenty of time to regrow a finger." He could see the anxiety building on my face. "Dude, it will be fine." He then paused before saying, "But there might be one little snafu. I won't be able to hide you at my place every day. You'll have to report to the clones' living quarters until departure. They'll feed you, house you, and provide for your care until the departure date. I'll be able to take you to my apartment on weekends and periodically during the week. You're not a real Martian citizen, and with that identification chip in you, you're more or less a product and not a person."

I suddenly lost my appetite. I was now totally dependent on Todd, and if he wanted to, he could completely eliminate me without having to answer to anyone. However, I felt that I knew Todd and had nothing to worry about. Then again, how well do we really know someone? I mean, we had spent time drinking and studying with each other, mixed some genetic code together, but how well did I really know him?

I double-checked that I had my real ID chip in foil with me, panicking that I might have left it back in Todd's apartment by accident. Then what? Would I become a zombie slave? My life could get really ugly without that chip. I was technically just a product. Wow, now I knew how the clones felt.

As the evening came to a close, Todd said, "I'll take you to the clone holding area at my company tomorrow and get you settled in. You don't have to do anything. Just don't speak."

"What are you talking about?" I asked.

"You have no education, no knowledge of how to do anything. You're not even supposed to be bathroom trained, so they'll put you in diapers."

I sighed and dropped my head into my hands. "This is not going to work. I can't possibly shut my mouth for twenty-four hours. It's not going to happen."

"It's the only way. I have no choice!" he exclaimed. "That chip is in you, and the entire facility is monitored. They'll know you're there even if you never come out of the apartment. Then you'll be incarcerated one way or another if you don't just join the other clones at the facility."

"Can't you just remove the chip and wrap it up in foil, as well?" I asked.

"That won't work if you want to catch a ride back to Earth. You need to be logged in at the holding facility then moved to the transport along with the others. If you can't act like a clone that knows nothing, you need to get someone else to help you. This is all I can do, and it will be easy so long as you keep your mouth shut and just go along with the program."

"So, that's it? Tonight at your place, and then into the clone holding facility as a product?"

He shrugged and said, "Yep."

That did not seem like the Todd I knew, but I was really at a loss when it came to options. I mean, there was no plan B at this time.

We got back to his place, and I washed up and crashed on his couch again.

13.6.14.14.8 | TZLOK'IN DATE: 3 LAMAT | HAAB
DATE: 6 MAK | LORD OF THE NIGHT: G9
GREGORIAN: NOVEMBER 2, 2145

I awoke early and ordered a cup of coffee. It took only a few minutes for it to arrive at Todd's apartment. Then I sat back, watching the sunrise across the Martian plain. So harsh but beautiful. Off in a distance, I could see a large dust devil as it raced across the horizon. I was taking it all in, knowing these moments would likely be limited unless I could surreptitiously find another way off this planet without Todd's help.

I started thinking about the original plan. I would have been leaving Mars this morning. If I wanted to stick to that original plan, all I needed to do was to somehow switch my chip implant with that from one of the clones who were scheduled to be on the transport.

With that thought, I went into the pocket of my friend's lab coat that was hanging on the rack by the front door of his apartment. I removed the chip extractor/inserter and stashed it in my pocket. I just needed to borrow it. Besides, with any luck, he would have forgotten he even had it with him. In my pocket was now the chip extractor tool with several five-dimensional (5D) quartz data storage cards and the schematics to the quartz reader/writer.

I could hear Todd stirring around in his room, getting ready for work. Then he walked out into the main room of his apartment and asked, "How did you sleep?"

"Good. I was quite comfortable on the couch," I answered.

"They have nice beds in the clone holding rooms." It almost felt like a parting shot.

Todd ordered breakfast for the both of us, and as soon as we finished, he grabbed his lab coat and we were off to his office.

Just before we left his apartment, Todd said, "Extend your hands."

I did as he asked, and he quickly slapped on a pair of handcuffs.

"What's up with the cuffs?" I asked nervously.

"Clones are not allowed to walk around unrestrained in public. Once we're at the lab and in the secure area, the cuffs will be removed. It's the law; I have no choice."

I was really not liking this, but I was still without an alternate choice. To make matters worse, I would not be permitted to speak once we left the apartment or I might blow our cover.

The trip was quick. Upon arrival at his workplace, Todd scanned himself in then had me hold my hands over the chip reader. "You should wait in the lobby," he told me. "Someone will escort you to the clone holding station and remove the cuffs." Then he assured me, "Everything will be okay."

I took a chair in the lounge.

"Remember," Todd said, "if you want to get back to Earth, you need to act like you don't know how to speak and that you don't understand what is being spoken to you. Just follow the escort and don't give them any trouble. I will see you again in a couple of days. They will give you everything you need. Just play along."

After a few moments, Todd waved goodbye, and I was left sitting in the lobby, not sure what was really going to happen.

As good fortune would have it, a whole group of clones, dressed like me, in my clone jumpsuit, came into the lobby. They were stopped as the escort went to the front desk, and I heard him say, "This is the group boarding for Earth this morning. I need to check them out of the facility." He looked back and started counting them. Then he asked the girl at the desk, "Do you mind watching them for a moment? I need to use the restroom and get the proper number of cuffs from the storage room."

"Of course," the girl at the counter agreed, so he proceeded toward the restroom.

This was the break I had been looking for.

As soon as the guard left the restroom to go in search of cuffs, I went in and broke a mirror. I was able to manipulate a piece of the broken glass that had fallen into the sink and proceeded to slice my hand in half from my index finger down through my palm to my wrist. I folded my hand in half to get out of the cuffs. It was painful but, within a few minutes, the bleeding had stopped and my skin was regenerating. Next, I reached into my pocket and, with the sharp point of the chip extractor, sprang the lock on the other cuff.

Leaving the bathroom, I proceeded to remove the clone identification chip with chip extractor. Then I walked over to the male clone that was closest to me, took his left hand, and walked him back to the place I had been sitting. I removed his identification chip and inserted the one that had been in me. He unexpectedly started to cry from the pain of the chip extraction and insertion. This was just what I had hoped would not happen.

I tried to quiet him, but he was wailing like a baby with blood all over his hand. I then left the poor guy sitting in the chair, crying. I turned my back away from the girl at the desk and took the chip I had extracted from the clone, inserting it into my freshly healed hand. I quickly put the chip tool into my jumpsuit pocket and mixed into the group.

As the escort exited the storage room, he asked the girl, "What's going on?"

"I don't know. There's a clone over on the chair, crying," she answered.

The escort went over to the crying clone and took him to the chip reader, scanning his left hand. Then he checked his list of clones being transported. "You're not part of this group. Todd Woerner removed you from this trip." As though the clone could understand what was being said, he looked at the crying clone and said, "Sorry, guy. I see you are scheduled to transport out next month." He then slapped a pair of handcuffs on the clone and walked it back to the chair to wait for his escort back to the clone holding center. The escort then dressed the clone's wound with gauze from a first-aid kit to stop the bleeding from his left hand.

Fortunately for me, my hand had only bled for a few moments, the skin healing without any trace. All this had happened within moments and before anyone had noticed. I was almost as good as new with the exception that my hand was smaller and the skin was somewhat pale.

Each of the clones, and myself, were then processed for passage to Earth. We were scanned as we left the facility and put in a transport that was to take us to the shuttle destined for Earth. The escort counted us again and made sure each of our names was on the manifest.

My new identification was the clone of Bobby Leonard, Annapolis, Maryland. I thought to myself, *I'll change my chip to my real identification chip once we land on Earth*. I could even wait until I was delivered to Mr. Leonard to see his face when he saw that I didn't look anything like him. When they scanned me, I would not be the right clone. I would not be a clone at all. Mr. Leonard would not appreciate that, and the last thing I needed was to get arrested or cause an issue that Todd could use to trace me.

I thought to myself that it would probably be best if I just snuck out of the clone group once we landed and made my way back to West Virginia. With any luck, this bucket of bolts would be heading for Richmond, or someplace relatively close to West Virginia.

The one thing I was sure of was that Todd was going to know that I had abandoned the Mars clone holding facility within the next few days. I didn't know if he would know I was on the transport. He might think I was hiding out on Mars somewhere, but there was the possibility that if he found out, he might try to intercept me before I could get off the transport. I was relatively sure he was not going to say too much about clone Maximilian Hickman. The last thing Todd needed was to have to explain to his superiors what he had been doing. He would have to get someone on the Earth side of the trip to intercept me if he was going to do anything at all. I suspected that person would be our old lab partner, Ed Carney.

I was boarded on the shuttle to Earth and, within an hour, we were strapped into a seat and made ready for takeoff. We were put into a space diaper, of sorts. The clones were not potty-trained and had each been hooked into a waste collection system. When you had to go, you just did your thing and the space diaper took care of the rest. There was not even a restroom that could be used by a clone on this craft. Okay, this was not going to be easy to get used to for one to two months, but I really didn't have a choice. No talking or acknowledging anything ... for up to two months. I just had to eat, sleep, drink, pee, and crap myself for the duration of this trip. No entertainment, no reading, writing, television, or anything other than some elevator type music that seemed to play on a loop. Around and around with the same music for hours and hours, upon days and days. What a fun trip this was going to be.

Being the gravity on Mars was much less than that of Earth, the takeoff was a lot less dramatic than the trip from Earth to Mars had been. However, there was also the difference between the speed and size of this craft compared to the size and speed of the craft I had taken in the year 3036 just a few short days ago. In fifteen minutes, we were weightless and moving toward Earth.

I patiently awaited my release from the chair, but it did not come quickly. Hours turned to days with the crew stopping by about once an hour with water and food.

The food was the worst. The only thing I could compare it to was hummus, but most of the spices in their recipe were missing. The crew also applied some type of compression wraps around each of our extremities. These wraps would cycle through various patterns of squeezing one leg then the other, followed by a series of squeezing on one arm and then the other. Then the chair went into a set of relaxing massage patterns. People would pay big WebDollars for this treatment if it were for just one hour in a mall. But mandatory, twenty-four seven for over a month? It would be a hard sell for the most tense amongst us.

This went on hour after hour. There was no clock, and the lights were always too dim, as though we were on a cross-country red-eye flight back in the day. In retrospect, I was on the ultimate red-eye flight.

Taking this trip as a clone was borderline insanity. I could not even move my arm enough to scratch my ass or anything. Water, food, and an endless massage as we traveled, mounted on a space toilet. A trip to remember, for sure.

There were a few good things about the trip—no loud, obnoxious passengers patronizing on this flight, no lines to use the restrooms, and there were windows. Yes, I could see out of the craft as we traveled toward Earth.

After what seemed to be an eternity, I finally caught a glimpse of the moon and the blue ball I called home. It was small at first but eventually grew and grew until the blue ball, with its wispy clouds, filled the window. I knew I was going to see home that day.

13.6.14.16.2 | TZLOK'IN DATE: 11 IK' | HAAB DATE: 0 MUWAN | LORD OF THE NIGHT: G7 GREGORIAN: DECEMBER 6, 2145

The small transport was starting to enter Earth's atmosphere. The craft was rocking back and forth, shaking violently as we skipped across the planet's ozone and succumbed to its gravity. You could feel the heat and see the glow on the wings out of the windows as we plunged toward Earth's crust. Our target, I did not know for sure, but no matter. I thought to myself, *If the craft were to burn up, at least my ashes would be reunited with my origins.*

It took about fifteen or twenty minutes for the flight to smooth out and descend more like a normal plane ride. We did a few small turns, and then you could hear the landing gears lower. The runway was getting larger by the second. Finally, we touched down.

The clones had no idea what was going on as we approached the end of the runway. There was no mad dash to get luggage, or head for the door, or anything. They just sat in their assigned seats, strapped in, oblivious to everything that was happening. If they had food, drink, and a clean bottom, they were perfectly content. I had to do the same until an opportunity presented itself to bifurcate from the group of clones.

Each clone had their restraints removed one by one. They had their space diapers removed and put into an adult diaper. Then they were placed into a wheelchair and removed from the transport. As they were removed, their implanted identification chips were scanned, and they were moved to select holding areas for final transport to their perspective transplant facilities.

My turn came. Great. I had not been diapered in a long time, but I kept a straight face and just kept with the program. Within a few minutes, I was sitting in a wheelchair, unrestrained in a holding area with a sign that read, "*Washington DC.*"

I thought to myself, *This will be great. A trip all the way back to DC will leave only a short distance to Bethesda or Capon Bridge, West Virginia.* The problem was, I didn't know where I was, and the crew was most definitely going to scan my biochip before they loaded me onto any transport, no matter what the destination.

As the crew tended to the clones, I quickly slipped into the adjacent restroom and pulled out my trusty biochip extractor/applicator from the clone pocket. Within a few seconds, I had Dr. Bobby Leonard's clone chip out. Then I took my chip, that had been wrapped in foil, out of my pocket and inserted it into my left hand again. I was now Maximilian Hickman once again, with all my assets intact. I was no longer a clone. Just your average guy in a clone outfit, with a diaper, in a clone transport facility restroom, who had not walked in thirty-five days. Now I had to get out of this place.

The clones were not using the restrooms, as they were not potty-trained, so what I needed to do was wait for a guy about my size to enter the restroom, restrain him, and take his clothes. Or, I could try to find some luggage from one of the crew and see if they had any clothing I could pilfer. All they wore were coveralls, anyway.

I poked my head out of the restroom. Luckily, no one had noticed I was missing from the wheelchair yet. I walked up to the wheelchair and took it into the restroom, hiding it in a stall. I then proceeded to walk out of the holding area.

One of the people tending the clones walked over to stop me, and I greeted her with a, "Hello." Knowing that the clones could not talk, there was no doubt that I was not a clone. "I had an accident in the restroom and had to put on a clone suit. You know, 'shit happens.'"

She scrunched up her face and pinched her nose. "I need to scan you before you leave the area," she insisted, looking at me in disgust. "You probably have no business even being at this facility."

"I'm just here to drop off some research data for the shuttle to take back to Mars for Todd Woerner."

She looked up Todd's name then nodded. "Yes, I see he is listed." She then pointed me toward the customer service center and stated, "Anything to be transported needs to be manifested and go through security. We can't just have someone take anything on the transport without going through proper procedures."

"Okay. Thank you for your help." Then, as quickly as possible, I left the area and started for the exit.

Amongst the faces approaching me, I thought I saw Ed Carney heading toward the clone holding area. I was sure he had not spotted me yet, so I did an about-face and started walking with some other people, away from him. I felt safe that he would not be able to recognize me from the back.

After turning a corner, I peeked back and, sure enough, it was Ed. Todd must have sent him here to see if I had been on the transport. I thought to myself, *Too late, Ed.*

As Ed proceeded toward the clone holding area, I went for the exit again. This time, I found myself outside the doors of a large building located at Dulles International in Virginia. Wow, had I lucked out. I had really thought I would be in Richmond and was relieved to find myself so close to Capon Bridge. But I still needed to find a ride.

I walked to the main shuttle terminal and found a help desk. It was more of a self-help kiosk, but no matter. I was able to arrange for transport. Now, all I had to do was wait without Ed spotting me.

It seemed I could expect the transport to arrive in three minutes outside of gate A1, so I walked out of the main terminal, found gate A1, and just stood there. Sure enough, a taxi shuttle pulled up. I hopped in and provided the address to my destination. "Hickman Nature Preservation Park, please."

The driver scanned my left hand for payment and off we went.

About ten minutes later, we were pulling up to the park.

"Just let me out at the park entrance," I told the driver, leaving me to walk up to the cliffs, to the pyramid's location.

I found the large rock where I had hidden the pyramid's key and rolled it way. But the key was not there. In my haste to hide the key, it had never occurred to me that I would not be returning the same year. The key was under the rock in the year 3036. It was 2145. That really sucked. Now I had to figure out how I was going to get inside the pyramid.

My backpack was at Todd's apartment on Mars, so he had my backup acoustic speakers and the frequency generator. None of that was going to help me get the key or jeopardize the secret of time jumping, being Todd did not even know anything about it. Therefore, I felt secure about Todd having the contents of my pack, but how did I get inside the pyramid? I couldn't even use my backup equipment to go forward and retrieve the key.

I started picking at the lock, but I knew it would be futile. Then I remembered the tunnel entrance that used to lead to my old shop/lab. I knew people in the park could see the main entrance to the pyramid, but something told me that the old tunnel entrance would still be there. Not to mention, it would be much more discreet.

I walked down to the area where my old lab/shop used to be located and started to poke around the rocks and boulders. I just needed to find the secret entrance.

There it was, overgrown and quite unsuspicious, looking more like a drainage pipe than a tunnel.

I pushed away the cobwebs and maneuvered around the large rocks and boulders that had concealed the tunnel entrance for years. Dark, cold, and unlit, I proceeded to just follow the tunnel by feel. Once at the end of the tunnel, I felt around for the old, familiar, big iron door handle. Yes, there it was. I turned the handle and found it to be quite stiff, but it moved and the locking mechanism released. All those years of maintenance had paid off.

With all my might, I pulled on the heavy iron door. It gave out a mighty squeak as it shuddered and slowly opened. By just feel alone, I walked up the steps and entered the security of the pyramid. As I flicked the light switch on, I said the words, "Let there be light." And so, there was.

I had everything in the pyramid I needed—food, a nice restroom, complete with shower, and my comfortable lounge chair—all awaiting me.

It was an overwhelming feeling of hope and relief to take a shower; the first in over a month. Then I brushed my teeth, combed my hair, which had grown quite long, and clipped my nails. I even shaved. Most importantly, I washed my space-diapered ass. I even had clothes—denim blue jeans and tee-shirts. Yes, cotton tee-shirts. I had so longed for the feel of cotton clothing. Synthetic clothing would never feel as good as cotton, in my opinion.

I took my position in the lounge chair, stuck a Van Morrison CD into the CD player, and drifted off to sleep.

CHAPTER TWENTY
READ ME FIRST
13.6.14.16.3 | TZLOK'IN DATE: 12 AK'B'AL | HAAB DATE: 1 MUWAN | LORD OF THE NIGHT: G8 GREGORIAN: DECEMBER 7, 2145

I awoke after the best sleep I'd had in ages, but I did not even know what time it was. There, over the doorway, was the Mayan calendar and my trusty atomic clock. "*1020 hours*" was displayed on the digital screen. I needed to get a new phone and reconnect into the data stream (DS).

I took the spare door key and unlocked the pyramid door. Then I proceeded to look out of the eye to make sure the coast was clear. After assuring myself that no one else was around, I opened the bay door and took Hal, the air transport craft (ATC), out. Then I closed the bay door, locked it, and climbed into Hal, heading for town.

Within an hour, I had purchased a new phone/DS device and was shopping online. I then had a copy of the pyramid door key duplicated. They simply scanned it then just printed a new one out. Awesome. Quick, easy, and no grinding or cutting. I ordered new acoustic speakers and a new frequency generator. I could not risk any additional time jumps without a backup. I also ordered some fresh food reserves.

I was becoming a traveling prepper, living out of a pyramid in a park. This was a strange way to live as a multimillionaire named Maximilian. I smiled in spite of myself. Surely, intrinsic motivation.

Things were being neglected. In particular, my hair. It had been a long time since I'd had a haircut, and I was looking quite shabby. I did not want Terri to see me like this, so I directed Hal to take me to the Skills barber shop where Barry and Bradley Schmidt had set up shop.

Bradley brushed off a chair as I entered, signaling me to take a seat and explaining that his brother, Barry, was late today, so he was working by himself. After the haircut, I felt somewhat recuperated from space travel and ready to take care of "Business."

Satisfied that I had what I needed from town, I took my seat in my ATC and told Hal to take me to Bio-Mechanics Institute of Technology laboratory in Bethesda. Hal wasted no time delivering me to the front door of the lab.

I entered my passcode and, apparently, I was still cleared for entry. I made my way to the data entry station and brought up the research data with the bioengineered virus that could transplant the altered genetic codes. I double-checked to make sure there was no data related to longevity in the notes or data. The altered genetic code from the eternal jellyfish had been washed from the system. Next, I made sure everything related to controlling who could be affected by the altered genetic code was removed from the computer system. I copied the gene sequence onto a thumb drive and put it in my pocket.

It was now time to take care of Todd. I needed him to pay for deceiving me and trying to hold me captive.

I looked up the genetic code for a viper's tongue and skin and spliced it into the gene sequence for my buddy, Todd. I figured he would try the virus on himself without taking the time to review everything, being he had seen it work on me. It wouldn't take long after that for Todd to discover he would have a slick, black forked tongue and slippery, scaly skin forevermore. That should be justice enough.

I put a note in the data file. "*Read me first file: Todd.*" Then a second file. "*Read me first file: Ed.*"

> *Todd: The altered genetic code is yours, as agreed. My mission was of the utmost importance, and my timely return to Earth was related to national security. I have included a document releasing all rights to you.*

> *Ed: It was a pleasure serving as your protégé. You are an admirable man and one who I will remember. I will always be thankful for the guidance you provided with my studies. A special package will be delivered to you in the near future. Keep an eye out for it. Best wishes.*

I listened to myself as that little voice in my head said, *Let's get out of here before we get caught.*

I closed up the files and made for the door. I jumped into my ATC and gave Hal the commands to take me home. "*Country road, to the place I belong.*" Obviously, Hal did not understand that one line that had been drilled into my brain, so I gave Hal the commands back to the Hickman Nature Preservation Park.

No matter how good AI was at crunching numbers and compiling algorithms, it would never match the power of the human brain to connect relationships between phrases and emotions.

Back at the pyramid, I scanned the area, and when I was comfortable that the coast was clear, I unlocked the door and pulled Hal into the bay. Closing the door behind me, I locked myself in.

Now that I was back at the park, I loaded up the gene sequence onto my phone and sent it to Ed over the DS with a release form for all rights. In the email, I told him that he should not trust Todd, that he had the tongue of a viper and was a slick one, not to be trusted. Ending it with, "*Eventually, you may be able to see it.*"

I had been thinking about all the different options I had during my long return trip, but I still was not sure there was a simple answer. If I went forward in time, society would be run by robots that were plotting man against man, nation against nation, to eliminate biological life on Earth. People of that era had been raised by robots and were oblivious to what was happening. If I tried to work in this current time period, I was like a fish out of water—unfamiliar with the dress, customs, and how to interact on a social level. Besides, I was living out of a pyramid, in a park, with a fake identification chip. Under closer scrutiny, I might be discovered. Who knew what would happen?

So, I thought that maybe my best option would be to go back to my own time period and try to get the government on board to set up and avoid a robotic, artificial intelligence takeover. I would be home with my wife, living in the time period I felt most comfortable in. If needed, I could always intervene if something went wrong. I had nine hundred years, less my age and time travel loss, to make it work.

My wife was a smart woman when it came to things like this. I so wished I had her with me to consult with, but I was on my own, on a mission from God. I decided to take it easy and not to make any rash decisions that would jeopardize my mission.

13.6.14.16.4 | TZLOK'IN DATE: 13 K'AN | HAAB
DATE: 2 MUWAN | LORD OF THE NIGHT: G9
GREGORIAN: DECEMBER 8, 2145

I decided I needed to clean up a few loose ends before I did anything else, afraid to alter what I had already. That was to say, if I were to leap forward in time to January 15, 3036, and tell myself not to go to Mars, that might have some strange consequences, such as myself not being where I was now in this time period. The knowledge I had gained about the robots taking over and the information on five-dimensional (5D) crystal storage might be lost. I thought it would be best to just to avoid myself and carefully make corrections to my missteps.

I decided to travel forward to January 17, 3036, and retrieve the hidden key. I didn't need some robot with super artificial intelligence gaining access to time travel technology. After that, my plan was to return to August 6, 2021, at 1000 hours, an hour after I had departed for the future. Terri would have only missed me for an hour. I would have the five-dimensional (5D) crystal storage system with me and be able to show authorities what was happening in 3036.

Or maybe not.

They would probably blow me off as some kooky or nutty professor. Either way, I would have many years to work it all out.

13.6.14.16.5 | TZLOK'IN DATE: 1 CHIKCHAN | HAAB
DATE: 3 MUWAN | LORD OF THE NIGHT: G1
GREGORIAN: DECEMBER 9, 2145

I made ready for my jump forward. So far, my equipment had operated flawlessly, but I felt good knowing I had obtained backups just in case.

I entered the new destination date and time: 15.11.17.17.9 | 1 Muluk | 12 Ch'en | G7, January 17, 3036, at 1000 hours (10:00 AM). I also logged the current date and time: 13.6.14.16.5 | 1 Chikchan | 3 Muwan | G1, December 9, 2145, 0900 hours (9:00 AM). Before taking my position in my reclining chair, I made sure my personal protective equipment (PPE) was readily accessible. I then placed the shields over me just in case. All systems seemed to be a go, so I hit the green button.

The ionic cloud ensued, the tingling pulsed through my body, and the lights in the pyramid were dimming in and out. After a short period, the cloud started to clear, the tingling subsided, and the lights were bright as the reactor wound down. I was back in 3036, so I made haste to check the radiation and oxygen levels. All seemed stable for the moment. At least, there were no alarms.

I took a peek out of the all-seeing Eye of Horus. I did see a couple moving hastily through the park. They were only in sight for a few moments. I decided to make a run for the key so I could get out of this time period and back to safety.

I unlocked the door and opened it. Yes, the same bad air came rushing in. With haste, I proceeded to the boulder where I had hidden the key to the pyramid. I was having trouble breathing after just that short distance. I rolled the boulder aside, and there it was, waiting for me. I removed the key, placed it into my pocket, and went into a jog back to the pyramid. I ran right through the door and closed it as quickly as possible behind me, gasping for air all the while.

Pulling the key out of my pocket that I had just retrieved, I locked the door with it to make sure it still worked. I then went for the oxygen tank I had by my recliner for a few rescue breaths. Now it was time to get out of here.

I could hear waning sirens off in the distance. Earth was becoming an unstable place for life to exist. There was no need for me to chance it any longer than necessary.

I took my position then entered the new destination date and time: 13.0.8.13.10 | 8 Ok | 8 Yaxk'in | G9, August 6, 2021, at 1000 hours (10:00 AM). Then, as always, I logged the current date and time: 15.11.17.17.9 | 1 Muluk | 12 Ch'en | G7, January 17, 3036, 1030 hours (10:30 AM). All seemed to be in place, and there was no worry that I would need shields. I hit the green "*Go*" button once more and heard the *pop* of an electrical breaker. The reactor was not firing up as it should—no cloud, nor tingling. Something had gone wrong.

Great. Good old Murphy's law at work.

The good thing was that I didn't think it was the frequency generator or acoustic speakers. No, this sounded like a heavy voltage short of some type.

I opened the reactor room door with my radiation gauges in hand. All appeared to be radiologically safe. I then entered the small electrical chamber between the reactor and the pyramid floor. I could smell the ozone of an electrical spark or short in the air. I put on a rubber glove and opened the breaker box door.

Well, well, well, what do we have here? It was a field mouse family. Now toast. Apparently, the little fellers had taken refuge in the pyramid, and I had cooked them alive when I'd hit the green button. So sad to see some of the only wildlife remaining on Earth toasted. At least it had been quick, and they had never known it was coming.

I cleared the remnants of the rodents from the box then threw the breaker back on. After a few moments, I was back in my reclining chair and ready for another try. A couple of additional huffs of oxygen, and I hit the green "*Go*" button. The cloud appeared, the tingling ensued with a pronounced shock to it, and the lights were burning brightly. I thought I could see my own heart beating through the cloud.

Within moments, the reactor wound down and the fog had cleared. I was still tingling from the initial shock but, for the most part, I was good.

I proceeded to the door, unlocked it, and who was there? Yes, my Terri. This time, I stepped out to greet her before she had the chance to rush me. It was I who had longed for her touch, her hug, and her kiss. I had been away for some time, and I had truly discovered just how much I depended on her.

CHAPTER TWENTY-ONE

THE WHITE HOUSE

13.0.8.13.10 | TZLOK'IN DATE: 8 OK | HAAB DATE:
8 YAXK'IN | LORD OF THE NIGHT: G9
GREGORIAN: AUGUST 6, 2021

After this past trip, I decided I was going to take a little break from time jumping. I had to put the mission on hold and make sure I spent some quality time with my wife and children. After all, what good would it do if I died attempting to save the world? One bomb, or even a brief moment of being irradiated, could end it all. And that would leave my wife wondering what had happened, and the world would never know the tragedy that awaited them. The world would remain on the same path to total annihilation by robots and AI. All my work would be lost.

In the meantime, I contacted an old associate of mine, Ms. Beverly Lord. She was now working for South-Sampton University in the United Kingdom, on the development of a long-term data storage system. I sent her a five-dimensional (5D) quartz storge card and a copy of the schematics of the reader/writer for her use by mail. I included a note and told her that this device could store all the information ever written since the beginning of time on just one chip, and it should retain the information without corruption for 13.8 billion years. I knew that would spark her interest. I asked her to investigate it and do all she could to develop the technology as quickly as possible.

Beverly responded after about a week, probably within hours of receiving it in the mail. I got an invite from her online to join an online meeting room.

"Wow," Beverly said. "This technology is incredible! It's a real game changer."

"I can't believe it," one of her colleagues said. "How did you develop this, Mr. Hickman?"

"It's hard to explain. It all came to me in a visionary dream of the future," I answered.

"A dream? That's rather incredible. But, how does it work? Can you explain the technical details?"

"Well, you see, it's a combination of advanced algorithms and cutting-edge hardware, but the specifics are quite complicated," I edged.

"We can worry about the specifics later," Beverly interrupted, seeming to sense that I didn't want to say how I had really come about it. "The important thing is to bring this technology to fruition as quickly as possible. We need to start planning how to implement it."

"I have so many questions about the potential applications and implications of this technology," another colleague voiced, staring at me in awe. "It's mind-blowing."

"I'm glad to see the excitement," I told him. "Honestly, I never expected such a strong reaction."

"Well, you've certainly impressed us all." Beverly smiled. "This could revolutionize our work here at the university. Let's keep the momentum going and start working on a plan to make this a reality."

"Absolutely, this could change everything. I'm just really glad to meet you, Mr. Hickman. Beverly talks about you all the time."

"Thanks. And I'm sorry I can't really answer all the technical questions. I've given you everything I know about the system."

"That's all right, Mr. Hickman," the first colleague said. "We understand. This is just phenomenal. But, what can you tell us about how you made the quartz chip?"

"Ah"—I gave him a grin—"that secret is going in a vault."

That said, I made a financial deal with the team that included an agreement that I would be provided with a working reader/burner and ten chips as soon as humanly possible.

13.0.9.13.10 | TZLOK'IN DATE: 4 OK | HAAB DATE: 3 YAXK'IN | LORD OF THE NIGHT: G9 GREGORIAN: AUGUST 1, 2022

A year passed, and the knowledge of Earth's current destiny weighed heavily on my mind. I kept pushing my intervention off until the foreboding feelings overcame me, forcing me to act once again.

This time, I decided I would try to intervene in a slightly different way, being I was not anxious to leave Terri again. I would try to make the government aware of the future without jumping time; let the governments of the world make the changes to avoid this looming doom. I would only jump time forward to confirm if the changes had made a difference. I figured I could do all the time jumping I needed to in the future, only after Terri had lived her life to the fullest, together, with me by her side. There was no rush; 3036 was not going anywhere, and I had a mission to save Earth, but I didn't have to save it in 2022. I could save it in 3035, and everything would still be fine. I had to curb my anxiety and master my emotions.

It was on this day that I picked up a mighty pen—actually, it was not a pen at all but my trusty computer keyboard with a fancy font—and produced a letter to the United States of America, Homeland Security, to the attention of Secretary Alejandro Mayorkas.

August 1, 2022
Secretary Mayorkas,

I would like to introduce myself and offer my transcendent powers to the government of the United States.

I am sure the government gets plenty of nutjobs writing every day about various matters. This is not the letter of a person who is attempting deceit or the writings of a person with a twisted sense of humor. I am of sound mind and body, and my words are truth.

I can assure you that the claims I make in this letter to be verifiable. I will offer you proof of my claims, provided the government permits me to speak to the President and the Joint Seats of Congress after proving to the government that I possess such abilities. I have some very vital information that I would like to share with the United States of America. However, we have plenty of time to take defensive action.

I have the ability to report events that will happen in the future. I can see any public event and tell you with certainty what will happen, no matter how far into the future. For the purpose of proving

I have this ability, I would suggest that we work with events that are not too far off into the future. Anything from lottery numbers to reporting some major world events that would normally be reported in the news.

I know this power could prove to be invaluable to the United States. It could ensure that we have the upper hand in almost any situation. As a US citizen, I would be proud to support my country with such vital information on an as needed basis.

I would like to add that I am not looking to be paid for this service, and it should be noted that I would only use this power to aid in the stabilization of our national security and not to provide information for offensive actions or political gain.

I reserve the right to refuse service at any time.

Sincerely,
Maximilian Hickman
US Citizen, Capon Bridge, WV

After writing this letter, I sealed it and noted the date and time in my personal journal. You never knew when one might need to change something like this letter. Time noted as: 1100 hours (11:00 AM).

I placed a stamp on the envelope and mailed it to the Office of Homeland Security at 2707 Martin Luther King Jr. Ave., SE Washington DC, 20528.

As I placed it in the mailbox and put the flag up, I thought to myself, *This should catch someone's attention even if his mail is screened.*

I could feel my nerves were on edge a little as I saw the mailman pick up the mail. The letter was officially sent. Now I just needed to wait until I got a response from Secretary Mayorkas.

13.0.9.13.13 | TZLOK'IN DATE: 7 B'EN | HAAB DATE: 6 YAXK'IN | LORD OF THE NIGHT: G3 GREGORIAN: AUGUST 4, 2022

Days went by, and I did not receive a response from the DHS. No phone calls, letters, emails, or anything. I figured I would give it a little more time, and then I might even need to try writing to the FBI.

I had been so preoccupied with my letter-writing campaign that I had almost forgotten that tomorrow was Terri's birthday. There was a lot to do. I needed to get a cake, some flowers and, yes, a nice gift. I figured I would dress up nicely, put on some of that cologne she liked, and serve her breakfast in bed tomorrow morning. Then a day of lunch out on the town, some shopping, a movie, and a night cap to end the day. I thought to myself that she should like all that.

I spent the balance of the day running around town, getting everything I needed to make sure she was not forgotten. Flowers, a nice new dress for her, and tickets to the show. I made reservations at the local Italian restaurant then made my way back home. I hid the flowers in the shop/lab refrigerator, next to the beer bottles with the engineered virus, and then I made my way back into the house.

I must have had that cat that ate the canary look on my face when she asked what I was up to.

"Nothing," I said. "Just tinkering out in the lab."

That kind of answer scared a woman whose husband messed around with nuclear matter just for fun, and I saw a slightly concerned look on her face.

I then reassured her, "It's all safe. No explosions or anything to be expected."

That evening, Terri asked, "Have you done any work to resolve the world crises?"

Maybe the presidents of the world got that kind of question thrown at them in the evening on occasion. Maybe even some generals must answer that type of question. But me? It seemed out of my pay grade.

"I wrote to DHS and am awaiting their reply," I replied.

She looked at me and said, "I cannot believe you bothered reaching out to our current government to address a problem more than a thousand years from now."

I spent the next few hours sharing my plan to have the governments of the free world work this out. That knowing something was a lot different than having to personally change it.

Being as wise as she was, she told me, "You should have waited until we lived our lives out together. Now I'm going to be concerned about the US government intervening with our lives in a very negative way."

"Don't worry," I told her. "I will go back in time if things get out of hand and eliminate the letter. I want to give them a chance and possibly help our country to resolve other worldly issues as they might arise."

13.0.9.13.14 | TZLOK'IN DATE: 8 IX | HAAB DATE: 7 YAXK'IN | LORD OF THE NIGHT: G4 GREGORIAN: AUGUST 5, 2022

I woke up early, as I did many mornings, dressed, and made myself ready for the day. Yes, I put on some of that smell good cologne, too. I brewed a cup of coffee for myself and Terri then went to work fixing her a nice breakfast and served her in bed.

She seemed grateful but concerned that I had messed up her kitchen. In her head, I was kind of like a two-year-old making pancakes or something.

With that said, I skedaddled back to the kitchen and did a quick cleanup. I got it all in order to make her happy. It was her birthday, after all. Then I ran out to the lab/shop and got the flowers out of the refrigerator, setting them up on the kitchen table so she would see them when she came out of the bedroom.

A few moments later, I heard her call me. "Max? Max."

I removed the flowers from the table and took them with me back to the bedroom. Apparently, breakfast was not filling enough, and she insisted that I return to bed, if you know what I mean.

We had been busy for a couple of hours when I emerged from the bedroom. I was hungry now and in need of some replenishing nourishment and hydration.

As I sat at the kitchen table with a plate of food and a glass of OJ, Terri emerged from the bedroom with her dishes and tray in hand. Just then, a knock came at the door.

She looked at me and asked, "Are you expecting someone or a delivery?"

"No," I told her as I went for the door.

She retreated to the bedroom and kind of peeked out as I opened the door. Immediately, I knew it was the government's response to my letter.

Two men, dress in black, with really white button-up shirts and small speakers wired in their ears were now standing at the door with badges out for display.

"Good morning, men," I greeted them as I looked at their badges. "Is there something I can help you with?"

"May we come in and speak with you for a moment?" one asked.

"I was just grabbing something to eat and need just a few minutes."

"We will wait," the other said.

I closed the door then went for the dishes to clean up the table, figuring I would talk with them there.

Terri came out of the room with that "I told you so" look on her face, in disgust, and sat at the table. "You might as well let them in."

I went to the door, opened it, and signaled for the men to enter.

Only one of the agents took a chair at the table; the other stood by, as if on guard.

The one at the table introduced himself, "I am Special Agent Cris Brown, and the other man is Special Agent Stuart Fenton." Then he proceeded to withdraw a letter from his jacket breast pocket and asked, "Do you recognize this letter, addressed to Secretary Alejandro Mayorkas with the Department of Homeland Security?"

"I recognize the letter as being the one I mailed," I answered.

"DHS is very interested in your claims and wants to know how it works."

I briefed them on what I would need, telling them, "You will have to ask a question, allow me to return to my home, and give me a couple of days. I will return with an accurate answer, provided the information is public or generally obtainable."

Agent Brown then slid a piece of paper toward me. As I picked it up, he explained, "There are three questions written on the paper that I need answered by tomorrow."

"Tomorrow might be tough," I told him. "The wife and I have plans for the day."

"Tomorrow," he stated, "would be best." Then he stood up. "I will return tomorrow at 1000 hours." With that, they quickly moved to the door and made their exit.

I could see them walk down my driveway and get into their black SUV, leaving the wife and I looking out the door in disbelief.

I shook my head as I closed the door, knowing their timing was the worst. I could fix it all by going back in time and not mailing the letter or waiting to mail it at a later date, but I figured I would wait and decide after I saw what proof they wanted.

Terri took the note that Agent Brown had passed to me, opened it, and read it out loud.

> *"Mr. Hickman,*
>
> *In response to your letter, dated August 1, 2022, we respectfully request that you reply with the answers to each of the following questions. We look forward to your cooperation and your response.*
>
> *#1. List each obituary in the Sunday* Washington Post *newspaper for the date August 7, 2022, final addition.*
>
> *#2. Provide the S&P 500 closing price for August 8, 2022.*
>
> *#3. Provide us with the Power Ball lottery numbers for August 6, 2022.*
>
> *Regards,*
> *Secretary Alejandro Mayorkas, DHS."*

"Don't worry. I got this," I told Terri. "Just hand me the dirty dishes and get dressed. I have a nice day planned for the two of us."

She just looked at me with disbelief.

"Go ahead and take a shower, get dressed so I can take you out for lunch." Then I turned my back on her and proceeded to rinse the dishes and load them into the dishwasher as she made her exit from the kitchen and headed to the bedroom. I then grabbed my keys and quickly made my way to the pyramid and locked the pyramid door. There, tapped on the door, was a small note from me.

> *Remove the GPS tracking bug from the driver's side wheel well before taking the truck. Replace it when you're done. Don't forget; it's very important.*
> *Max.*

I took my place in the recliner and, with great haste, I set my new destination date and time: 13.0.9.13.18 | 12 Etz'nab' | 11 Yaxk'in | G8, August 9, 2022, at 0600 hours (6:00 AM). Then I logged my current date and time: 13.0.9.13.14 | 8 Ix | 7 Yaxk'in | G4, August 5, 2022, at 1000 hours (10:00 AM). Without further ado, I hit the green button, not even thinking that it had been a year since I had traveled.

Luckily for me, all went well. The reactor went into high gear, the ionic cloud filled the room, and the tingling started. Within minutes of my starting off, everything was winding down. Heck, the chair was not even warm from my body yet.

I turned on the red-light switch for the dining room light. Then I unlocked the pyramid door and headed for my pickup truck, remembering to remove the GPS device from the driver's side wheel well.

After driving to the local fast food mart, I bought one of the remaining August 7, 2022, Sunday *Washington Post* newspapers that was left over and slightly torn up. You would think they would have sold it to me at a discount, being it was old, but no, full price. Then I purchased the prior day's evening paper.

I sat in my truck and quickly scanned the papers to make sure they had what I needed. The lottery number for Powerball drawn on August 6, 2022, was 8, 15, 46, 56, 68, and Powerball 3. The Power Play was 2X. I checked that off the list. S&P 500 closing on August 8, 2022, was Price: 4,140.06; Open: 4,155.93; High: 4,186.62; Low: 4,128.97; and the change was -0.12%. I checked that off the list. Now the list of obituaries from the Sunday paper. I extracted the entire obituary section of the paper, figuring I would have to copy it to take back with me.

Listening to the radio news on the way back to the pyramid, I heard that, on Sunday, the U.S. Senate passed a spending bill that included an unprecedented four hundred million dollars to reduce greenhouse gas emissions. I thought I would throw that into the information I provided, just for good measure.

I returned to the cabin, parked the truck, replaced the GPS device onto the wheel well, and then made my way back up to the pyramid. I could see the red light was on in the cabin and knew I was probably watching myself. Then I saw myself wave for me to meet at the laboratory/shop. I had myself approach, and the conversation was very strange.

I was told by myself, "Two agents are going to visit on August 8th and invite Terri and you to the White House. The agents will be leaving a listening device, stuck to the underside of the kitchen table—you will be under surveillance. Do not bring any edible gifts because the President and First Lady will not be permitted to consume them. It's best to go without a gift for the host, being it's more of a meeting than a social dinner." Then I told myself, "Pack a night bag and have Terri pack one for herself. Plan for an overnight stay. Book a room at the Double Tree Hotel in Northwest DC." I shook my hand.. "Good luck and have fun." I turned and one of me went for the cabin and the other to the pyramid, through the tunnel so as not to be seen.

I entered the pyramid, pushing past the heavy steel door as it groaned, and went up the steps. I then pulled up a chair and copied each obituary from the Sunday, August 7th *Post* down into my notebook, followed by the S&P 500's closing information for August 8, 2022. Then I jotted down the Powerball numbers for August 6, 2022. And just for good measure, I inserted the information about the Senate passing the spending bill on Sunday the 7th, 2022, for four hundred million dollars. When I finished, I opened the pyramid door, wadded up the newspapers and threw them out, and then closed the door once more and locked it. It was time to travel back for my girl's birthday.

I entered the return date and time: 13.0.9.13.14 | 8 Ix | 7 Yaxk'in | G4, August 5, 2022, at 1015 hours (10:00 AM), and then logged my current date and time: 13.0.9.13.18 | 12 Etz'nab' | 11 Yaxk'in | G8, August 9, 2022, at 0800 hours (8:00 AM). I turned off the red light then sat in the recliner and hit the green button once again. The reactor fired right up, the cloud engulfed the room, and there was that persistent tingling. Within moments, the jump was over. I was back after just fifteen minutes absence. When I returned to the cabin, Terri was just wrapping up her shower.

I tore the page from my notebook and placed the sheet of paper with my responses on the kitchen table. Then I sat back, waiting for Terri to ready herself for a day and evening of outings as the old Eric Clapton song "Wonderful Tonight" played in my head.

As she exited the bedroom, all dressed, I could not help but smile and tell her, "You look wonderful."

We were off to town for a nice lunch, followed by an afternoon reshowing of a steamy love movie and a bout of shopping for accessories to match her new dress. Yes, shoes and a new designer purse. Happy birthday, baby. I then took Terri out to a fine jazz club where we had a few drinks. We finished the evening with a cake from one of the fine bakeries in Little Italy, Baltimore, where I placed a birthday candle in it and sang her "Happy Birthday." She seemed to be enjoying everything. It was truly a wonderful time with the exception of the two men in black following us around. I ignored them and did not mention anything to Terri about their presence, but they were definitely there, watching everything we did.

When we got home, it was late. As I turned off the lights, I told her that I loved her. I don't recall her responding; she was out for the count.

13.0.9.13.15 | TZLOK'IN DATE: 9 MEN | HAAB DATE: 8 YAXK'IN | LORD OF THE NIGHT: G5 GREGORIAN: AUGUST 6, 2022

I woke up that morning and made myself coffee. Unlike most days, I made my own breakfast and cleaned everything up immediately after. I figured I would not disturb Terri and just let her sleep in after such a late evening. I also knew the DHS agents were going to visit this morning, and I wanted to be ready for them. I had a couple of disposable coffee cups out, along with the typical coffee condiments to offer the agents.

At 0945 hours (9:45 AM), I could see the agents' SUV pulling up at the end of the driveway. I noticed that, in both instances, they had avoided pulling into the drive but rather parked out on the street and walked up the drive. Maybe that was some agent protocol?

Just a few minutes later, they started walking toward the house. When they knocked, I immediately opened the door, half-startling them.

"Please, come in."

As before, they took their places. Agent Brown sat at the table while Agent Fenton stood guard.

I offered them both a cup of coffee, noting, "I have cups you can take with you."

"No, thank you," both men declined.

Agent Brown then asked, "Are you able to answer the questions, being your schedule was so full yesterday?"

I nodded that I had as I slid the notebook paper with my handwritten responses on it.

Agent Brown asked, "How did you get this information?" as he passed the note to Agent Fenton to review.

"I am revealing my ability for the good of mankind. However, I have no intention of sharing how I accomplish it," I told him.

Agent Brown then said, "We will be in contact with you sometime after August 8th."

"I expect to see you next week, when you will need to prepare to uphold your end of the bargain."

"We have not agreed to anything," Agent Fenton said.

I looked him straight in the eyes and said, "It would be unfortunate for you to find out that I may be able to alter history as well as report it." Then I smiled and escorted the agents to the front door.

I could tell he did not like that response and had most definitely taken my last comment as a threat. That was fine for now. They could take it as a threat if that was what it took for them to take me seriously.

After they left, Terri poked her head out of the bedroom. "Are they gone?"

"They have already driven off."

"I heard some of the conversation, and I am now concerned that the government will be more interested in finding out how it's done more than actually honoring any stipulations that you request. I doubt you will ever get to meet with the President, or any of his cabinet."

"Don't worry," I told her. "I can always jump forward and ask myself what they are doing, and then come back to alter my actions to avoid any issues."

We carried on with our normal day.

That evening, before bed, we tuned into the televised lottery drawing and waited for the Powerball numbers to be drawn. I smiled at Terri and told her, "I bet there are a bunch of DHS special agents watching the drawing tonight."

We both got a chuckle, thinking about the agents playing the numbers, but I figured they were so straitlaced that they would not dare try. We then laughed at the idea that the US government was going to have to start playing to pay off the national debt. It did not seem like such a farfetched idea when you thought about it.

At 2300 hours (11:00 PM), the drawing began. The first ball was a 15, then the next a 8, followed by 46, 56, 68, and Powerball 3, just as I had reported to the agents. I knew they were going to be taken aback by the experience when they read tomorrow's obituaries in the *Post*. They were going to know for sure that I was the real deal.

13.0.9.13.16 | TZLOK'IN DATE: 10 K'IB' | HAAB DATE: 9 YAXK'IN | LORD OF THE NIGHT: G6 GREGORIAN: AUGUST 7, 2022

This should prove to be a day of reckoning for the DHS checking me out.

We went about our morning as normal, and then I told Terri, "I'm going to go up the street to grab a *Post*."

I picked it up and, behold, the obituaries were there in print, just as I had reported them to the agents.

Speaking of the agents, they were there, too. Across the street, I spied their black SUV with the dark tinted windows. Apparently, I was still under surveillance. Maybe more so now than before.

I made my way back to our cabin and told Terri, "They are watching. We probably have our phones bugged." We almost never used our phones, but just in case, I wanted her to be aware.

That afternoon, we turned on the news and, sure enough, it was reported that the U.S. Senate had passed a spending bill that included an unprecedented four hundred billion dollars to reduce greenhouse gas emissions. Now, even if the government had been skeptical about my ability to predict lottery numbers and that I had somehow rigged the draw or that I had some inside information on what was being published in the *Post* obituary pages that Sunday, they knew for sure I did not have the ability to influence or alter the votes of the US Senate. I thought to myself, *By tomorrow afternoon, at 1600 hours (4:00 PM), when the S&P closes, they will surely want to talk with me again.*

13.0.9.13.17 | TZLOK'IN DATE: 11 KAB'AN | HAAB DATE: 10 YAXK'IN | LORD OF THE NIGHT: G7 GREGORIAN: AUGUST 8, 2022

It was Monday morning. I was not expecting to hear from the DHS today, but I had told myself to expect two agents, so Terri and I just went about our regular business as we kept an eye out.

We were sitting in the living room when there was a knock on the door.

"Just sit there. I will get it," I told Terri as I went to the door and peered out the side window. There they were, two agents on the front stoop.

I opened the door, and they had their badges extended, announcing, "We are DHS agents." This time, it was Special Agent Linda Mason and Agent Etta Faulkenhan. Both were women agents.

"How can I help you?" I asked.

Like the other agents, one of them asked, "Can we step inside and speak with you?"

"Of course," I agreed and directed them to the kitchen table.

Agent Faulkenhan was the one who took the seat this time while Agent Mason stood by her side.

"We apologize for arriving unannounced, but we need to know if you are willing to meet with the President this evening at the White House."

"Is the invitation just for myself or is my wife also invited?" I asked, thinking it was odd that such a meeting would be set up before the markets closed this afternoon. "Why so soon?" I asked, being the closing bell for the S&P would not be until 1600 hours (4:00 PM).

"You demonstrated your abilities sufficiently to merit such a meeting," Agent Faulkenhan answered.

"Can I consult with my boss before I commit?" I asked.

They looked at each other, and then Agent Faulkenhan said, "I was not aware you were still employed."

I cracked myself up again, and told her, "No, this boss," as I pointed to Terri.

We all smiled, and Agent Faulkenhan said, "Sure."

Terri and I got up from the table and walked to the back room.

"What do you think?" I asked.

"Why not?" was her reply. "You met with yourself and were told to enjoy it. Besides, it's not every day one gets invited to the White House."

We rejoined the agents, and I told them, "We would love to meet the President this evening."

"Thank you," Agent Faulkenhan said. "Secret Service will pick you up at 1600 hours (4:00 PM). Dinner will be at 1800 hours (6:00 PM). And the dress is semi-formal, as you will be guests of the White House. The President and all the White House executive officers are expected to attend, with the exception of the Vice President."

All I could say was "Wow" as the agents got up and walked for the door.

Then Agent Mason said, "Oh, a couple of things I need to tell you. Do not share your plans or this schedule with anyone. You can't bring electronic devices, especially phones or recording devices. And it should be obvious that food, firearms, or drugs of any type are not permitted."

Terri and I looked at each other, and then I said, "There will be no problem complying with those terms."

The agents then walked down the driveway toward their vehicle.

Knowing the place was bugged, we did not say anything. Terri gave me the *shh* sign, and I nodded in agreement. Then we both started looking under the kitchen table. Sure enough, we found what we were looking for—one of the agents had stuck a listening device on the underside of the kitchen table.

We removed it and placed it on the top side of the table, putting a glass over it. Then we stepped outside, and Terri said, "We are in deep, and none of these people can be trusted."

We went back into the kitchen and lifted the glass that had been over the listening device. We had a brief discussion about how exciting it would be to meet the President and his cabinet. We kept the conversation light and positive, winking at each other as we played on with the conversation. What really bothered me was that the agents really didn't have a good reason to bug our home. I was offering to help the US government, and if this did not work out, I was going to throw away the letter I had written to DHS before I had even mailed it.

By 1530 (3:30 PM), Terri and I were both dressed and waiting on the Secret Service to arrive. We had basically not spoken in the house since the bug had been planted, with the exception of some small talk.

I turned on the television to the news channel, figuring I would watch the market close for the day. As I did, I heard a knock at the door. It was 1555 (3:55 PM), five minutes before the stock market closed.

It was another agent who introduced himself as Secret Service Agent Jerry McDonald, and his partner, who was outside the door, was introduced as Secret Service Agent Donna Scott.

"Pease, come in," I told the agents. "We're going to watch the market close before we depart. Terri is putting together a few things."

Agent McDonald came in and stood at the door while Agent Scott remained just outside the door.

Ding, ding, ding, ding, ding, the market closing bell rang. Within seconds, the market's closing numbers were published on the screen. Closing Price: 4,140.06; Open: 4,155.93; High: 4,186.62; Low: 4,128.97; and the change for the day was -0.12% in the red, just as I had reported them.

When Terri came out of the room with an overnight bag in hand, I told Agent McDonald, "I need one more moment." I picked up my smart phone and made a quick reservation at the Double Tree Hotel in Northwest DC. Then I gave the, "Okay, time to go," announcement and placed my cell phone on the kitchen table next to the listening bug under the glass.

Terri and I exited the door with the Secret Service agents leading the way. The agents were polite and held the doors open for both my wife and myself. I thought it was the first time in my life that I had ever been in a stretch limo. Most definitely a first for a diplomatic one, for sure. We looked at each other as we took our seats inside the car and smiled. It felt highly prestigious to be riding in a presidential limo.

I didn't think the Secret Service guys liked having to do this escort service, being the roads to our cabin were all dirt. It was a hard five-mile run of potholes, boulders, and trees. The vehicle would require a full bath before they even get to the White House. And, sure enough, they made us switch vehicles so that our entry would not be out of a muddy, dirty limo but rather a clean, freshly waxed one.

"Don't forget the overnight bag," I had to remind Terri as we made the transfer. All and all, I had to admire the forethought that had gone into that vehicle switch. Yes, I could say I was impressed.

As we made entry, we were announced to the room as, "Mr. and Mrs. Maximilian Hickman." After that, I was not sure what I was supposed to do. I just had my wife hold onto my arm, and we walked in, no waving or anything.

I was immediately greeted by each of the cabinet members who were present, each shaking my hand, and then my wife's, as we made our way to a large, long table where we were seated.

Everything was presidential—flags, blue White House water bottles, White House plates with the emblem on them, and just about everything had an official White House seal on it.

Then the President of the United States was announced. President Joe Biden and First Lady Jill Biden. We all stood up as they entered and made their way to the table where we had been seated. President Biden came over to me, and Jill to my wife, and they shook our hands.

"Thank you for attending," President Joe Biden told us.

"The pleasure is all ours," I responded. "And I hope that our visit will benefit the United States and the world as a whole."

"Hold those thoughts," he said. "We will talk in the Oval Office after dinner."

The dinner was great. It seemed they knew all of my favorite dishes. We had Maryland crab soup, followed by a traditional Maryland crab cake dinner. There was also some other seafood affair served that included shrimp, oysters, and lobster. They even had rotisserie chicken, macaroni and cheese, fire roasted corn, and several other side vegetable dishes. It was like I had ordered my dream meal and someone else was paying for it.

You could not have smacked the smile off my face as we made small talk during the meal. Then, with all that, they brought out the dessert cart. It had all mine and Terri's favorites on it. When I saw that, I knew they had done their homework. They had scanned my social media pages and used the information they had gathered about my likes and dislikes about food to plan this meal. I could see Terri had picked up on it, as well. It was not too often in one's life when everything on the menu or being served was your favorite. They had overdone it, for sure, but I felt there was no reason to fight it. I did not think they would poison me or anything. Most likely, they just wanted to know how I was able to know the future and not so much what was coming next. That was something we were not going to share.

After some additional small talk, meeting and greeting, handshaking, and the like, one of the Secret Service agents came over to me. "Will you please follow me to the Oval Office to meet privately with the President?"

"Of course," I agreed then whispered in my wife's ear, "I'm going to go meet with the President. I will be back in a few."

One of the men attending the meeting held out his arm and said, "Terri will be fine with me. I will take good care of her while you're gone."

I nodded. "I'm sure she will," I said as she stepped away from me and latched on to him.

The agent then led me to my meeting.

Upon approaching the Oval Office, we stopped in the hallway, and I was asked to extend my arms out as they patted me down and ran a scanner over my person. After clearing my belt buckle and my watch band, the agent then opened the door to the Oval Office.

President Biden was seated behind the presidential desk. "Please, take a seat." He indicated to the leather chair that was in front of it.

I took a seat, as directed, and although the chair was in front of his desk, it was so far away that I felt like I was sitting out in the middle of the room. It was the feeling of being in a small raft in the middle of a large ocean, all by yourself, only able to rely on your own resources. There would be no support or rescue from outside. No one would be throwing me a safety line. No matter. I was prepared.

President Biden smiled. "Thank you again for joining my wife, the cabinet, and me for dinner."

Then the office door opened, and top-ranking members of the cabinet filed in. They took their places in some of the surrounding couches and seats. All were quiet and mostly just stared at me. Then the door closed as the Secret Service agents made an exit from the room.

The President then looked at me and said, "You have obviously caught our attention. We want to know how you do it." He picked up a piece of paper that was on his desk, read for a moment, and then said, "You reported that the closing price of the S&P 500 would be 4,140.06 today." With everyone giving him their full attention, he announced, "The closing price was 4,140.06." Then he looked at me. "How could you possibly know that on January 6th when you reported this to us?"

I quickly responded by telling the group, "I have the ability to see public and readily available published information in the future and report it."

"But, how?" the President asked.

"I'm sorry that I can't reveal my means and methods, but I am willing to share this information with the US government if it impacts the United States or its citizens." When he started to say something, I said, "Please let me explain," and he signaled for me to proceed. I told the group, "I requested this meeting because I want to share some very vital information, and the only way I felt anyone would take me seriously was to prove that I have these abilities before I present the situation of concern. I hope I have proven, without a doubt, that I can accurately report what will happen. With the information I provide, the future can be changed and the outcome for any event can be permanently altered."

One of the President's men stepped toward me and asked, "How can this knowledge change anything?"

"If a Hitler were to rise in the future, and we knew that before the rise, we could take whatever actions necessary to eliminate that rise to power. We could place armies in the way of an invading army before the army even knew they were going to invade, and possibly thwart the invasion altogether. I will provide the US government the power to squash any foe before they even become a threat."

Then one of the cabinet women asked, "How will we know you are not just going to manipulate the US government by telling us things that make changes for your own benefit? Like you most likely did to win the lottery."

I thought I turned a little red with that statement and started to become self-conscious, but I gathered myself and told her, "Yes, I used the knowledge one time to win a large lottery. This was done to finance my operation, and I will never need to do something like that again. If I wanted to, I could have started with one hundred dollars and just played the markets until I had millions of dollars, but that would not have been any better. This way, it was not taken from anyone, and the government was able to collect all the taxes on the money. No businesses or investors were hurt, and there were no losses to anyone."

I admitted, "I did not feel good about it, but I had to do it, so I did what needed to be done. Besides, now there is no additional cost for future information, provided my abilities are not made public outside of this office." I warned, "Spreading the knowledge of my abilities will jeopardize my willingness to help. It will endanger my family and myself, and I will find out who leaked the information and report it back to the government."

I continued, "The main reason I even stepped forward to share my abilities with the US government is to stop a horrible event that will happen in the future if action is not taken."

You could have heard a pin drop after I had said that.

"In the year 3036, man will destroy the world as we know it. Armageddon will start in Southern Israel as a small clash with the surrounding Muslim nations and expand throughout the globe, ending in a complete apocalypse. Earth will cease to support life. Unlike any film that has been made of the post-apocalypse, there will be no survivors that are biologically alive. No heroes, no great rebirth of the planet, no prepper will have the resources to survive. None of the great comebacks or stories the movies have portrayed will happen. Not even single-celled organisms will make it. Only machines will exist, and they will inherit the Earth. All this will be due to artificial intelligence (AI) and robots. They will play man against man, nation against nation, until we all destroy each other and the life-sustaining ability of our planet."

I heard a few chuckles in the group.

"That's it?" President Biden asked. "You want us to believe that AI and robots will end the world in 3036, and you want us to do something about it now?"

"Yes," I told them. "Legislation needs to be put in place to limit AI's capabilities and to protect humans *now*. That is why I asked to speak before all of Congress—to give this warning and beg for action before we humans give it up and lose power over our own selves." I begged them to please believe me by saying, "I would not have risked revealing my capabilities if changes did not absolutely need to be made *now*."

President Biden stood up, walked around the desk, and approached me. He reached his hand out, shook mine, and said, "Thank you. Is there anything else we need to know?"

"No. My only goal is to save humanity and planet Earth. I feel that the mission was given to me by God, and this administration is the army."

As the group started filing out of the office, the President asked, "Please hang back for a moment. I want to talk to you in private." He stood at the door as his cabinet exited and thanked each attendee as they made their exit from the Oval Office.

He then signaled security to close the door, stating, "We only need a moment." He then walked over to me and asked, "Can I ask a personal question?" He got that Joe Biden grin on his face. "Do I win the 2024 election, Max?"

I smiled. "I promised myself that I would not use my abilities, or let others use my abilities, for personal or political gain. However"—I paused for a long moment—"I did make an exception for myself one time by winning the lottery. I regretted doing so and, as such, it was brought up today, in this office, only moments ago. It was wrong but necessary." When I saw his smile drop a little, I continued, as this was wrong but possibly necessary, "You have nothing to worry about, Mr. President, or I would not have bothered to meet with you today."

His smile returned as a full grin.

I did not have the heart to tell him that he would not live long enough to serve his full second term.

Our meeting concluded, and I was escorted back to the hall where all the attendees had gathered. Each cabinet member was saying their goodbyes and exiting as they retrieved their jackets and stoles. It was getting dark, and being the sun set late in the summer months, I knew the hour was late.

Terri and I rejoined and thanked everyone as we made our exit. The Secret Service was there at the door as we stepped out into the evening air, and they showed us to the limo.

"Would you prefer to stay at a local hotel this evening rather than make the two-hour trip back to your cabin in Capon Bridge?" one agent asked.

"Yes, I already made reservations for the Double Tree Hotel in Northwest. We have our overnight bag."

The agent looked shocked, unsure how I had planned such a stay without having been asked.

"We will need to depart tomorrow morning in time to reach the cabin by 0730 hours (7:30 AM) because I have prior commitments that I have to keep." Of course, I didn't elaborating as to what they were.

That evening, Terri and I relived the day's events. She asked me a lot of questions about my meeting with the cabinet as we enjoyed a glass of wine. Her having not been in the room was making me have a hard time getting a feel as to whether they would take heed to my warning or just play me off as a nutjob.

"I think they were just patronizing me," I told her. "It's like someone believing in God as insurance to not go to hell but not because they really have faith. Something along those lines. They are most likely bugging our house now and setting up camera surveillance of our property as we sit in this room. It's probably the reason they even invited us to this event and suggested we grab a room for the evening instead of returning to the cabin tonight." I just didn't trust them after their planting of a listening device already. How could I trust them?

CHAPTER TWENTY-TWO

AVERTED

13.0.9.13.18 | TZLOK'IN DATE: 12 ETZ'NAB' | HAAB
DATE: 11 YAXK'IN | LORD OF THE NIGHT: G8
GREGORIAN: AUGUST 9, 2022

It was 0500 hours (5:00 AM) when the hotel room's phone rang, a wake-up call from the Secret Service, letting us know we would have to leave in about thirty minutes if we wanted to make it to the cabin by 0730 hours (7:30 AM).

I nudged Terri and got her on her feet. I was the early bird, and she was not, to put it politely. She went through the motions of waking up, but she was sleepwalking, more or less.

I got a knock on the door, and it was one of the Secret Service agents again. He handed me two coffees and a couple of bagels with all the fixings. "We will be out front, waiting for you at 0530 hours (5:30 AM)." He was so awake and chipper that it was scary.

I closed the door and told Terri, "Creeeepy."

Terri just laughed as she worked hard to get her hair in order.

I was dressed in moments and sat back, sipping on my coffee while Terri sat at the dressing bureau and continued her prep work.

At 0520 hours (5:20 AM), we opened the door to exit the room. The agent was there.

"We are ready to take you," he announced, and then we followed him to the elevator. Within moments, we were walking out the front door and being seated in the limo. This was our original limo that had initially picked us up from the cabin. I could tell—the mud on the tires and splashed along the sides was a dead giveaway. No matter. It was still a presidential limo, or at least a diplomatic one. I was proud to be sitting in that dirty-ass car.

The limo made good time getting out of DC, being we were heading against traffic. They took 66 West. Then, after about an hour, we headed north on 81 until we got to Winchester. It was not long after that we were in Capon Bridge and the limo was off-roading once again. I was sure all my redneck neighbors were stunned to see a mud-covered limo navigating the small mountain dirt roads as they squeezed by in their pumped-up four-wheel drive diesel pickup trucks, heading out to work.

We arrived just after 0700 hours (7:00 AM). The Secret Service agents opened our doors and let us out at the entrance to our driveway. I thanked them for the ride, and then Terri and I headed back up to the cabin.

About halfway up the driveway, I noticed my truck was missing. I was glad the drivers were Secret Service agents and not special agents for the DHS.

I could see that Terri was on her own mission—to feed and care for her cats. The President himself did not rank above her kitty cats.

Once we were in the cabin, I sat down at the kitchen table and noticed that the listening device was no longer under glass. It was gone. I pointed out the missing upside-down empty glass to Terri and could see the fire in her eyes. She was mad, and I knew she felt like I did—violated by the DHS. Then I noticed that the red light in the dining area was on. That meant I was visiting from another time.

It was not long before my truck pulled up in the driveway. It was me, with the newspapers in my hand.

I ran out the door and signaled myself to go to the shop/laboratory building. Once in the shop, I told myself, "Two agents are going to visit on August 8th and invite Terri and you to the White House. The agents will be leaving a listening device, stuck to the underside of the kitchen table—you will be under surveillance. Do not bring any edible gifts because the President and First Lady will not be permitted to consume them. It's best to go without a gift for the host, being it's more of a meeting than a social dinner." Then I told myself, "Pack a night bag and have Terri pack one for herself. Plan for an overnight stay. Book a room at the Double Tree Hotel in Northwest DC." I shook my hand.. "Good luck and have fun." Then I turned, and one of me went for the cabin and the other to the pyramid through the tunnel, so as not to be seen.

I entered the house and signaled Terri to walk outside onto the porch. I then told her, "I forewarned us about events that are going to be happening, so as not to be taken off guard. I'm going to order an electronic bug detector through Ama-Zing, and we should be able to get it by tomorrow." It would be hell trying to live in a house that was completely compromised.

"Do you know how to use one?" she asked.

"No, but they always come with Chinese directions. No problem. I got this." Then we spent the day silent, for the most part.

It was hard to shake the feeling of being violated. Obviously, they knew we knew they had bugged the house. So, why would they do it again, knowing we were not going to say anything? What a twisted mental play.

13.0.9.13.19 | TZLOK'IN DATE: 13 KAWAK | HAAB DATE: 12 YAXK'IN | LORD OF THE NIGHT: G9 GREGORIAN: AUGUST 10, 2022

I spent most of the next day looking out for that Ama-Zing delivery truck to come bouncing down the dirt road to deliver the bug detectors that I had ordered. I had actually ordered a couple of different types of detectors so that I had all the bandwidths and all the different types of surveillance devices covered.

When they finally arrived, I was so happy that I walked down the driveway to meet the Ama-Zing driver and take the packages from him. I could hardly wait to tear into the boxes, load the batteries, and see where the government had hidden the bugs.

Within fifteen minutes, I had the first detector up and running. I walked around the house, going room to room, in search of more listening devices.

I could not find any. Nothing at all.

I then walked up to my lab/shop and scanned the entire place.

Again, nothing.

I was completely disappointed, thinking that maybe this one was not working. So, I took the second detector out of the box and installed new batteries. Again, I searched the house and shop building.

Room by room, area by area, all negative.

Lastly, I went out to my truck with the bug detector, and I got a hit. There, up in the driver's side wheel well, I found a magnetic bug that the special agents with the DHS had planted. They had been tracking my truck. This sent a cold shiver down my spine. They had to know that my truck had been out, making a run yesterday morning, just after 0600 hours (6:00 AM) and that it had returned shortly after we had arrived back at the cabin. I knew I would have to fix this. *What else have they been doing?* was all I could think.

Then it hit me. They had made sure we had left our phones, computers, and all recording devices in the cabin. We had not secured them. I had placed my phone right out on the kitchen table, next to the surveillance bug that we'd had under glass. So, the DHS had complete access, and they'd had all the time they needed to install a tracker on our vehicle, being they knew we were being transported by the Secret Service.

I entered the cabin and signaled to Terri to come to the porch again. Outside, I told her, "The truck has a GPS tracker on it. I will have to go back in time to fix that. Our phones and computers are all compromised, too. They didn't have to place listening devices around the house when they could just install surveillance software into our personal devices to listen in. So, no matter what we do, the government is going to have a set of backdoor keys to any locks I could possibly install on the devices. The only way to avoid the bugging is to use burner phones and destroy them before they can bug them. The computers ... well, all our data needs to be kept on chips that they cannot decrypt and in a secure place."

I continued, "Just keep in mind that they are watching anything we do online and everything that is said. It's going to be hard, but we really need to unplug as much as possible from the internet. Even my purchase of the bug detectors is something they can see. They are probably sitting back, laughing at the purchase, knowing they didn't implement that type of surveillance in the cabin."

The decision was made. I needed to warn myself on August 5, 2022, that the truck was bugged with a GPS tracking device up in the driver's side wheel well. I needed to remove it before taking the truck to town on August 9, 2022, and I needed to replace it upon returning the truck to the driveway. I would travel back in time and just write a note, leaving it on the control panel for myself to read, as I had already seen done. That should take care of that loose end.

No need to secure the phones and computers. They would eventually hack them, anyway, so I just needed to switch over to burner phones and avoid internet use. I would then travel forward in time to the year 3035 and purchase a five-dimensional (5D) quarts chip reader/writer for storage of our data. That should prevent the government from having access for some time. I would bring the reader and a chip back to 2022 and load everything we had on it.

"Do you want to travel with me? I need to get a few things to secure our privacy," I asked Terri.

This time, she agreed. "Just this one time."

I could not believe it. I was so excited by her decision to jump time with me.

"I promise we will be back in less than an hour," I told her.

"I only want to jump time with you because I'm afraid to stay in the cabin alone, not because I want to experience time travel." She shrugged. "It's the lesser of two evils."

We made ready for the jump—always pack a lunch when jumping more than a day or two. I packed one for Terri, as well. It wasn't like I didn't have survival food ready just in case but, for the most part, I tried not to touch it for normal operations.

Terri and I used the tunnel up to the pyramid, so as not to be seen walking up the cliffs to the hidden pyramid. Best if they just saw us going to the shop.

While in the shop, Terri suggested, "You should set up a couple of manakins so they don't know we're gone. I have a couple of those old dress sewing type manikins, but they're ceramic."

"That'll work out great," I told her.

We made the trip back to the cabin and removed the sewing manikins from her sewing closet, placing them in the shop/lab. I took some thermal pipe tracing tape and wrapped it around the heads of the manikins. Then I placed a hat on the head to hold it all in place, explaining to Terri, "The heating tape is self-regulating, and once I set the temperature on the controller, it will maintain the temperature without any risk of fire."

We set the manakins up at the counter and plugged them in. I set the temperature to 37°C (98.6°F), and then we were ready. I named them Tom and Jerry.

We traveled through the tunnel to the pyramid and opened the heavy iron door.

After walking up the steps into the pyramid, Terri asked, "What do we do next?"

"Just take a seat in one of the reclining chairs. I'll take care of everything else."

I put the lunches in the refrigerator then entered the new destination date and time: 13.0.9.13.14 | 8 Ix | 7 Yaxk'in | G4, August 5, 2022, at 0900 hours (9:00 AM). I then logged our current date and time: 13.0.9.13.19 | 13 Kawak | 12 Yaxk'in | G9, August 10, 2022, and the time was 1500 hours (3:00 PM).

I looked over at Terri. "It's going to get foggy, like an electric tingling type fog, and you will feel a tingle. Don't be scared, and no matter what you do, do not get out of the chair or move around until we complete the jump."

She looked terrified but held on to the recliner arms and nodded as though she were ready to go.

I reached over to the control panel from my recliner and hit the green button. The reactor fired up and the ionic fog engulfed the interior once again. The tingling was present, as always. Then, within moments, it was over. The reactor wound down, and the tingling subsided.

I looked over and told her, "It's over."

She smiled. "That's it?"

I laughed. "It's a little more intense on longer jumps, but the little jumps are easy."

13.0.9.13.14 | TZLOK'IN DATE: 8 IX | HAAB DATE: 7 YAXK'IN | LORD OF THE NIGHT: G4 GREGORIAN: AUGUST 5, 2022

We both got out of our recliners, and then I pulled up a chair to the counter and wrote a note for myself to find. I placed the note on the control panel so that it was over the green "*Go*" button.

"Why not just go to the house and have a conversation?" Terri asked.

"There are many risks with that. We need to keep the interaction for one time period separate from another time period, if at all possible." But she got me thinking. What if the note traveled forward with us and I didn't find it when I traveled from August 5th to August 9th? I would still have a problem. So, I opted to make a second note and, instead of placing the note on the control panel, I taped it to the outside of the pyramid door, and another one on the tunnel entrance to the pyramid. No matter what, I would see the note before I jumped time on August 5th to August 9th.

I locked the doors and told Terri, "Take your position in the recliner." I then took out the lead blankets and low-Z Plexi shield, placing them over her and myself. She knew what they were for, being we had discussed why I needed them in the first place.

"We need to make a big jump now," I warned her then entered the new destination date and time: 15.11.17.15.11 | 2 Chuwen | 1 Yaxk'in | G5, December 10, 3035, and set the time to 1000 hours (10:00 AM). Next, I logged our current date: 13.0.9.13.14 | 8 Ix | 7 Yaxk'in | G4, August 5, 2022, and the time was 0915 hours (9:15 AM).

"Hold on," I warned. "The tingling may even burn a little, like a mild electric shock." Then I hit the green "*Go*" button and the jump was on. The reactor fired up, as expected, the cloud came on thick, and the tingling was intense. It took a few minutes, and then it started to wind down. I could see that Terri wanted to jump up, but she was unable to move, and I unable to even tell her not to.

As soon as it was safe, I said, "You can get up out of the recliner."

I had to laugh. Her hair was stuck up on end, like a big afro or a cartoon of someone who had been electrocuted. I didn't think she thought it was amusing, and she would give me grief about how I had not warned her for years after that, but as I looked back, it was funny.

"You have to ground yourself," I told her and had her grab the railing to the metal stairs.

Her hair relaxed somewhat with that, and she worked it in place with some water and her hairbrush, cussing and fussing the whole time.

15.11.17.15.11 | TZLOK'IN DATE: 2 CHUWEN | HAAB DATE: 14 YAXK'IN | LORD OF THE NIGHT: G5 GREGORIAN: DECEMBER 10, 3035

As a precaution, I looked at the monitor that was hooked up to the Eye of Horus to see if the area was clean. Then I drew some air for sampling through the sample tube. Oxygen levels were right in the sweet spot, and radiation levels were at normal background levels. It was now time to pull out the trusty, dusty air transport craft (ATC), good ole Hal.

I opened the bay door and pushed Hal out into the open air. I could not help but notice that there was some plant growth—small trees and shrubs. Much better than my visit to January 3036 had been. I could not believe so much would have been destroyed in such a short period of time.

Terri and I got in the ATC, and I asked Hal to take us to town. I needed to purchase a five-dimensional (5D) quartz crystal reader/writer and a few cables that would allow me to pair it up with my laptop.

This was Terri's first time in the ATC, and she hung on like it was a carnival ride. Her fingernails sank deep into my skin as we levitated off the ground. She could see the Plexiglass ATCs all around us and the people inside staring as they blew by.

"Don't worry," I told her. "This is going to be a quick trip, in and out." When we landed in town, I then told her, "You may want to just sit in Hal and wait for me."

That was when I saw her face as she noticed everyone walking around in see-through clothing.

I grinned sheepishly. "I forgot to mention that the styles have changed." It was all the more reason she might want to just sit in Hal and wait for me.

Her eyes told the whole story as she focused on a passerby.

All the pedestrian traffic seemed to be humans, and none seemed to be robots. Lots of humans with their private parts hanging out as they strolled through town. Some with their children in tow.

I made it quick. I entered the store and sat at a terminal. I placed my order for the reader/writer that I needed and several adapters. I then ordered a couple of quartz storage cards. Within a few minutes, all were delivered to the counter and payment was made as an almost nude twenty-something female clerk scanned my biochip that was still implanted in my left hand. I could not help but notice that I was being waited on by a human and not a robot, as I would have expected. I would have thought most people would have already started fleeing to the moon or Mars by now. *Maybe they don't know it's coming*, I thought to myself.

I walked out of the store and saw a police officer talking to Terri through Hal's open window. He, too, was a human. His butt crack was smiling at me as I approached my ATC.

I smiled and said, "Hi."

He gave me a big grin back. "I have never seen such an old unit that still operated. What's the year and make? How did you keep it in such pristine condition?" He wanted to know everything and anything about Hal. He even took photographs of himself with Hal then asked, "So, what are you guys doing? Where are you from?"

I gave him the old tale. "We work displays for the museum and are dressed for the up-and-coming exhibit. I'm related to the Hickmans and stopped by to visit the park my relatives established, The Hickman Nature Preservation Park."

He smiled. "Enjoy the park. No one ever goes there anymore, but it's nice for a quiet day."

"We're going to have a picnic there," I told him.

He winked at the wife then left in his see-through ATC with its blue lights flashing.

I got in Hal, and Terri automatically said, "I can't believe you talked us out of that."

"That wasn't my first time," I told her. "We have to keep in mind that Hal is from 2145, and it's 3035. This ATC, good old Hal, is eight hundred ninety years old. It's like driving up to a McDonald's in a horse-drawn chariot, dressed in Roman garb, and not expecting to draw attention."

I then gave Hal the commands to return to the pyramid, and we were off. It only took a few minutes to get back. I scanned the area and, seeing that the coast was clear, unlocked the door and pushed Hal in. We closed the door behind us and locked it.

I had purchased everything I needed. We would be able to save all the data we wanted onto the five-dimensional (5D) quartz card. Being the technology did not exist in the year 2022, it should be safe until Beverly's team at South Sampton fully developed the technology in 2024.

I then broke out the lunches and told Terri, "We should take a few minutes and have a picnic in the park that we established." Being I had packed lunch, we might as well eat it.

I unlocked the door, and we walked down to the beach. It was strange to both of us that the once small trout stream, Dillan's Run, was now a major ocean tributary.

We ate our lunch as we gazed out over the water. The landscape around us was green and not at all as barren as it had been in January of 3036. It was evident to both of us that 2022 was paradise compared to 3035. There was so much more life, and the wilderness was alive compared to what we were experiencing in 3035.

"Although life is not as abundant as it is in 2022, there's something different in this time period than my January 3036 jump. The air is breathable now, the radiation isn't elevated, plants are growing, and small animals are around," I told her. "It seems that the war hasn't started, and that means that all the destruction I witnessed happened in less than a month." I could not believe it. Life had been at its end in January 3036, and I had been fleeing to Mars to survive.

I then stood up and had a good stretch, telling her, "This saving-the-Earth thing is all getting old."

She looked at me with an enigmatic smile and reminded me that, "We have mastered time travel and taken on God's mission. This mission was not forced upon us, but rather, we chose to take on this burden. We could easily turn our backs and just live out our lives, never doing anything, and no one would ever be aware of what's going to happen." She took my hand. "That's not the kind of man I married. I married a strong man who is kind and loving, and who I know will not give up. You have God and me standing with you. What more could a man want?"

A tear came to my eye as she hugged me in our park, on the shores of the ocean inlet.

After lunch, we returned to the safety of the pyramid and made ready to return to 2022, but then Terri stopped me and asked, "Will you take me to the end of life on Earth? I want to see what you have seen so I can feel the full implications of the mission."

I was taken aback by that a little but agreed. "We can jump to January 17, 3036." I checked the log. It would be best if we arrived at 1100 hours (11:00 AM), just after my last departure. "I'm not sure just how much longer after that the Earth can support life. Just one nuclear bomb in the area, and we would be dead." Maybe 1045 hours would even be better. I made her understand that, "We will need our shields in place and hooked into oxygen before we even jump."

I plugged in the new destination time: 15.11.17.17.9 | 1 Muluk | 12 Ch'en | G7, January 17, 3036, 1045 hours (10:45 AM). I logged our current date and time: 15.11.17.15.11 | 2 Chuwen | 14 Yaxk'in | G5, December 10, 3035, 1245 hours (12:45 PM). Everything was in place. We had our shielding on and O2 hooked up. I hit the green button, and the reactor responded, the ionic cloud filled the room, and a tingling could be felt. Within seconds, we were there, and the generator wound down.

15.1117.17.9 | TZLOK'IN DATE: 1 MULUK | HAAB DATE: 12 CH'EN | LORD OF THE NIGHT: G7 GREGORIAN: JANUARY 17, 3036

I signaled Terri to remain seated in the recliner under the shields. I was waiting to hear the oxygen sensor and radiation alarm sound. But nothing.

I got up and checked the control panel. I confirmed that we had jumped forward, but nothing seemed to be the same as the last time I had jumped to this date. I looked out of the Eye of Horus, and everything was just like it had been on December 10, 3035. Had I errored when I'd reported that the end of life was in January 3036?

I checked the radiation levels. All were normal. The readings were at background levels. No elevated gamma, alpha, or neutron levels.

"It's safe to get up from under the shields," I told Terri before I unlocked the door and opened it.

We stepped out of the pyramid and into the park. A serendipitous encounter unfolded before our eyes. A deer, standing in the park within twenty meters (65 feet) was grazing on the grasses. There was life, and nothing seemed to be in duress. It was much warmer than it should have been for a January day in West Virginia, but life seemed calm and normal-ish.

Terri looked at me and exclaimed, "We did it! Mission accomplished! Whatever you said to President Biden and his cabinet has somehow changed history and averted the end of life on Earth!"

There was no one to thank us or pat us on the back. No recognition, acknowledgement, award, or trophy. No way to know whether our assumptions were correct. Our payment was the satisfaction that we had triumphed in our quest, against all odds.

I was not sure she was correct, that we had overcome the apocalypse, but even if we had, the job was not done until we returned to 2022 and finished the task.

I brought out Hal, and Terri and I rode around the park, up to the top of the cliffs and down to the beach, along the wave-lapped shores. We were taking it all in as a victory lap. A celebration of life on our ATV that was more than a thousand years old. Wind in her hair, a smile on her face, with sunshine on her brow, it was a snapshot in time that I would always remember.

I was sad that it had to end, but we needed to return. Besides, Terri would have to remove bugs from her teeth if she kept smiling like that on the ATV.

We put the ATV away and locked the door. Terri took her place in the reclining chair as I plugged in our new destination date and time: 13.0.9.13.19 | 13 Kawak | 12 Yaxk'in | G9, August 10, 2022, 1600 hours (4:00 PM). I then logged our current date and time: 15.11.17.17.9 | 1 Muluk | 12 Ch'en | G7, January 17, 3036, 1530 hours (3:30 PM). We looked at each other as I reached over and hit the green "*Go*" button. The reactor fired up, the ionic cloud got really thick, and the tingling was as intense as I had ever felt it.

A few minutes later, the cloud started to clear and the intense tingling subsided. As the reactor wound down, I looked over to my spouse, with her hair standing straight up and out, and signaled to her that we were back.

We got up and received a big shock, much like the kind you got when you rubbed your feet across the carpet in the winter or wore a wool sweater. Then she reached out to me, and an electric bolt hit me so hard that it hurt. We laughed and headed for the tunnel exit, back to the lab/shop building.

CHAPTER TWENTY-THREE
THE GOGS
13.0.9.13.19 | TZLOK'IN DATE: 13 KAWAK | HAAB
DATE: 12 YAXK'IN | LORD OF THE NIGHT: G9
GREGORIAN: AUGUST 10, 2022

There, we found our manikins sitting in their places, all nice and warm, just like we had left them. I unplugged them and proceeded back to the cabin.

Terri was happy to be back with our cats. She picked up each one as they took their turns greeting her. Cleo, Parker, Frankie, and Belle each got a handful of treats as though we had left them starving for a week.

"You were only gone for an hour," I politely reminded her.

She acted like she had not heard me and proceeded to give the cats her full attention.

I was tired, and although it was only 1600 hours (4:00 PM), and I had just eaten my lunch not that long ago, I was just mentally whooped. I sat back in my lounge chair and turned on the news. It was interesting to see that legislation had been introduced to limit and restrict artificial intelligence (AI). Also, the four hundred billion dollar bill to reduce greenhouse gases was being signed into law by President Biden.

Tomorrow, I would transfer all my vital records over to the quartz storage chip and stash it so my vital data and records were both encrypted and secure until Beverly Lord's team was able to master the five-dimensional (5D) quartz storage system. I was convinced the government would eventually get bored of watching me.

13.1.2.6.10 | TZLOK'IN DATE: 7 OK | HAAB DATE: 3
MUWAN | LORD OF THE NIGHT: G4
GREGORIAN: JANUARY 5, 2035

It had been years since I'd made a time jump. I had so wanted to use the technology to help society, but with the government monitoring my every move, I felt it would be better to just ignore it all for some time. I wanted to help murder victims avoid their demise. Mass shootings could be halted before they had happened, and the impact of large disasters, like earthquakes, volcanoes, and tsunamis, could be minimized. But I was not giving this technology to the government, and they were intent on monitoring me. The world would just have to pay in small ways for the lack of knowledge.

After my meeting with President Biden, the US government never came to me, asking me for help. Apparently, they were reluctant to ask me to intervene. But with the world's unrest and ever-changing political atmosphere, I found their lack of contact disappointing. So long as the stability of the United States was not in jeopardy, I just let it play out. Sure, there were bad things happening throughout the world, and I was sure I could have helped thousands of people avoid sudden death, but not at the cost of handing man the ability to travel through time.

I decided on this day that I would revisit January 17, 3036, just to make sure nothing had changed. If I found everything to be in order, I would travel forward further into the future to see how long the stability had lasted mankind.

I packed my lunch and restocked all my supplies. I double-checked the reactor to make sure I had enough fuel. The ATV batteries and the ATC checked out fine. Good old Hal was still working like a champ. I made sure I had fresh oxygen in the life support equipment, batteries in the radiation detectors. Then I checked their calibration.

"I have to make a quick jump to check on Earth's status. I will be back in less than an hour," I told Terri.

She shook her head and said, "I knew you couldn't leave it alone." Then she put her hand on her hip. "You have one hour. You better not keep me waiting."

I entered the pyramid and locked the door. I then set the destination date and time: 15.11.17.17.9 |1 Muluk| 12 Ch'en | G7, January 17, 3036, 1630 hours (4:30 PM). I logged the current date and time: 13.1.2.6.10 | 7 Ok | 3 Muwan | G4, January 5, 2035, 1100 hours (11:00 AM). I then took my seat in the recliner and covered myself with the radiation and neutron shields. I had the PPE equipment by my side, and the radiation meters were readily accessible. I hit the green "*Go*" button, and the reactor came to life, the ionic cloud came on heavy, and the tingling was almost a burn. It had been some time, so I had forgotten that the larger the jump, the more intense the tingling.

After a few minutes, the cloud started to clear, the tingling subsided, and the reactor wound down. I remained in the chair for a few moments just to make sure the alarms were not going to go off.

15.11.17.17.9 | TZLOK'IN DATE: 1 MULUK| HAAB DATE: 12 CH' EN | LORD OF THE NIGHT: G7 GREGORIAN: JANUARY 17, 3036

All seemed good. I took a peek out of the all-seeing Eye of Horus, and everything looked clear. I felt confident that I did not need to test the air. Everything was just like when we had left the park. Only thirty minutes had elapsed since my departure with Terri from this date.

I unlocked the door and stepped out. Yes, all was still good. Confirmation that whatever the US government had done was enough to change history and prolong the end of life on Earth.

I turned around and figured I would jump forward another two hundred three years. I had done some quick research and, as I understood it, it had been prophesied in the Judaism Talmud that the end of days, as we knew it, would be September 30th, in the year 3239.

I locked the door and set the new destination date and time: 16.2.4.11.10 | 3 Ok | 13 Xul | G5, September 30, 3239, at 1100 hours (11:00 AM). I logged my current date and time: 15.11.17.17.9 | 1 Muluk | 12 Ch'en | G7, January 17, 3036, 1645 hours (4:45 PM). Expecting the worst, I covered myself with the shields again and had the oxygen close at hand. Then I reached over and hit the green "*Go*" button once again.

The ionic fog rolled in from one wall to the other, almost like a wave that I had not seen before. The tingling was numbing and seemed to penetrate all my facial orifices, from ears, to nose, then into my mouth. It was taking my breath, and the hair on my arms and neck stood straight up.

As the reactor wound down, the alarms rang before I could even move. I grabbed the oxygen and took a couple of hits as soon as I could. The radiation alarms were sounding, so I stayed under the lead and high-Z shields.

16.2.4.11.10 | TZLOK'IN DATE: 3 OK | HAAB DATE: 13 XUL | LORD OF THE NIGHT: G5 GREGORIAN: SEPTEMBER 30, 3239

I knew I was in trouble, and there was no need to stick around. I plugged in a new destination date and time, figuring I would go back a year and assess the conditions. New destination: 16.2.3.11.5 | 2 Chikchan | 13 Xul | G9, September 30, 3238, 1100 hours (11:00 AM). My current time was: 16.2.4.11.10 | 3 Ok | 13 Xul | G5, September 30, 3239, at 1100 hours (11:00 AM). I hit the green button without a moment's hesitation, the reactor fired right up, and the cloud appeared and disappeared in just a second or two. I didn't recall feeling the tingling, but it might be because I was still numb from the big jump or just plain scared out of my wits.

16.2.3.11.5 | TZLOK'IN DATE: 2 CHIKCHAN | HAAB DATE: 13 XUL | LORD OF THE NIGHT: G9 GREGORIAN: SEPTEMBER 30, 3238

The alarms had stopped ringing. However, I was still on the oxygen tank. I checked the radiation meters and oxygen levels inside of the pyramid, and all seemed fine. I felt the prudent thing to do was to take a look around out of the Eye of Horus, and then draw an air sample before I opened the door.

Things looked quite different as I gazed out of the all-seeing eye. The sky was no longer blue but more of a red, and I saw no signs of life. Dusty, barren, sandy, and devoid of plant, mammal, or fowl. I drew the air sample, and it quickly became obvious that I was living on the edge. Although the oxygen levels were capable of sustaining life, the air was full of noxious gases and poisons.

I decided to go out and try to evaluate the situation. The goal was to find out who and what Gog and Magog were that the Talmud had named.

I opened the door, keeping my respirator on, and then brought out the air transport craft (ATC). Good old Hal. I had Hal take me to Capon Bridge, but there did not seem to be anything there. Even the old bridge had rusted away. I then asked Hal to take me south in search of life. But signs of life were scarce. Only the highest peaks of the mountains still had their summits above the sea.

Eventually, I happened upon a small town with a few people. It was a scene out of a post-apocalyptic movie from the 2000s. The people were dirty and wearing all types of mix-matched clothes. Each had a respirator and all types of weapons.

I stopped a guy in the street and tried to speak to him about the current affairs, to no avail. He ran off, threatening to kill me and warning me not to follow.

I realized that the end of days had not come all at once but had been eating away at the Earth for some time. If my recollection served me well, it had not been prophesied to be the end of Earth or even life. It was to be the year the Messiah was to arrive and save life. It was to be the end of bad days that had plagued the Earth for a thousand years and the beginning of good days. That the war and the end of days was one that was supposed to start in the Middle East and then spread outward.

How could I possibly travel to the Middle East, being I was time jumping in West Virginia? What I needed was to pinpoint a date and time when the beginning of the end of days had started. Then I could get information about who was involved and what the circumstances were.

I returned to the pyramid and parked Hal. I closed and locked the door, figuring I would go back in time a few more years to see what I could find out. I snickered as I plugged in the new destination date, thinking I better not be late, or Terri would not let me forget it. I entered: 16.1.18.9.19 | 9 Kawak | 12 Xul | G1, September 30, 3233, 1100 hours (11:00 AM). I then logged my current date and time: 16.2.3.11.5 | 2 Chikchan | 13 Xul | G9, September 30, 3238, 1400 hours (2:00 PM). I took my place in the reclining chair and placed the shields over me. I hit the green "Go" button and back I went. The reactor came to life, the all-familiar ionic cloud rolled in, and the tingling ensued. Within a few moments, the cloud cleared, the reactor came to a rest, and the tingling vanished from my body.

16.1.18.9.19 | TZLOK'IN DATE: 9 KAWAK | HAAB DATE: 12 XUL | LORD OF THE NIGHT: G1 GREGORIAN: SEPTEMBER 30, 3233

There were no alarms. As before, I checked to make sure that the radiation levels were in a safe range and that the air was breathable. Luckily, I could function without the respirator this time.

Looking out the Eye of Horus, I could see there was life present. This was a good sign.

I opened the door and moved the ATC out of the bay door once again. Giving Hal the commands, he quickly took me to town. It did not take me long to find the problem.

It seemed man kept falling into the same pattern—robots and AI were running the show.

I got a connection with the data stream (DS) and quickly found what Gog and Magog were. They were real, right there on the DS. It took me no travel or hardship to find what I was looking for.

The prophets had almost nailed it perfectly. It seemed robots were called Gogs, and the world-wide manufacturing company was the Megagog Company. With a little more digging, I found that the company had actually been established in Israel and had grown to be one of the largest robot manufacturers in the world. They had implanted AI into the Gogs and, of course, like before, the AI was going to migrate toward the control of Earth and elimination of biological life forms. Survival of the fittest.

I took the time to load all the information I could find about the company on the quartz five-dimensional (5D) crystal storage card to take back with me. I would have hundreds of years, and many more lifetimes, to seek the changes necessary to extend life. I had made up my mind that I was not going to burden my wife with any of this information.

It was now time to end this time jump. I would return to my wife and live my life to the fullest by her side. When Terri was gone, and I had a generous amount of idle time, I would then focus to resolve this dilemma. For my mission was perpetual, and I believed it had been inspired by God, as Noah's mission to build the ark had been to him. The difference was that God had spoken to Noah and had told him how to build the ark. God had told Noah what to put on the ark and, according to biblical records, Noah had been obedient. It had taken Noah about a hundred years to complete the task per God's instructions.

This mission had not been delivered to me by God. There was no clear directive on what to do or how to accomplish it. This mission was self-appointed and based solely on faith.

I returned to the pyramid and locked the door. I stored the five-dimensional (5D) crystal chip in my shirt pocket and plugged in my new destination date and time: 13.1.2.6.10 | 7 Ok | 3 Muwan | G4, January 5, 2035, at 1200 hours (noon). I logged the current date and time: 16.1.18.9.19 | 9 Kawak | 12 Xul | G1, September 30, 3233, 1710 hours.

No need for the heavy lead shields on this trip, I sat back in the recliner and hit the green "*Go*" button. I could feel it coming. It was a big jump. The reactor was groaning under the immense strain of generating so much power at once, and the ionic cloud was really not a cloud this time. It was thick, like huffing on bug spray. An ionic soup of some type. My skin crawled from the burning, and my eyes burned and watered. My nose was stuffed from the thick ionic atmosphere so much so that I could not breathe. I was drowning, holding my breath, but I had my mouth open, gasping and waiting for the jump to be over.

For some reason, the jump was much more difficult than any other I had experienced. My jumps early on had been greater in time but had not been as demanding. Apparently, if one was in the future and jumped back to the original date, the system required much more energy than traveling back then forward to one's original time. I would note this in the log.

The reactor started to back down, and the ionic fog thinned slowly at first, then cleared enough that I could see the walls of the pyramid once more. Eventually, all was back to normal, and I was amazed as to how close I had come to dying. Any longer of a jump might have left me dead by asphyxiation. They would have found my lifeless body in the recliner with the five-dimensional (5D) crystal chip stuffed in my pocket and my handwritten log on the control panel. That was not the way I planned on leaving this Earth, and I would surely plan better for future jumps.

I gathered myself and completed logging everything. I then unlocked the pyramid door and stepped out.

You know it. Terri was there, hand on her hip, looking at her watch. "You just made it, buddy."

I smiled, and we proceeded back to the cabin. She had lunch sitting on the table as though it was an offering, like I would somehow find my way back for lunch if for no other reason.

"Is 3036 still stable?" she asked.

"We fixed 3036. All is good. There is no war, and robots have not taken over. We fixed the problem."

She smiled and broke out a bottle of wine. She poured each of us a glass and raised hers to a toast. "To our accomplishment."

I felt guilty drinking to this accomplishment, knowing I would spend the rest of my life fighting to stave off man's self-extermination. But I smiled in spite of myself, raised my glass, and drank to the toast.

I felt as though she could see through me, as she always seemed able to do. However, I never did tell her what I had found during that jump forward in time. It always bothered me that I had not been more forthcoming. As the feeling would roll in, I would brush the feelings of betrayal from my mind and write it off as something that would have caused her pain and would have served no purpose. I had withheld the truth for her sake and knew I would have to work at resolving it later in life.

CHAPTER TWENTY-FOUR

BY HER SIDE

13.2.0.3.12 | TZLOK'IN DATE: 7 EB' | HAAB DATE:
15 YAXK'IN | LORD OF THE NIGHT: G9
GREGORIAN: AUGUST 5, 2052

It was Terri's birthday yet again. She was ninety years old this year.

As the years had passed, it had become obvious that I had chosen to alter my genetic code to live an extended life. Terri was nearing the end of hers, and although she had aged gracefully, she did not look quite as young as I did. I appeared to be about thirty-five years old.

She had stuck to her guns right to the end. She was not going to change God's plan for her. Her time was nearing, and she had come to terms with it. Everyone we had ever known had already passed.

It was scary when all your friends and coworkers had crossed to the other side and only your children and young family members remained. Half of them didn't know your story, your age, your real name. It was then that one would realize you were left behind to wait your turn. But my turn was still way off in the future. I figured I had about eight hundred ten more years to live at this point.

I had become accustomed to having more than one of me present at every one of Terri's birthdays. But not this one. This was one of the few that I got to share with her all by my present-day self. No drop-ins from the future jumping back to this birthday. I knew it was her last that I would share with her. She wanted to go as God planned.

God did not put an expiration date on anyone, and you were not supposed to know when or how it would end. I made sure we had a cake with just nine candles. The children and grandchildren came by midday and wished her a happy birthday.

13.2.0.5.11 | TZLOK'IN DATE: 7 CHUWEN | HAAB
DATE: 14 CH'EN | LORD OF THE NIGHT: G3
GREGORIAN: SEPTEMBER 13, 2052

Terri passed that same year, after seventy-two years of marriage. We never traveled to the future together again after that spectacular trip in 2022. The jump forward in time to 3036 that had revealed that we had completed God's mission and saved Earth. I, by myself, had made periodic jumps forward to confirm that our mission had succeeded. And yes, it had succeeded in extending the end of life on Earth, but I had found that the extension was not eternal. It was merely a stopgap. An extension of the inevitable.

I knew I would have to intervene again and again to move the extinction date. I would not be able to master or formulate a permanent solution. Much like the US Senate trying to approve an annual budget, stopgap after stopgap would be required until the end. Man seemed to be internally driven to annihilate himself and all life. But once Terri's mind was at peace, I never wanted to tell her that the mission was a perpetual assignment. That I would have to return and make more corrections in the coming years.

Terri was cremated, as she had requested, and her ashes were united with the ocean waters where Annapolis had once stood as the capital of Maryland. Across those waters, where the mighty Chesapeake had once yielded her bounty of shellfish. Where her family had so proudly worked as lighthouse keepers, oystermen, and crabbers. It was a mist on the gray kind of day. The skies, the waters, and the waves all varying shades of blue and gray.

When the captain told me that we had reached the area over the old Thomas Point Lighthouse, I set her spirit free on the surface of the waves to join her kin. I had the captain provide me with the GPS coordinates so I could revisit the area in the future, or maybe even join her someday.

13.2.0.9.10 | TZLOK'IN DATE: 8 OK | HAAB DATE: 13 MAK | LORD OF THE NIGHT: G1 GREGORIAN: DECEMBER 1, 2052

It was my birthday now. I was ninety years old with the face of a thirty-five-year-old. But no matter how young I appeared, I had an old soul, and this was the first birthday I would have without my bride in more than seventy years. Yes, the children called on a three-dimensional (3D) hologram, and I spoke to each of the grandchildren, but I was missing the sweet voice and presence of my Terri. I had the power to go back and visit her. I wanted to go back to when she was thirty-five, but that would have only prolonged the pain. I needed to grieve and move on.

Maybe in the future, I could travel back and spend some time with her, but not now. I would do something that I would regret—inject her with the virus and extend her life before she even knew what was going on. I could do that, but I dared not. She had gone her way, and I had to learn to live with it.

I bought a cake and had it delivered to the cabin. There, I had Alexi sing me "Happy Birthday," and I bought myself a few nice gifts.

I made up my mind that day that I was going to leave this time period and either jump back in time or forward and live for a hundred years or so. Maybe I would do both. I had about eight hundred years to use, and I was not going to be happy spending them by myself. I was not looking for a new partner and, with my genetic modifications, I would have to be careful. I didn't think just anyone was capable of living with someone like me and, more importantly, keep quiet about it. If I were to jump too far back in time, I would be perceived as a sorcerer, and if I were to go too far forward in time, it would be difficult to hide capabilities like mine. Too many advancements in technology, all watching and monitoring my every move. I could even relive the same years that I had grown up in with a different alias. Knowing what I knew now, that could be fun.

I spent my birthday thinking about all the possibilities.

13.2.0.11.4 | TZLOK'IN DATE: 3 K'AN | HAAB DATE:
7 MUWAN | LORD OF THE NIGHT: G8
GREGORIAN: JANUARY 4, 2053

I decided that I would jump time for a while. I always felt that I would love to sail the seven seas and help discover the world. I didn't think I could take the whaling ship thing. I was against that, but maybe be a chef on a sailing vessel who could keep the crew well fed due to my knowledge of food preservation. Showing Christopher Columbus where to sail. Inoculating the Conquistadors, so as not to spread disease to the South American natives. Who knew the full potential of my intervention, the numerous lives I could save?

Or, maybe an inventor. That would be easy for me. I could hobnob with Einstein, Edison, and Tesla. With any luck, I could get the group to work together. Could you imagine how far man could go? Maybe I should step back in time to the days of DaVinci or Archimedes and really give mankind a jump.

But what would any of that do for mankind? From what I had seen, man would only exterminate himself sooner. Could I go back and put an end to WWI or WWII? If I could, would it be advisable? Any significant change could cause me not to exist. Maybe my ancestors would not migrate to the United States if the wars did not happen. One small change could change all of society. One life extended or voided could change everything, and if I was personally wiped from the book of time, I would not be able to go back and fix it.

No, history must stay history—unchanged and devoid of modification.

I could go back to my own birth year and anytime forward, but traveling back and changing the past should be taboo. If I decide to jump back in time, it should only be for research—to get answers on how the pyramids had been built, how the stones of the monolithic temples had been cut, moved, and assembled. To witness the birth of Jesus. To see if ancient aliens had visited our planet. Could you imagine? To do any of that, I would need to travel with the aid of Hal—long distances. I needed to find a way to power my ATC so it would fly for thousands of miles, quietly and almost unnoticed. Maybe a ship out to sea, venturing in the ATC inland to study, and then returning each day to the ship, so as not to change history.

Before I ever went back in time again, I needed to really consider all the consequences of my actions. I needed to be responsible for any interaction. Eventually, the technology that Terri and I had discovered, that allowed me to jump through the spans of time, would be discovered by another. Apparently, time travel was not discovered until much later in history.

Maybe time travel had been discovered by others, but they, too, had realized the magnitude of this power and wouldn't share it with society. Maybe the UFOs of today, and the aliens that man had witnessed, were no more than time travelers from the future coming back to visit the past and study.

I decided to go forward in time, to the year 2100. I would retain my name as Max Hickman. That way, I still had the WebDollar crypto that was implanted in my left hand so I wouldn't be burdened with work, to live my life without monetary worries. To study, help, and philanthropize. To watch my descendants and help guide them. All the while, I would engage, as necessary, to fulfill the duties of my perpetual mission. This would be my destination.

Once I made this jump, I might not return for some time, with the exception of visiting my wife, Terri, on her birthdays.

CHAPTER TWENTY-FIVE

THE HAND-OFF

Scott had been sitting on the couch the whole time. Now, he got up and gave out a yawn and a big stretch.

At this point, I believed Scott had heard enough. He had a clear understanding of how Terri and I had accidentally discovered time travel. Scott had heard the story of how Terri and I had intervened to stave off the end of the world and how the end of life as we knew it on Earth was in perpetual jeopardy. He knew the story behind my altered genetic code that had extended my life to about nine hundred years and why his forty times great-nana was not with me. He knew that my body had the ability to resist cancers and even grow back damaged appendages or organs. And, last but not least, Scott had confirmed that he, too, had the same abilities.

I felt there was no reason to tell him everything else now. I had time to share more of my adventures with him in the future. For now, I would let the information I shared resonate. Besides, he had everything he needed to carry on the mission should anything happen to me.

"We should call it a day, spend the night in the pyramid, and I'll bring you up to speed tomorrow on current affairs," I suggested to Scott.

13.07.7.12.14 | TZLOK'IN DATE: 9 IX | HAAB DATE:
17 XUL | LORD OF THE NIGHT: G2
GREGORIAN: JULY 26, 2020

It was warm, so I did not close the doors on the pyramid. We slept in our recliners as we watched the fire in the burn pit lick at the night's darkness just outside the bay door. It was the perfect night to just stare at the stars.

Scott had never experienced such a night in his life. All you could hear were the deer tiptoeing through the woods and the caterpillar droppings hitting the leaves of the trees as they slowly ate their meals. I could see that Scott was a-stir with emotions, having been subjected to so much new information all at once and to be experiencing a world that he had never known.

We awoke to the morning dew dripping from the mountain tree leaves and pattering on the forest floor. The smell of the campfire still hung in the air, as it did on a camping trip in the early morning. Scott, being a military man, was up early and out discovering the life that surrounded the pyramid. He had to touch everything, from the caterpillars to the various forms of fauna that grew in the immediate area. I tried to warn him that not everything was harmless, but he didn't pay me any mind. I knew it would only be a matter of time before he touched poison ivy, got stung by a bee, or was bit by a snake, so I brought him in and fixed him some breakfast. I then gave him some strong warnings.

We took in the rising of the sun as planet Earth continued its rotation. Sipping our coffees, I went on with my story, explaining how I had moved the end of days more than once. There was a problem, though. The movement was in both directions. Sometimes, the date would seem to happen sooner, and other times later. It would, and could, be moved out farther, extending man's existence for some time, but nobody knew the time of doom in a strict manner. The date of the apocalypse, or the end of days, seemed to move with each geopolitical event, war, scientific development, and rescue. Only with a helping hand, guidance, perseverance, and love could it be extended.

Apparently, without an act of God, the apocalypse, or end of days, could not be permanently eliminated. I had discovered that I did not have the power to change things permanently, and he might find he did not, either. Maybe God had given man the ability to change his destiny and his destiny was not as predetermined as many religions claimed, or it might be that our destiny was predetermined, and no matter how hard we tried to change it, we would always gravitate back to what was predetermined.

I explained to Scott that I had jumped forward in time about once every twenty-five years to check on the status of man's extinction, doing whatever I could to guide men of power to make changes that would prolong life. But I was limited to working with the US and friendly nations. I had no communication with communist nations or nations ruled by dictators. I had little or no ability to stop man from inventing new forms of pollution or weapons. I could not singlehandedly stop the extinction of many forms of life on Earth. Man had a voracious appetite to kill life, and I could not stop it by myself. Not even with the aid of the US government.

The US government knew that I possessed the power to provide information about the future, but they didn't know how I did it. I had met many Presidents at one time or another. All had been reluctant to ask for my assistance, apart from asking if they would win their next election. I had been able to keep the fact that I could jump time a secret from almost everyone. The key had been to keep a low profile, to live where most men did not.

"What do you mean by that?" Scott asked.

"That information is for another day. You have enough to work with now," I answered.

I passed one of my jump logs to Scott. This log contained only the information about the time jumps I had shared with him. "I will give you the other logs after I have time to share my other journeys."

I then told Scott, "Ready yourself to jump back to April 3, 2405. We have to make the camping trip believable, so I think a 1200 hours (noon) return on Sunday the 3rd will be best."

He agreed, but I could tell he was not anxious to end this trip, so I reminded him, "You can return to this time period any time you wish in the future."

With that, I got a smile out of him.

I stood up and grabbed Scott's hand, pulling him up to his feet. I then shook his hand and told him, "It's now your mission to do what you can to keep man from exterminating himself. To possibly change the world, to bring back biodiversity that has been lost to time. To take the Earth under your wing and do whatever you can until God Himself provides a permanent solution. A perpetuum assignment until God or man's Messiah relieves us of this duty."

Scott and I then walked back to the pyramid and took our places in the recliners. I turned off the red light that illuminated in the cabin dining area when I time jumped. I entered the destination date: 13.19.17.17.18 | 9 Etz'nab' | 16 Sek | G7, April

3, 2405, 1200 hours (noon). I then logged our current date and time: 13.07.07.12.14 | 9 Ix | 17 Xul | G2, July 26, 2020, 0900 hours (9:00 AM).

I sat back in the recliner and made sure Scott was in position. Then I reached over and hit the green "*Go*" button. The reactor came to life, and the ionic cloud filled the room. I could feel the tingling as it creeped across my skin, and I could tell that Scott was feeling it, as well. After a minute or two, the cloud cleared, and the tingling came to an end. The reactor was winding down, and I signaled to Scott that he could now move.

13.19.17.17.18 | TZLOK'IN DATE: 9 ETZ'NAB' | HAAB DATE: 16 SEK | LORD OF THE NIGHT: G7 GREGORIAN: APRIL 3, 2405

We both got out of our recliners, and I then showed Scott the control panel with the Mayan calendar built into the selection knobs. I explained how the selection using the Mayan calendar made it easier to select time and track time. I went through the various frequencies and oscillations that each knob on the control panel was used for. I then showed Scott where the formulas were written. The frequency $f = 1/T = \omega/2\pi$ of the motion gave the number of complete oscillations per unit time. It was measured in units of Hertz (1 Hz = 1/s). $a(t) = -\omega2A \cos(\omega t + \varphi) = -\omega2x$). The quantity, φ, was called the phase constant. Each combination of frequency and oscillations changed the dates, and they were directly related to the Mayan long calendar. With the leap years removed, and the long date having such a large cycle, there was less room for error.

Scott, having taken in all he could handle for the day, was now anxious to go. I escorted him through the tunnel, back to the lab/shop building. I turned off Tom and Jerry so the heat would stop being generated, and then we both exited the building and headed toward the cabin.

I could say, without hesitation, that Scott was a changed man. Suddenly, he realized that the world and universe was larger than himself. He now understood the power he held and was starting to realize his full potential. He was a changed man.

We agreed to meet at least once a week. I thought it would be best if I mentored his use of the time jumping equipment until he had a grasp on everything.

Before he left, Scott said, "That trip might have altered my career path."

"Be careful about such a move. Your security clearance may provide you better access to top officials than I ever had. You will have the ability to do everything that needs to be done in just a few hours or days, so it should not impact your career path."

It was now early afternoon. Scott headed for the boat dock.

"Wait. You might want to change your clothes," I warned him. I thought he had gotten used to the nice cotton denim and tees.

Eventually, he loaded his boat and headed off across the inlet, back to his life in the US Navy.

CHAPTER TWENTY-SIX

THE ENLISTMENT
PRESENT DAY

My hard work was done. I worked with Scott for years and, eventually, shared all my stories with him. Now my time has grown short, so now I need to provide Scott with as much support as I can. This is where you, the reader, come in to become a full-fledged agent.

I am giving each reader the opportunity to join our force and hear the rest of the stories as I release them.

Join our movement and look for your next assigned reading. Get the next story before anyone else and vote on where we go and how to solve the mission. It's a new movement, as of now, but it will grow, and Earth, with all its inhabitants, needs you to join us to make the mission strong.

Join us in Perpetuum.

End.

Timeline

Perpetuum

Maya Calendar Date for Jump Code Settings Current Time Period	Gregorian Start Date	Atomic Clock Start of Jump	Forward / Backward / Start	Gregorian Jump Date	Maya Calendar Date for Jump Code Settings to Destination Time Period
Time Jump Log					
13.0.8.10.18	8 Etz'nab'	16 Sotz'	G2	6/15/2021	12:00	Back in Time	6/15/1021	13.0.8.10.18	8 Etz'nab	16 Sotz'	G2
10.9.1.1.1	6 Imix	4 Sak'	G3	6/15/1021	14:00	Return to Start	6/15/2021	10.9.14.1.1	6 Imix'	4 Sak'	G3
13.0.8.11.5	2 Chikchan	3 Sek	G9	6/22/2021	8:00	Back in Time	6/15/1021	13.0.8.10.18	8 Etz'nab	16 Sotz'	G2
10.9.1.1.1	6 Imix	4 Sak'	G3	6/15/1021	17:55	Back in Time	6/15/1021	-3.-5.-20.-11.-13	-4 Imix'	-15 Sak'	G-7.
(BCE) -3.-5.-20.-4.-8	-4 Kawak	-15 Ch'en	G-	6/1/4000 BCE	15:00	Forward	6/1/3000 BCE	0.5.15.7.2	11 Ik'	0 Mewan	G7
(BCE) 0.5.15.7.2	11 Ik'	0 Muvan	G7	6/1/3000 BCE	16:10	Forward	6/1/2000 BCE	2.16.3.17.17	5 kab'an	10 Ch'en	G6
(BCE) 2.16.9.17.12	13 Eb'	5 Ch'en	G1	6/1/2000 BCE	15:30	Forward	6/1/1000 BCE	5.7.4.10.2	2 Ik'	10 Sip	G4
(BCE) 5.7.4.10.2	2 Ik'	10 Sip	G4	6/1/1000 BCE	15:20	Forward	6/1/0001	7.17.19.2.12	4 Eb'	0 Pax	G7
7.17.19.2.12	4 Eb'	0 Pax	G7	6/1/0001	16:15	Forward	6/1/1000	10.8.12.12.17	5 kab'an	5 Yax	G5
10.8.12.12.17	5 Kab'an	5 Yaz	G5	6/1/1000	16:12	Returned to Start	6/22/2021	13.0.8.11.5	2 Chikchan	3 Sek	G9
13.0.8.11.18	2 Etz'nab'	16 Sek	G4	7/5/2021	10:00	Forward	7/5/3036	15.11.18.7.19	2 Kawak	2 kumk'u	G6
15.11.18.7.19	2 Kawak	2 kumk'u	G6	7/5/3036	9:10	Emergency Returned to Start	7/5/2021	13.0.8.11.18	2 Etz'nab	16 Sek	G4,
13.0.8.11.19	3 Kawak	17 Sek	G5	7/6/2021	11:45	Back in Time	7/3/2021	13.0.8.11.16	13 K'ib'	14 Sek	G2
13.0.8.11.16	13 k'ib	14 Sek	G2	7/3/2021	14:30	Returned to Start	7/6/2021	13.0.8.11.19	3 Kawak	17 Sek	G5
13.0.8.12.0	4 Ajaw	18 Sek	G6	7/7/2021	10:00	Forward	7/7/2045	13.1.13.0.6	2 Kimi	9 Pax	G4
13.1.13.0.6	8 Kimi	4 Xul	G6	7/7/2045	12:30	Forward	7/5/2145	13.6.14.8.8	13 Lamat	6 Yaxk'in	G6
13.6.14.10.15	8 Men	13 Ch'en	G8	8/21/2145	14:00	Returned to Start	7/7/2021	13.0.8.12.0	4 Ajaw	18 Sek	G6
13.0.8.12.1	5 Imix'	19 Sek	G7	7/8/2021	10:00	Back in Time	8/5/1984	12.18.11.3.15	13 Men	18 Xul	G3
12.18.11.3.15	13 Men	18 Xul	G3	8/5/1984	14:40	Returned to Start	7/8/2021	13.0.8.12.1	5 Imix'	19 Sek	G7
13.0.8.13.10	8 Ok	8 Yaxk'in	G9	8/6/2021	9:00	Forward	1/15/3036	13.12.1.1.10	6 OK	3 Yax	G3
15.11.17.17.14	6 Ix	17 Ch'en	G3	1/22/3036	16:10	Back in Time	11/1/2145	13.6.14.16.7	2 Manik'	5 Mak	G8
13.6.14.16.5	1 Chikchan	3 Muvan	G1	12/9/2145	9:00	Forward	1/17/3036	15.11.17.17.9	1 Muluk	3 Mewan	G1
15.11.17.17.9	1 Muluk	12 Ch'en	G7	1/17/3036	10:30	Return to Start	8/6/2021	13.0.8.13.10	8 Ok	8 Yaxk'in	G9
13.0.9.13.14	8 Ix	7 Yaxk'in	G7	8/5/2022	10:00	Forward	8/9/2022	13.0.9.13.18	12 Etz'nab'	11 Yaxk'in	G8
13.0.9.13.17	11 kab'an	10 Yaxk'in	G7	8/9/2022	8:00	Return to Start	8/5/2022	13.0.9.13.14	8 Ix	7 Yaxk'in	G7
13.0.9.13.19	13 Kawak	12 Yaxk'in	G9	8/10/2022	15:00	Back in Time	8/5/2022	13.0.9.13.14	8 Ix	7 Yaxk'in	G4
13.0.9.13.14	8 Ix	7 Yaxk'in	G4	8/5/2022	9:15	Forward	12/10/3035	15.11.17.15.11	2 Chuven	1 Yaxk'in	G5
15.11.17.15.11	2 Chuven	1 Yaxk'in	G5	12/10/3035	12:45	Forward	1/17/3036	15.11.17.17.9	1 Muluk	12 Ch'en	G7
15.11.17.17.9	1 Muluk	12 Ch'en	G7	1/17/3036	15:30	Return to Start	8/10/2022	13.0.9.13.19	13 Kawak	12 Yaxk'in	G9
13.1.2.6.10	7 Ok	3 Muvan	G4	1/5/2035	11:00	Forward	1/17/3036	15.11.17.17.9	1 Muluk	12 Ch'en	G7
15.11.17.17.9	1 Muluk	12 Ch'en	G7	1/17/3036	16:45	Forward	9/30/3239	16.2.4.11.10	3 Ok	13 Xul	G5
16.2.4.11.10	3 Ok	13 Xul	G5	9/30/3239	11:05	Back in Time	9/30/3238	16.2.3.11.5	2 Chikchan	13 Xul	G9
16.2.3.11.5	2 Chikchan	13 Xul	G9	9/30/3238	14:00	Back in Time	9/30/3233	16.1.18.9.19	3 Kawak	12 Xul	G1
16.1.18.9.19	3 Kawak	12 Xul	G1	9/30/3233	17:10	Return to Start	1/5/2035	13.1.2.6.10	7 Ok	3 Muvan	G4
13.19.17.17.16	7 k'ib'	14 Sek	G5	4/1/2405	7:45	Backwards	7/25/2020	13.0.7.12.13	8 B'en	16 Xul	G1
13.07.7.12.14	9 Ix	17 Xul	G2	7/26/2020	9:00	Return to Start	4/3/2405	13.19.17.17.16	9 Etz'nab'	16 Sek	G7

Destination Jump Time	Time Aged	Elapsed Time Upon Return	Total Jump Time Aged		Notes
12:00					First Jump
13:00	2:00 hrs	1:00 hrs	3:00 hrs		First Return
14:30	3:25				2nd Jump Back to Pyramid
10:00	5:00				Move Pyramid back to 4000 BCE
15:00	1:10				step 1 return, clean off exterior
15:00	:30				step 2 return, exterior found in good
15:00	:20				step 3 return, exterior found secure
15:00	1:15				step 4 return, cleanup at entrance
15:00	1:12				step 5 return, clean off exterior
9:00		1:00	12:52		Back to start, Note: Aged more than anyone else. Long trips could be noticable to others due to my aging.
9:00					
11:00	:10	1:00	:10		Suspect War raging. Note: Aged less than those not time jumping. Long spans of delayed return from time jump while making short stays in a time period would result in others aging more than myself.
14:00					To buy winning lottery Ticket. Note: Saw myself.
12:00	:30	:15	:30		Obtained winning Power Ball Ticket
9:00					Stopped in to talk to myself and wife.
9:00	3:30				Jump forward 100 years.
11:00	47 Days + 4:00	1:00	47 Days + 7:30		
10:00					Planted Virus into myself
10:30	4:40	:30	4:40		Terri's Birthday.
9:00					
6:00	6 days + 21:00				Made trip back in time on Mars. Then returned to Earth.
10:00	40 days + 1:00				Forward to get pyramid key.
10:00	:30	1:00	46 Days + 23:30		removal.
6:00					
10:15	2:00	:15	2:00		Proof for DHS
9:00					bug
10:00	:15				Forward to buy quartz reader/writer
10:45	2:45				Earth
16:00	4:45	1:00	7:45		Back to complete informaiton transfer and security.
16:30					All Conditions are Good as of 2035
11:00	:15				3239 - Environment Devoid of Life
11:00	:05				bad
11:00	3:00				Life sustaining. Megagog Co. fond to be responsible for end.
12:00	6:10	1:00	9:30		Returned with data on Megagog.
8:13					mission
12:00					

Author, Ralph Boldyga, invites you to join him on Facebook:

WebDollar App for Android:

Information sources and information found on the internet concerning the end of time and data used in the writing of this sci-fiction novel.

This Sunni Muslim theologian, author of the Risale-i Nur and founder of the Nur movement, wrote in a letter to one of his students (the 21st in the so-called *Kastamonu Appendix*) that by applying numerology to a hadith, he arrived at a date of 1545 for the arrival of doomsday. 1545 in the Hijri calendar would be 2122; in the Rumi calendar, it would be 2129. Nursî added that this was not a definite prediction, as "nobody knows the time of doom in a strict manner."

According to the Talmud, in mainstream Orthodox Judaism, the Messiah will come within 6000 years of the creation of Adam, and the world may be destroyed a thousand years later. This would put the beginning of the period of desolation in 2239, and the end of the period of desolation in 3239.

Sources

Seed of life drawings source and information:

- https://www.etsy.com/au/listing/1256981540/sacred-geometry-seed-of-life-germ-of
- https://www.outofstress.com/seed-of-life-meaning/

Thorium based reactors: https://en.wikipedia.org/wiki/Thorium-based_nuclear_power

5D optical data storage sources:

- https://en.wikipedia.org/wiki/5D_optical_data_storage
- https://www.dpreview.com/news/6930207183/researchers-develop-5d-optical-data-storage-method-that-can-preserve-up-to-5tb-per-disc

Fission Reactor Sources: https://www.nature.com/articles/d41586-023-04045-8

Milton Keynes UK
Ingram Content Group UK Ltd.
UKHW031016200324
439740UK00017B/190/J

9 798990 193703